DEADLY RIVALRIES

NICO ARGENTI
BOOK 6

KEN TENTARELLI

1

WEDNESDAY APRIL 16, 1466

THE ROAD TO CALENZANO

"Everything must be perfect for Marco's betrothal celebration," Simona said — for the fourth time by her husband's count. Her last words were nearly lost as the carriage veered off the well-traveled Florence-Prato road and onto the bumpy track toward the town of Calenzano. Antonio attributed his wife's chatter to her anxiety at returning to the family's villa.

Their son Marco had asked that his betrothal be announced at the villa, and his parents had agreed to his request, despite his mother's trepidation.

One year ago, during Antonio's birthday celebration, smoke from the fireplace's blocked chimney had filled the villa's salon, ruining two prized tapestries. A year before that, Marco's sister, Giuliana, suffered a broken leg when she was thrown from a horse while riding on a trail near the villa. And those were only the latest ill-fated incidents. The villa was fashioned like an ancient Roman Domus, and a series of misfortunes experienced during its construction had stone masons remarking, only half in jest, that the Roman styling attracted Fauns, those mischievous creatures of Roman mythology. Simona wasn't a believer in ancient lore, but the long history of hapless occur-rences had made her uneasy. While she agreed that the villa's peristyle was an ideal setting for the betrothal dinner, she would have preferred that it be held at their palazzo in Florence, where happenings were always predictable.

Simona Ridolfi insisted on arriving early so she could personally inspect the preparations and verify they were completed exactly as she had instructed. She flashed a quick nod to Camello, the caretaker, before rushing past him to view the arrangements in the peristyle.

After his wife scurried away, Antonio chatted with the care-taker. "Did I see you inspecting the vines?" he asked.

"Si, Signore," Camello replied. "It's still early, but the grapes are already swelling. We should have a bountiful harvest this year because we've been blessed with fit weather. The clusters are heavy, so I was making sure the vines are anchored firmly to the trellises."

"Will you be taking guests to the vineyard?" Antonio asked.

"Yes," Camello replied. "Signora Simona requested we keep the guests occupied before the dinner by showing them the vats where we crush the grapes and the wine-aging casks in the cellar."

After the two men discussed work being done at the villa, Antonio went in search of his wife. He passed through the villa's formal entrance hall to the quiet interior garden, flanked on both sides by bedchambers. A dining salon at the far end of the garden had enough room for family dinners, but not for all the guests invited to the betrothal celebration. The celebration dinner would be held in the large open peristyle, where Antonio found his wife questioning the chef.

Simona's mere presence intimidated the small man. His neck quivered nervously as he spoke. He coughed; then attempted to hide his insecurity by deepening his voice. "As you requested Signora, all the food is coming from the finest restaurant in Florence, the Uccello. The Uccello staff will prepare antipasti and desserts at the restaurant and bring dressed pheasants. Signor Donato Argenti, the restaurant owner, will be here to supervise the service personally." Smiling, the chef added proudly, "I will roast the pheasants and ensure they are cooked to perfection."

Simona tried to think of incidentals she could question, but none came to mind. Although satisfied with the chef's report, she rubbed her hands together anxiously, unable to dispel her fear that something might go awry. Antonio crossed the peristyle and approached his wife. "Is everything satisfactory, my dear?"

"Mmmm," she muttered and walked away to scan the tables, searching for anything out of place. She stood behind the head table picturing the setting: her husband and Daniela's father will sit next to each other at the center. She will be seated at one end of the table with son Marco and daughter Giuliana, and Daniela will be seated with her mother and brother Polito at the opposite end. The arrangement pleased her.

Simona walked among the tables readied for the guests; at one she pulled a wilted blossom from a flower arrangement, shook her head, and said, "Must I do everything?" She raised her eyes to examine the sky above, where a single puffy cloud floated overhead. Not having cause to complain about the weather, she called to her husband, "Marco should have come with us. It will be shameful if he isn't here before the guests arrive."

"I'm sure he'll be here in time, my treasure," Antonio responded and moved to a side-table, uncorked a wine flask, and poured himself a drink. "It's going to be a long day," he muttered to himself.

A stable in Florence

A stableboy saddled two horses and handed their reins to Marco and Lazo, both handsome men with strong features looking more like brothers than cousins. Marco wore the expression of one who thrust through life like an arrow speeding toward a target while Lazo took time to absorb all the world had to offer.

Marco, the more experienced horseman, climbed aboard his mount, cued the horse into a trot and headed toward the city gate that would put him on the road toward Prato. Lazo set his horse at a walk initially and fell behind until he felt comfortable enough with the animal to increase its pace; then he eased the horse alongside Marco's and said, "I find you to be surprisingly calm, dear cousin. Most men approach their betrothal with either anxiety or fervor."

"Betrothal is just a business arrangement and the commitments have already been made," Marco countered. "The dowry has been decided and notaries have drawn up the marriage documents. The only reason for this announcement celebration is to please my mother ... and maybe Daniela's parents. My mother planned today's event meticulously. Leave nothing to the hands of fate, she repeated incessantly. I've heard her recite the details countless times, making it feel like I've already lived through the day."

"But, dear Marco, betrothal is more than business," Lazo persisted. "It's also the commitment of you and Daniela to share a bed and a life together. She's a delightful woman, beautiful and charming. You're the most fortunate man in Florence. Other men would battle demons to claim Daniela as their life's companion. Don't you become warm when you look into her eyes and doesn't your heart speed when you touch her hand?"

Marco returned a smile and replied, "Everything you say

about Daniela is true, and I'm eager to have her hand in marriage. Daniela has been special to me for as long as I can remember. I've always loved her ... as a sister when we were children ... and now as the woman who lives in my heart. But betrothment ceremonies are merely extravagant events. Daniela's father will offer his daughter and a bountiful dowry. Next, my father will graciously accept with a speech about the joy of our families being united. Decorum will keep him from mentioning the business profits he expects from the union. Daniela and I will have no part in the exhibition other than to sit apart from each other and appear happy."

As youngsters, Marco and Lazo had been almost inseparable. Their fathers, Antonio and his younger brother, lived in the same town and saw each other frequently, eventually hiring the same tutor for their sons.

Before his business became a thriving success, Marco's father, Antonio, had been close to his brother. In time, business success drew the two men apart. As an international merchant, Antonio gained a status that had him socializing with Florence's elite, the Bardis, the Medicis, and other prominent families. His brother had become a carpenter taught by an artisan to build tables and chairs. With practice, the talented apprentice surpassed the tutor and opened his own shop, where he honed wood with precision using awls and chisels. His shop earned a reputation for producing finely crafted pieces. Carpentry, however, ranked among the bottom tier of Florence's trades, which limited his family's social status. Although Lazo hadn't yet gained his father's skill at shaping wood, he contributed to the shop's success with a keen eye for finding wood with straight tight grain among uncut lumber at the mills.

Antonio Ridolfi's isolation from his siblings caused Marco to drift away from his other cousins, but not from Lazo. The two men met regularly for drinks at a drab tavern in their old neighborhood, and occasionally dined together at a trattoria where they enjoyed each other's company, griped about the Signoria's latest rulings, relived the recent games of Florence's athletic competitions, and critiqued the performances of visiting musicians. Marco's parents valued social standing, but class mattered little to Marco, who insisted that his best friend, Lazo, attend the betrothal ceremony and serve as his groomsman at the wedding.

The two men guided their mounts to the side of the road and waited for an oncoming farm wagon to pass. Lazo slowed his horse and fell in behind Marco. "This is going to be an interesting day," he told himself.

2

Casa Argenti, Florence

Alessa burst into the dining salon, strutted to the table where Nico was seated, and scolded, "Was I dreaming, or did I hear Donato say you're going with Francesca Pitti to Marco Ridolfi's betrothment celebration?"

Before replying to his sister, Nico shot a frosty glance across the table to Donato, who was munching on a raspberry pastry. "I didn't intend for Donato to announce it to the world, but yes, you probably heard him mention it." Chuckling, he added, "Although maybe you dreamed it. You do sometimes have very prophetic dreams."

Alessa squared her shoulders, set her hands on her hips, and fumed, "How can you be so foolish, dear brother, to disrespect Bianca by cavorting with Francesca Pitti?"

Nico filled a mug with cherry water, pulled a chair out from the table, and said, "Come, sit, have a drink and let me explain." Alessa angled the chair to let her face Nico, took a swig of the cool liquid, and waited for Nico's justification. He began, "I am not cavorting with Francesca. I agreed to be her escort to the ceremony at Bianca's suggestion. Francesca's father is the Ridolfi family's banker. He was invited to the event, but he can't attend because he's in Venice tending to a matter of the Ridolfi's business, so Signor Ridolfi asked Francesca to attend as her father's representative."

Requesting a young unmarried woman to stand in for her father was remarkable, but Francesca Pitti was an extraordinary woman. She was the strong-willed daughter of banker and Florentine aristocrat Luca Pitti and the person who had introduced Nico to Bianca, the woman who made his heart beat faster. Bianca understood Francesca needed an escort, and she assured Nico that she had no qualms about him accompanying Francesca to the betrothal celebration.

Nico leaned back in his chair and folded his hands in his lap. "Signor Ridolfi must know that Francesca is no ordinary woman, and this won't be her first time serving as her father's proxy. The betrothal is between Marco Ridolfi and Daniela Martone. I was told the Martone family's banker will attend, so Signor Ridolfi felt his banker also needed to have a presence. He asked Francesca to represent her father, and she agreed, but she couldn't possibly attend without an escort."

Scowling, Alessa pressed, "Doesn't Francesca have other gentlemen friends whom she could have asked... *unattached* gentlemen friends?"

Alessa's mention of unattached gave Nico pause. He and Bianca had never discussed the extent of their relationship. They weren't betrothed, but he was committed to her, and he knew she was committed to him. Maybe it was time for them to have a serious talk about their future.

While Alessa's comment distracted Nico, Joanna, Donato's wife, said to Alessa, "I may be able to answer why Francesca invited Nico. The Ridolfis and the Martones are among

Florence's most prominent and influential families. Some men would use an invitation to the celebration and closeness to those elite families as an opportunity to elevate their own social status. I've watched men make fools of themselves in similar situations, and Francesca may have wisely wanted to avoid enabling that possibility."

Donato laughed. "Are you saying she chose Nico because everyone knows he has no interest in social status?"

Joanna gave Donato's arm a halfhearted slap. "No, my dear husband, I'm saying everyone knows Nico can respect social etiquette. And Bianca knows he can be trusted."

Comforted by Joanna's explanation, Alessa asked Nico, "When do you leave? Is Francesca sending a carriage for you?"

Reaching for another pastry, Nico said, "I'll leave as soon as I finish this *torta*, and no, Francesca isn't sending a carriage. We'll leave from her palazzo." Turning to Donato, Nico asked, "Since the Uccello is supplying food for the dinner, will you be going to the villa?"

"Some of my staff should already be at the restaurant, packing wagons with food items, and when they've finished, they'll be traveling to the villa. I'll go later with a chef to be sure there are no problems with the food service. The chef at the villa intends to prepare the roasted pheasant main course himself, but I doubt that he's ever cooked for so many guests. If the dinner isn't perfect, it could reflect on the Uccello, and I can't let that happen."

After finishing his torta and brushing away a wayward crumb, Nico stood before Alessa and asked, "Am I suitably attired for a dinner with Florentine elite?" He had donned one of his finest tunics for the occasion, a deep blue silk fabric with silver buttons and trimmed with white embroidery. Alessa nodded as she inspected her brother and pulled lightly to correct the drape of the garment on his shoulders.

"Francesca should have sent her carriage for you. Since she didn't, take care to keep clear of horses and wagons splashing mud as you walk to Palazzo Pitti," Alessa cautioned. Nico smiled, thankful to have the support of a loving sister.

Outside the Chancery offices, Florence

The Florentine archbishop's elegant carriage drew the attention of everyone in Piazza della Signoria. It stopped at the Chancery offices where a coachman set steps alongside the carriage and opened its door. Moments later, Chancellor Scala appeared, climbed aboard the coach, settled into a plush red velvet seat, and greeted his friend the archbishop. "Buon giorno, Giovanni. Thank you for offering to let me travel with you." Scala scanned the coach's exquisite appointments. "I can't imagine a more comfortable means of transport."

Archbishop Diotsalvi let his gaze drift over the carriage's opulent interior. "It is a luxury I inherited from my predecessor. Its stability and your company will make this journey to Calenzano a pleasure."

Scala smiled at the compliment and asked, "Are you close with the Ridolfi family?"

"No, not at all," Diotsalvi replied. "If my memory is correct, I've met Signor Ridolfi only twice, but he's a very generous donor to the Church, so I am happy to oblige his request that I bless the betrothal of his son Marco."

The carriage passed out of the city through the Porta al Prato gate, where tax collectors were inspecting wagons coming into Florence. The taxmen stopped to gawk at the fancy vehicle heading north toward Prato. Scala returned the smile of a grinning boy seated next to a woman, probably his mother, aboard a wagon in the queue awaiting inspection. The chubby boy pointed at the stylish coach until the woman pulled his arm down and scolded him. Scala heard her say, "Not polite."

Diotsalvi asked, "And you, Bartolomeo, how did you become acquainted with Antonio Ridolfi?"

Scala waved a hand dismissively. "We are not acquainted at all. I've seen him at some public events, but we've never spoken; however I have had interactions with Marco. He's a supporter of the confraternity that donates blankets to the poor. He's a very generous and caring young man."

"Is that reason enough for you to be invited to the betrothal dinner?"

"I've asked myself that question," Scala responded.

The archbishop, who appreciated the vagaries of Florentine politics, said, half in jest, "Perhaps Antonio Ridolfi wants something from you."

Chuckling, Scala replied, "What an uncharitable comment coming from one who represents the Almighty. I have little to give, and there's little that Antonio doesn't already have. He built one of Florence's most successful merchant businesses, importing sugar."

"Merchants are always pressing for tax relief. He may intend to seek your help to lighten his burden," the archbishop suggested.

"Perhaps, but he'll be disappointed because the Chancery doesn't set tax rates."

"The Chancery may not set tax rates, but as Chancellor you have influence with those who do." Changing the subject, the archbishop asked, "Does this betrothal surprise you?"

"Not at all. It will bring together Marco Ridolfi and Daniela Martone. Nozzo Martone, Daniela's father, is an equally powerful international merchant who built an import business comparable to that of Antonio Ridolfi, but the two families don't compete because Martone imports spices, not sugar. The families will soon be dynasties because both sons, Marco and Daniela's brother Polito, are instrumental in their family businesses. The families can gain significant advantages by combining their businesses. Their partnership will create an unrivaled merchant empire."

"Does that mean you believe the betrothal is purely a business matter?" Diotsalvi asked.

Scala shook his head. "Not at all. Joining the two families will certainly have advantages for their businesses, but Marco and Daniela have known each other for many years because their mothers, Simona and Lavinia, are close. Marco and Daniela shared the same tutors as children and now they see each other at guild events. It would have been surprising if they hadn't developed affections for each other." Laughing, Scala added, "Although I can't know for certain. The Chancery tracks many things in our republic, but not the passions of Florentine youth."

Archbishop Diotsalvi said, "The Chancery has informants everywhere, Bartolomeo, so you must know who else has been invited to the celebration."

Scala laughed, "I imagine the archdiocese has its own informants, Your Excellency, so your information might be better than mine."

The archbishop displayed a knowing smile as Scala continued. "Simona Ridolfi has a sister, as does Lavinia Martone. Their families will probably attend even though they're not fond of Antonio because they're among the relatives he's exploited to expand his business. Antonio isn't close to his brothers and sisters, so I doubt that they've been invited. The only non-relatives I'm aware of, other than us, are Cantore and Prizzi, the two consuls of the merchants' guild."

Diotsalvi raised an eyebrow. "Isn't Prizzi a competitor of Antonio Ridolfi?"

"They're not business rivals," Scala replied, "but they have opposed each other in guild matters. To the surprise of many, Prizzi defeated Ridolfi in the last election for guild consul. Rumors allege guild members may have been coerced."

Outside the Ridolfi villa

Four members of the Lenzi family climbed down from their modest carriage and headed to the terrace. Tessa Lenzi whined, "I've barely taken two steps and already my shoes are covered with mud. Why can't they have this affair in the city like civilized people rather than here in the wilderness?"

In a soothing voice, Mena, her mother, advised, "Try to watch where you step, dear."

Mena's husband Berto climbed to the terrace, surveyed the vineyard and grounds surrounding the hilltop villa, and groused with indignation, "We could have had an estate like this if your scoundrel brother-in-law hadn't reneged on our partnership."

Mena sighed, "That was years ago, Berto. Aren't you ever going to forgive him?"

"Look around, Mena. I'm sure Antonio invited us only to flaunt his wealth and make us feel like peasants."

"He didn't invite us. My sister Simona invited us."

A servant coming from the villa interrupted their squabbling. "On behalf of Antonio and Simona, I bid you welcome to Villa Ridolfi. There are drinks and viands here on the terrace to help you recover from the long carriage ride." He pointed to a building in the vineyard. "Some guests are down there inspecting the winemaking facilities. You may join them if you wish. Others are at the pond watching the ducks. And, of course, if you prefer, you may rest in the villa."

"Just wine," Berto snorted and hurried to the serving table.

Tessa made a sour face, looked down at her soiled shoes, and griped, "I'm not going through any more mud." She followed her father to the table where her brother Angelo was already pouring himself a glass of wine.

Angelo took a quick drink before filling glasses for his father and sister. He glared at the colonnade overhead and the white marble columns flanking the villa's entry. "Marco is a lucky bastard. He did nothing to deserve this, yet one day he'll have it all, and today he's going to have Daniela."

"Are you jealous?" Tessa quipped.

"Jealous? Of course I'm jealous. You've seen Daniela. She's beautiful."

"And maybe she's still a virgin," Tessa taunted.

Angelo emptied his glass and poured another. "She deserves a man, not a chicken heart like Marco."

3

THE RIDOLFI VILLA

Guests with wine glasses in hand were mingling outside the villa when Nico and Francesca arrived. They climbed to the terrace and exchanged perfunctory greetings with the other guests, none of whom Nico knew. Francesca chatted briefly with the women and accepted their compliments on her dress, an earthy red silk *cotta* topped by an embroidered almond colored *giornea* overdress. Most impressive were the cotta's slit sleeves, a new style trending in Paris that Bianca referred to as *finestrella*. Bianca had told Nico she had made the dress for Francesca inspired by the one she had created for Princess Joanna of Castile.

A servant offered to give them a tour of the winemaking facility, but Francesca declined. She told Nico, "I've seen how wine is made at my uncle's vineyard. Once, when I was a young girl, my father coaxed me into a vat to join my cousins who were stomping grapes. What I remember most from that experience is scrubbing my feet nearly raw to remove the purple grape stains. After that escapade, I vowed to leave wine making to others."

Nico and Francesca spent their time before the betrothal dinner strolling through the grounds around the villa. A pathway alongside the building took them to the stable behind the villa and to a field beyond, where two roan mares were grazing on tall grass. They stopped briefly to watch the horses before continuing along the path to a duck pond. "Does your family have a villa in the countryside?" Nico asked.

"My father bought a villa in Rusciano, a village a short distance south of Florence. He wanted changes made to the building and contracted with Signor Brunelleschi to make the renovations. However, Signor Brunelleschi has other obligations and my father devotes his energy to expanding our house in the city whenever he isn't traveling, so progress at the villa has been slow. I've visited it, but I've never stayed there." Francesca looked at the expansive white stucco villa on the hilltop. "This villa is lovely, but I doubt that the Ridolfi family uses it often because it's so far from the city."

"Do you know Marco's sister, Giuliana?" Nico asked.

"Whenever Signor Ridolfi signs an important contract, he hosts a celebration and invites my father, who coaxes me to accompany him. I see Giuliana at those events. She's pleasant enough, but she's quiet and keeps to herself, so I've not gotten to know her well. Since all the talk at those gatherings is about business with attention on Marco as Antonio's gifted son, she finds those occasions boring. I don't think she has much excitement in her life."

Nico smiled at another couple walking past him on the path, and said to Francesca, "I know none of these people. What can you tell me about Marco?"

Francesca stepped back to observe Nico and said, "Marco bears a slight resemblance to you in that he has wavy black hair and an athletic build, but he's not as tall as you, and he has a cunning face like a fox. He's always serious and has never shown an interest in anything other than the family business."

"He must have at least one other interest since he's about to be betrothed." Nico's comment elicited no response from Francesca.

They paused to watch a duck dunking its head in the water repeatedly, trying to catch a tidbit. After several futile attempts, the disappointed mallard paddled away. When they resumed walking, Nico asked, "Do you know Daniela Martone?"

Francesca's eyes brightened. "She's a charming girl, passionate about music. She's skilled at playing two or three different instruments and she has a wonderful voice. I heard her sing once at a reception hosted by her mother."

"You make it seem that she and Marco are cut from different cloth."

"They've always been close friends and they are each other's confidants. Everyone needs a confidant, but they've always been more like brother and sister than lovers, although it's possible their passion has blossomed."

"Women have little control over betrothals," Nico mused.

In a sharp tone, Francesca declared, "Some women might succumb without protest, but my father knows I would flee to a convent or a brothel, were he to pledge me to a man other than one of my choosing."

Managing to spit words out in the midst of his laughter, Nico said, "Ah, Francesca, I would expect nothing less from you."

A bell sounding in the cupola above the villa summoned guests for the betrothal announcement and celebratory dinner. The building's design details impressed Nico as soon as he entered the vestibule. Frescoes of country scenes adorned the two side walls. Below them, statues of cherubs stood with open arms to welcome those entering. The central fountain in the interior garden shot water into the air higher than his head. Droplets glistened on garden fixtures close to the fountain. Statuettes farther from the fountain were in shadow, their details obscured by the gray overcast that had replaced the morning's brilliant blue sky. The smell of coming rain tainted the air.

Upon entering the peristyle, a servant guided Signorina Pitti and her escort to their assigned table, where Chancellor Scala and Archbishop Diotsalvi were already seated. Scala registered only momentary surprise at seeing Nico with Francesca Pitti. The archbishop knew Francesca as Luca Pitti's daughter, and he remembered Nico as the man who had rescued boys taken from mountain villages by rogue mercenaries, but he didn't know their relationship to each other. He knew Luca had two sisters and assumed Nico and Francesca might be cousins. Addressing Nico, he asked, "Are you Corradina's son?"

Confused by the question, Nico hesitated, but Francesca grasped the archbishop's premise immediately and responded, "Our relationship is more distant." Her rejoinder only added to Nico's confusion, but it brought a mischievous smile to Scala, who knew the two were not related. Fortunately, a guest approaching the table to confer with the archbishop ended the wordplay.

After greeting Scala and the archbishop, Francesca took leave to talk with a woman at a nearby table. Noting Nico's unfamiliarity with the guests, Scala pointed out the two guild consuls seated at a table with Signor Martone's banker, then he identified the Lenzi family and relatives of Lavinia Martone at two other tables. Scala didn't know the four men seated at another table, but from their dress and staid behavior, Nico assumed they were business associates of Antonio Ridolfi. Nico couldn't help but notice Berto Lenzi's peculiar behavior. Despite his wife's persistent efforts to engage him in conversation, Berto only responded with a grimace and single-word replies. He seemed annoyed at having to attend the celebration. Francesca returned to the table wearing a self-satisfied expression. She leaned close to Nico and whispered, "I heard some interesting gossip, which I'll share with you later."

After all the guests had been seated, Daniela, her mother, and her father came into the peristyle and took their places at the main table. An awed silence yielded to murmurs of how lovely Daniela looked in her pale-yellow damask dress matched in color by the ribbons woven through her braided hair. She stayed close to her mother and refrained from making eye contact with anyone in the room, which Nico interpreted as signs of nervousness. Understandable, he thought. Moments later, Daniela's brother, Polito, appeared and seated himself next to his mother.

Antonio Ridolfi strutted into the peristyle, displaying an expression that some later described as officious. Behind him, Simona entered arm-in-arm with her daughter, Giuliana. Her gaze flitted across the room, still fearful she might find something amiss. Giuliana's eyes focused directly ahead, and she walked stiffly, as though in a trance. Could she find even this significant event boring? Marco wasn't with his family. Nico speculated that if Marco had inherited his father's vanity, he might intend to make a dramatic entrance.

Custom called for Nozzo Martone to begin the ceremony by pledging his daughter to Marco Ridolfi and describing the dowry he offered to bind the union of the betrothed. Antonio Ridolfi would then accept Signor Martone's petition on behalf of his son. But the ceremony could not begin without Marco Ridolfi being present. Antonio's frustration with Marco's absence intensified with each passing second. He could accept that commitment triggered anxiety in other men, but not in Marco, not in a Ridolfi. Antonio waited less than a minute before pounding his fist on the table and dispatching a servant to locate his tardy son. The servant beckoned two allies to help him search the villa.

Antonio was fuming when the servant returned, bent low, and whispered into Antonio's ear. Everyone heard the patriarch's retort, "That cannot be!" as he jumped up and bolted to the wing of the villa that held the sleeping quarters. Guests sat bewildered until another servant appeared and whispered to a third. Even though he spoke softly, people at a nearby table overheard his words and repeated them. Like lightning, the news flashed across the room: Marco Ridolfi was dead.

4

Simona Ridolfi stared with wide eyes at the servant, unable to believe what she had heard. Daniela shuddered and turned to her mother, Lavinia, who clasped her daughter's arm and pulled her close in a tight embrace. Nozzo Martone moved close to his daughter, put his arm around her, and searched in vain for words to console the stunned girl. Rumors and speculation racing around the room ended when Antonio Ridolfi's reappearance birthed a grim silence, filled only by his footfalls reverberating off smooth marble walls. He shuffled forward, his head down, his arrogance gone. "No. Oh, God, no," Simona wailed upon seeing her husband. With both arms extended toward Antonio, she willed an embrace that could vanquish the horror.

With other guests uncertain how to react, Chancellor Scala approached the servant who had brought the news and demanded to know what happened. In a quivering voice, the servant said, "We found Signor Marco on the floor in one of the bedchambers. His clothes are stained with blood."

Scala strode to the main table and conferred with Signor

Ridolfi. At Scala's urging, Ridolfi ushered his wife from the room, then Scala announced in a commanding voice, "Marco Ridolfi may have been killed." After the guests' shocked gasps subsided, Scala continued, "The village of Calenzano is outside the jurisdiction of the Florentine Guardia, so the investigation of this atrocity falls under the auspices of the Florentine Security Commission." Scala knew it was the army that had the authority to investigate crimes committed outside the city of Florence, but he also knew it would take hours for the army to be notified and respond. Action was needed immediately, so Scala pointed to Nico and said, "Messer Argenti is a member of the Security Commission. He will assume charge of the investigation."

When the Florentine Security Commission was formed two years ago, Scala had appointed Nico as one of the three members because he'd witnessed Nico's father, as a Florentine army legate, contend with foreign diplomats under trying circumstances, and he believed Nico possessed the same ethos. Scala's conviction was affirmed by Nico's boldness during commission assignments that had called for him to confront rogue mercenaries and insurrectionists.

Startled at being designated as the overseer, Nico collected his thoughts as he rose. All eyes fell on the tall dark-haired man, unknown to nearly everyone, who walked to the main table and stood beside Scala. The commotion had drawn servants from other parts of the villa and the kitchen staff to the peristyle. Surveying the crowd, Nico realized that if Marco Ridolfi had been killed, then one of the people facing him might be a murderer. Nico wasn't trained as an investigator, but he had seen his fellow Security Commission member and renowned Guardia investigator, Vittorio Colombo, take control at crime scenes. Recalling Vittorio's approach, he called to his cousin standing with the kitchen staff, "Donato, I need the names of everyone here at the villa: guests, staff, your workers, and the carriage drivers. Everyone. No one is to leave until you have their names." Donato nodded, but stood firm, expecting Nico might have more tasks for him.

Berto Lenzi pounded his fist on the table and bellowed, "You can't keep us here!" His outburst brought gasps from those near him and drew every eye in the peristyle, first to him and then to the young man standing beside Chancellor Scala.

Berto's first clue that Messer Nico Argenti had graduated in the first rank at the University of Bologna and knew the dictates of Florentine law came from Nico's firm retort, a defiant, "Yes, I can." Nico's assertive declaration surprised even himself. The room fell silent, waiting for Berto's response, which did not come. Stung by Nico's reproach, he lowered himself onto his chair and muttered through a bitter sneer. Berto had always dismissed stories of the Florentine Security Commission prosecuting Florentine citizens as exaggerations, but he had no intention of becoming the Commission's next target in the event those stories were true.

To forestall any further objections, Nico addressed the tall, brawny, bear-like member of Donato's staff. "Orsino, see that no one leaves the villa until Donato has recorded their names."

Orsino grasped what Nico wanted but was unsure how to fulfill the request. Seeing Orsino's uncertainty, Donato quietly gave a few instructions to the big man standing near him, who then made his way towards the back of the villa where the carriages were parked. From the group of servants standing together at the far side of the peristyle, Nico pointed to a powerfully built man. "What's your name?"

A husky voice replied, "Dego."

"Dego, go to the room where Marco Ridolfi was found and make sure no one enters that room." Dego gave a quick nod and scurried away.

As Donato began listing the guests' names, he purposely made his way through the room such that Berto Lenzi would be the last one he reached. Let the pompous cretin wait, Donato told himself. Hearing his cousin taking control brought a warm smile to Donato's face. He'd heard the accounts of Nico confronting assassins and mercenaries, but witnessing his cousin's leadership was a first for him.

Nozzo Martone had his arms wrapped around Daniela and her mother, attempting to comfort the two trembling women. Nico directed one of the female servants to take Signorina Martone and her family to a salon where she could settle her feelings; then he turned to Chancellor Scala. "No one is more adept at finding clues than Vittorio. I need to send someone to fetch him. A carriage would be too slow; it must be someone who can go on horseback."

Giuliana Ridolfi, who was sitting within earshot, announced, "I can go. I can ride as well as anyone." She looked up at Nico with determination in her eyes. Giuliana, whom Francesca had described as quiet and reserved, demonstrated astonishing strength in the face of her brother's murder.

Despite her apparent eagerness to find justice for her brother, Nico wasn't open to sending the young woman alone on a journey to Florence, but before he could dismiss her proposal, Francesca, who was also nearby, intervened. "I can go with her." Nico shot a quick glance at Chancellor Scala, whose expression confirmed the decision was Nico's. He hesitated, biting his lip, until the resolve of the two women standing side-by-side convinced him they could make the eight-mile ride to the Florentine Chancery safely.

Nico was about to urge caution when he noticed Francesca's sly grin. She expected his warning; nonetheless, he said, "Be careful and stop for no one." The two self-assured women hurried from the peristyle toward the stable behind the villa, detouring only briefly to Giuliana's quarters to change into riding clothes.

Feeling a presence behind him, Nico turned to face Archbishop Diotsalvi who said, "I need to bring the Lord's comfort to Signora Ridolfi, and I must give Marco a final blessing."

"Of course, Your Excellency. Chancellor Scala and I are going to view the body; you may join us and after you bless Marco, you can console the Ridolfi family." Nico regretted his words. He always thought it heartless to refer to a deceased person as *the body*, especially when the person was an acquaintance. He could take solace in believing that Marco's soul was with the Lord.

Dego was standing guard at the entry of the bedchamber where Marco Ridolfi lay when Scala, Archbishop Diotsalvi, and Nico appeared. The coppery odor of blood repulsed the men as soon as they entered the room. Following Nico's request, they touched nothing to avoid destroying any possible clues.

The archbishop leaned close, made the sign of the cross over Marco's forehead, and began reciting, "Per istam sanctam unctionem ..." Nico and Chancellor Scala stood back until the priest had finished administering last rites.

The body lay face down, stretched out on the floor alongside the bed. Blood from a wound on the side of Marco's head had pooled on the floor. A smear of blood covered the corner of the nightstand next to the bed. Vittorio might find other explanations, but to Nico's untrained eye, it appeared Marco had fallen and hit his head on the nightstand. Based on the descriptions he had heard from Massimo about soldiers killed in battle, Nico found it surprising that there was so little blood. Scala said, "A healthy young man doesn't suddenly fall and strike his head," and asked rhetorically, "What happened here?"

What indeed, Nico wondered, hoping the question would

be answered when Vittorio arrived. From the bedchamber, the three men went to the salon where Antonio Ridolfi was endeavoring to comfort his distraught wife. The archbishop entered the room, sat facing Simona Ridolfi and began reciting a prayer. Upon hearing his words, her sobbing lessened. Nico and Chancellor Scala remained outside the room, having decided it best not to intrude on Marco's grieving parents.

5

Giuliana returned to the villa with Vittorio. They left their horses with a servant, and she led Vittorio to the peristyle. Road dust blanketed her dress, and the wind had tousled her hair. She moved unsteadily, her shoulders slumped and her energy drained after two hours on horseback, but her determined expression showed satisfaction at having completed her mission. A maid took hold of Giuliana's arm, afraid the poor girl might collapse, and helped her to a room where she could recover. Francesca had elected to remain in Florence. Nico felt he couldn't detain all the guests, so most of them had already left the villa. They had been eager to leave the site of the tragedy as quickly as possible. Archbishop Diotsalvi remained at the villa, dividing his time between the Ridolfi and Martone families.

At the chef's urging, some servants had gathered in the peristyle to enjoy the food that had been prepared for the celebration dinner. Serving tables held trays filled with far more food than they could consume. The chef paced back and forth, fretting over what to do with the large amount of food that would remain after the servants had their fill. Feeling sympathy toward the poor man, Donato kindly offered to take the roast pheasants to the Uccello. He suggested that the remaining food be donated to the convent in nearby Calenzano.

While escorting Vittorio to the bedchamber holding Marco's body, Nico told his colleague what he had done after the body was discovered. "I prevented anyone from leaving the villa until we had a record of all their names, both the guests and the workers. And I posted a guard so no one could enter the room where Marco had been killed."

When Nico finished, Vittorio said, "You did well. It would have been helpful for me to have seen the guests' expressions and mannerisms. Guilty people often exhibit telltale signs, but I realize you couldn't have kept everyone here. The names you collected will tell us whom to question later."

A quick scan of the room where Marco had been slain assured Vittorio that there were no obstructions on the floor that Marco might have stumbled on. "He fell and struck his head on the side table," Vittorio said, confirming the conclusion reached by Nico and Chancellor Scala. "However," Vittorio cautioned, "when a person stumbles and falls, his arms are usually extended and his hands are away from his body. But that's not the case here. Marco's hands are under his chest as though they were holding something.

"His position, facedown with his head near the nightstand and his feet closer to the doorway, and droplets of water on the nightstand suggest he was facing the nightstand, possibly washing himself, when he fell. But if he was standing there washing, why did he collapse? And why did he fall to the side rather than forward?"

Vittorio knelt and scanned the floor, looking for clues, and noticed a snippet of cloth extended out from under the body. He pulled it gently to ease it free, held it up for Nico to see, and announced, "A washing cloth." Finding nothing else, he said to Nico, "Help me turn him over. Take hold of his arm and keep his hand in position as we turn him." The confined space between the bed and the nightstand made it awkward to rotate the body. Nico lay across the bed with his arms extending over its side so he could reach down and grasp the body. As soon as Marco was turned face up, Vittorio announced, "He was strangled." Pointing to a red mark wrapping across Marco's throat, Vittorio said, "That wound was made by something flat, not round like a rope. Judging from the width of the groove, I would say it was most likely made by a leather strap. Marco's hands were at his neck, trying to loosen the strap that was pulled tight by someone behind him ... by the murderer."

Nico stood and said, "Marco must have had a passionate enemy, someone vicious enough to turn his betrothal celebration into a spectacle."

In his customary non-committal manner, Vittorio responded with a simple "Perhaps." He took one last look around the room, then said, "We should speak with the person closest to Marco Ridolfi."

"That would be Antonio, his father," Nico said and led Vittorio toward the room where Antonio had taken his distraught wife.

They heard voices ahead and in a dimly lit alcove outside the bedchamber, they found the archbishop sitting with Antonio, who said, "Simona became nearly hysterical. I couldn't calm her, so I sent for a doctor from Calenzano. He's with her now. I'm not sure she will ever recover."

"And you?" Nico asked, "Will you come through this tragedy?"

Antonio pressed a hand against his forehead and exhaled forcefully. "I don't know. Marco was more than any father could expect in a son. He was thoughtful, kind, and insightful. I trusted his judgement in business more than my own. I may survive this tragedy, but I'll never be the same without him."

Nico introduced Vittorio, who pulled a chair next to Antonio. The villa, now devoid of all the guests, had become incredibly quiet, so that even the slight creaking of the chair as Vittorio settled onto it could be heard echoing in the confined space. The investigator began, "I know this is a difficult time, but if we are to find the person who attacked Marco, we must act quickly, and to do that, I need information." Antonio folded his hands in his lap and looked at Vittorio expectantly. "Did Marco have any enemies, someone capable of doing this?" Vittorio asked. Antonio's blank stare prompted Vittorio to press further. "Did he gamble?"

Antonio shook his head vigorously. "No. No. Marco had no life other than the business. Business was all he thought about. Even this partnership with the Martones was Marco's idea. He believed we could realize significant savings by sharing agents, warehouse space, and ships with the Martones."

"There must be other potential partners. Why did Marco decide on the Martones?" Nico asked.

"We and the Martones import different products, so we don't compete directly. They've been in business for many years, nearly as many as us, and they've always been successful. When Marco first suggested the partnership to me, he had records that showed the Martones' profits have been increasing. He believed by partnering with them, we could reap the rewards of their newfound efficiency."

Although betrothals motivated strictly by business were common, Nico wondered whether business interests were Marco's only motivation. "Daniela ..." he began.

Before Nico could frame his question, Antonio said, "Marco saw the betrothal as cementing the partnership. Daniela is a delightful girl. Her mother Lavinia and my wife are both active in a church group that helps the poor. Their friendship brought the two children together when they were toddlers. As the youngsters grew, so did their fondness for each other. While the business partnership may have sped up the engagement, I'm confident it would have happened anyway. Daniela and Marco picked the date, they chose to have the announcement celebration at the villa, and they decided whom to invite." Antonio's expression turned to anguish. He bent forward, supporting his head in his hands, and whimpered, "They would have had a gratifying union."

Antonio's phrase "gratifying union" stunned Nico. Whenever he dreamed of his future with Bianca, he imagined having a loving relationship, not merely a gratifying union. Surely Marco and Daniela must have expected an intimate relationship as well.

Antonio stated firmly, "I'm certain the intent of this horrific act was to prevent the partnership."

After considering Antonio's comment, Vittorio asked, "You control the family business, so why would someone attack Marco rather than you?"

"I may have the ultimate authority, but Marco has ... had a keen sense of the business. The partnership was his idea."

"Will the partnership be canceled?" Nico asked.

In a quavering voice, Antonio replied, "I don't know."

Vittorio said. "Someone who was here at the villa committed the crime, and all the guests were here at your invitation. Who among them might hold such strong opposition to the partnership that they would resort to violence to prevent it?"

Antonio spread his hands in a resigned gesture and repeated, "I don't know." Vittorio's expression showed his skepticism.

After offering their condolences, Nico and Vittorio made

their way back to the peristyle, each man mulling over Antonio's statements. Scanning the large space mostly empty now except for the few servants who were still eating, Nico observed, "It's disappointing that Signor Ridolfi wasn't helpful in identifying any potential culprits among the guests."

Vittorio pointed out, "It's always difficult for people to imagine their friends and acquaintances as killers. And the killer might not have been a guest. He might be a servant or a worker enlisted by an enemy of Marco or Antonio."

Nico asked, "Do you believe Marco was killed to prevent the business merger?"

"That's a starting point," Vittorio replied. "Antonio may believe the partnership was the motive, but he wasn't forthcoming in naming his enemies. No one builds a prosperous business like his without abusing competitors and attracting jealous foes."

A wave of doubt swept over Nico as he considered the potential breadth of the investigation. "How can we ...," he let his voice trail off and his question hang.

To ease Nico's concern, Vittorio said, "Since Antonio appears unable or unwilling to name his adversaries, we'll need to interview his employees to get that information."

Nico stopped in mid-stride, rubbed his chin, and said, "Do you suppose Antonio will try to find Marco's killer himself?"

"I'm certain he will, as soon as he recovers from the shock of his son's murder," Vittorio declared. "And if Antonio finds the killer before we do, it will result in further violence."

6

CALENZANO

To give Vittorio an understanding of the circumstances at the time of the murder, Nico closed his eyes to recall what the guests and servants had been doing when they assembled in the peristyle for dinner. Berto Lenzi's behavior toward his wife had drawn everyone's attention. One minute he totally ignored her and the next he was taunting her. Berto was also the person who had objected vehemently to being kept in place while Donato recorded the guests' names. Nico described those incidents to Vittorio and suggested that they question Signor Lenzi when they returned to Florence.

Vittorio said, "It would be good to gather more information before interviewing him. It's rarely helpful to interrogate suspects without knowing whether they're being truthful. Without a way to gauge their honesty, they simply deny having any involvement in the crime, and worse, when they realize they're under suspicion, they try to destroy evidence."

Vittorio gestured toward the table where the servants were eating and said, "I'm going to question those men before their memories fade." At Vittorio's suggestion, Nico opted to return to Florence to interview other guests who might know the reason for Lenzi's anger.

Vittorio listened to the men's conversation as he approached the table where they were eating. Their banter hinted at close friendship and strong camaraderie. He introduced himself as a member of the Florentine Security Commission and said, "You seem to know each other well. How long have you been employed by Signor Ridolfi?"

A man with graying hair and lines at his eyes responded, "We've been together since Signor Ridolfi bought this villa nearly six years ago."

"Do you all work here at the villa even when the Ridolfis are in Florence?"

"Yes, there are always chores to be done. Most of us keep busy in the vineyard; a few others care for the horses and the gardens."

"Are there any new workers who have joined you recently?"

The gray-haired man replied, "One man. Ugo. He works in the stable."

"How long has Ugo been working at the villa?"

"A few weeks. Maybe two or three."

"Is he here today?"

"I don't know, but the stable master could tell you."

"Are there any other new workers, or is Ugo the only one?"

The servants exchanged glances, nodded, then one replied, "None other than Ugo."

Before going to the stable, Vittorio had additional questions for Antonio Ridolfi. He found Antonio, Simona, and Giuliana on the terrace heading toward their carriage that would take them back to Florence. Upon seeing Vittorio, Antonio stepped away from Simona, approached the investigator, and explained, "My wife is impatient to leave. She has memories of other unpleasant incidents that happened here, and now she's become convinced the villa is cursed." He glanced around quickly, then said with a hint of regret, "I'll have to sell it because she'll never come here again." Still scanning the gardens, he said, "I've sent for a funeral director to take Marco's body to Florence, where we can have a mass for him at Basilica San Lorenzo."

Vittorio nodded respectfully. "I won't keep you. I have just a few more questions. Marco was in the room alone when he was attacked from behind. Why had he gone to the room by himself?"

"The dessert following the dinner was to be lemon custard. Lemon custard was Marco's favorite, but he was particular about the taste. It had to have just the right amount of lemon flavoring. Too much and it becomes bitter. We had just entered the peristyle when the chef brought a sample of the dessert for Marco to taste, to be certain it was satisfactory. Someone accidentally bumped into Marco, causing him to smear dabs of custard on his chin and neck. He went back to the bedchamber to clean himself."

Vittorio reasoned that the killer followed Marco to the bedchamber, so he must have witnessed the mishap, surmised Marco would be alone, and seized the opportunity. He asked, "Who bumped into Marco?"

"One of the servants. I don't remember which one. He was carrying a food tray," Antonio replied, then noticed his wife standing beside the carriage, glowering at him. "Excuse me, Signor Colombo, but my wife is growing agitated. If you have more questions for me, come to my office in Florence tomorrow."

Vittorio returned to the bedchamber for one last look at the body before it would be taken by the funeral director. He pulled the bed aside so he could get down on the floor to inspect the body. His close examination revealed three depressions spaced evenly along the wound. Studs, Vittorio realized. Metal studs were a popular way of styling men's belts. Unfortunately, it wasn't possible to tell what type of metal had made the marks. Servants' belts typically had bronze studs, while belts worn by the wealthy guests would have silver studs. Nonetheless, the finding confirmed Vittorio's assumption that the killer had seen Marco returning alone to the bedchamber as an opportunity and, lacking any other weapon, used his belt to strangle Marco. Vittorio placed a sheet of paper alongside the wound on Marco's neck and marked the paper corresponding to the distances between the depressions made by the studs. Then he made sketches of the diamond-shaped depressions. Although the sketches were crude, he thought they might be helpful in identifying the belt used to strangle Marco. Belts often featured circular shapes as their decorative designs. Diamond shaped designs were unusual.

7

When Vittorio had arrived with Giuliana, they'd dismounted at the front of the villa and left their horses with a servant, so he hadn't seen the stable, but he assumed it was at the rear of the villa. He began walking toward the front of the villa, intending to go outside and walk around the building. But before he left the peristyle, a servant intercepted him, pointed toward the kitchen and said, "There is a shorter way to the stable. The kitchen receives food through a rear entrance, which also provides access to the stable. Come this way." The man walked ahead, with Vittorio following.

The earthy smell of hay and the scent of horses enveloped Vittorio when he stepped into the stable. Sunlight seeping through gaps in the wooden walls illuminated dust particles suspended in the air. Sounds of horses shifting and snorting overlaid the soft creaking of the large wooden structure. Vittorio's footsteps rustling the straw-covered floor added to the ambient sounds. As he moved forward, his gaze shifted from one horse to another. Even his untrained eye could tell they were all well-cared-for animals.

Ahead, he heard someone brushing a horse and when he got closer, he recognized the horse as the one he had ridden from Florence. "Is this your horse?" the man asked when he spotted Vittorio. "I've watered and brushed him. He'll be ready for you as soon as I put on his saddle."

"Yes, it's my horse, but I didn't expect you to groom him."

The man gave a dismissive wave. "I know you rode him hard to get here as quickly as possible, and horses should always be cared for after they're ridden."

Vittorio asked, "Are you the stable master?"

"I am."

Vittorio introduced himself as a member of the Florentine Security Commission investigating Marco Ridolfi's murder and asked, "Did a man named Ugo come to work for you recently?"

"Yes, Ugo came here two weeks ago and said he needed a job. I put him to work, mostly mucking the stables."

"Is he here now?"

"He was here earlier, but he's gone now. I give him chores to do each day and when the chores are done, he leaves."

"What made him come to the villa for work? Did a member of the staff recommend him?"

"I think he just came on his own. He didn't say that he knew anyone working here."

"Where can I find him?"

"I think he said he has a room in Calenzano."

"What does he look like? Describe him."

"There's nothing unusual about him." The stable master studied Vittorio and said, "He's shorter than you ... and thinner. That's all I can say."

When the stable master finished tacking the horse, Vittorio rode downhill, crossed a small stream, then climbed toward Calenzano, a hilltop village fortified by a robust stone wall with angular towers and crowned with battlements. He passed through the town wall at Portaccia, the southern gate, and continued to the abbey adjoining the church of San Nicolò. The unattended vestibule held only a small table against one wall. Vittorio called out to announce his presence and soon heard footsteps shuffling toward him in an adjacent hallway. A priest wearing a gray robe that matched his smoky-gray hair appeared in the doorway and said in a fragile voice, "How may I help you, my son?"

"I am looking for a man named Ugo and I'm told he lives in Calenzano. Priests usually know everyone who lives in small towns, so I'm hoping you can tell me where to find him."

The priest shook his head. "There is no one named Ugo in my parish. It's possible he belongs to another parish." Cracking a slight smile, he added, "But as you said, priests eventually come to know everyone, and I don't know of anyone called Ugo. Even if he belonged to another parish, I would know of him unless he's new to the village."

"He's been working at Villa Ridolfi for the past two weeks, so he may be a newcomer."

The priest said slowly, "Ah, if he's a newcomer, he might be living with relatives outside the town." Rubbing his chin, he added, "Or he could be staying at the inn, Locanda Rustico." Noting Vittorio's quizzical expression, the priest said, "The inn is on the road connecting Florence and Prato. You passed it if you came from Florence."

Vittorio recalled seeing the large two-level stone structure near the turnoff to Calenzano. Rather than ask every family in the town and at nearby farms if they had a relative named Ugo visiting, he opted to begin his inquiry at the nearby inn. He dismounted at the front of the inn and walked around to the side where a woman picking vegetables in a garden greeted him, saying. "My husband isn't here, but I can help you if you're looking for a room."

"I'm looking for a man named Ugo who may have been staying here for the past two weeks."

The woman put down the basket she had been holding, wiped her hands, and said, "There was a man named Ugo staying here, but he's gone. He left earlier today. He said his mother had been taken ill, and he had to be with her." Rising to her feet, she inquired, "May I know why you're interested in him?"

Vittorio explained he was a member of the Security Commission investigating a murder at the Ridolfi's villa. The stunned woman instinctively blessed herself. "Mother of God!" she exclaimed. "In the village?" she asked.

"At the Ridolfi family villa."

"The stories must be true. The villa is cursed," she said and again blessed herself. Vittorio told her that Signor Marco Ridolfi had been killed. A mix of emotions played across her face from shock to deep sadness. Finally, in words heavy with the weight of the tragedy, the woman said, "That has never happened before in our community."

Vittorio waited until she regained her composure, then asked, "Do you know Ugo's full name?"

In an unsteady voice, she replied, "I think he said his family name is Fornelli. I'm not certain. He wasn't a talkative person and only mentioned his name once."

"Did he say where he was going?"

"No, only that he had to leave."

"Is he planning to return? Did he leave anything in his room, something that might tell where he went?"

"He didn't say whether he'd return." The woman lifted the basket of vegetables, headed toward the inn, and signaled for

Vittorio to join her. "We could see if he left anything." Vittorio followed her up a stone staircase to the inn's second level. "This was his room," she said as she pushed the door open. Vittorio stepped inside the sparse space and noted immediately there was nothing that would help him find Ugo Fornelli. There were no personal items, not even a scrap on the small desk in the corner of the room.

"Did Signor Fornelli say why he came to Calenzano?"

"He didn't talk much. He said only that he was looking for work."

"Calenzano is a small town. Do many people come here looking for work?"

"Men come to pick grapes in the vineyards around the town, but it's too early for that. The grapes won't be ready for harvest for another month."

Vittorio stepped out into the hallway, and, as he turned to leave, he asked a last question. "Is there anyone else who might have spoken with him?"

"Only my son. He took care of Signor Fornelli's horse. He's in the stable behind the inn." As Vittorio walked away, she said, "Please don't tell him about the murder." Vittorio assured her he would not.

A boy about ten years old was spreading straw bedding in a stall when Vittorio entered the barn that served as a stable. Noting the clean bedding in other stalls and grooming supplies neatly arranged in a corner of the barn, Vittorio said, "It's not easy for someone your age to take care of horses."

Without pausing, the boy said proudly, "I've been tending horses since I was little."

"Your mother said you looked after the horse of a guest named Ugo Fornelli."

The boy's eyes brightened. "I did and when he left, he

thanked me for taking care of his horse by giving me a denaro coin."

"Did he say where he was going when he left the inn?"

The boy's nose scrunched up in a puzzled expression and he said hesitantly, "He might have mentioned Florence. I was busy getting his horse ready, so I wasn't listening carefully."

Vittorio had scant information to begin an investigation. He wasn't sure whether Ugo had gone to Florence and he was uncertain about Ugo's family name, but Vittorio had begun investigations with less. When he had first joined the Guardia, he was tasked with finding a man who had viciously assaulted a woman. The woman had gotten only a brief glimpse of her assailant's face and remembered that his only distinguishing feature was a prominent mole under his right eye. With that little information, Vittorio's colleagues claimed it would be impossible to find the offender in the city of ninety thousand people. They claimed it would be wasted effort to hunt for the attacker, but Vittorio was unrelenting. He interviewed nuns at San Matteo hospital, where the woman was recovering, and they told him of another woman who had been attacked previously. Upon questioning the nuns further, Vittorio found that details of the two attacks were similar and led him to believe there might be more cases. He went to Santa Maria, Florence's oldest and largest hospital, where he learned of three other women who had been beaten while walking alone on one of the city's narrow streets. By interviewing all the women, he learned they bore scars from a weighty ring worn on the attacker's right hand, and that the thug reeked of alcohol and had slurred speech.

Knowing only that the man had a conspicuous mole, that he wore a large ring, and that he was a heavy drinker, Vittorio made queries in taverns throughout Florence until he found the culprit. That success earned Vittorio the title *Il Primo,* number one, among his peers. Bolstered by that accomplishment and his many achievements that followed, Vittorio was confident he could locate the man with a name like Ugo Fornelli.

8

FLORENCE

After discussing with Vittorio how best to approach Berto Lenzi, Nico opted to begin his search into Lenzi's background by meeting with Signor Cantore, one of the guild members who had attended the ill-fated betrothal dinner. Like Ridolfi and Martone, Cantore was an importer. His specialties were unique glass objects crafted by Venetian glassblowers. Florence had glassblowers, but they lacked the knowledge their Venetian counterparts had perfected and kept secret for two centuries. Cantore, Ridolfi, and Martone belonged to the same guild. Although known as the Physicians and Pharmacists Guild, its members also included barbers, funeral directors, and glassblowers, plus spice, sugar, pigment, and glass merchants.

Cantore owned a small shop away from the center of the city in the San Giovanni quarter. He had chosen the outlying location to avoid attention from Florentine glassblowers, who resented his importing of foreign glassware. However, even with his remote location, the affluent Florentine elite actively sought him out to purchase his exceptional products.

Upon entering the shop, Nico scanned the items arrayed on

shelves behind a counter and beyond the reach of any clumsy customer's hands. His gaze rested on a set of clear glass goblets. Venetian artists had developed a technique for making transparent glass, whereas Florentine glass always had a slight green tint. Florentine glassblowers claimed the transparency came from Venetian sand being superior to Tuscan sand. One shelf held a collection of animal figurines, each as shiny and clear as crystal. An apprentice approached Nico. "Buon giorno, Signore. I see you're admiring our beautiful goblets crafted by one of Venice's most experienced and talented artisans."

"They are beautiful," Nico agreed, "but today I'm hoping to speak with Signor Cantore."

"Certainly, Signore. He's in the next room. Please wait a moment while I get him."

Nico introduced himself when Cantore came into the showroom, although the introduction was unnecessary, as the merchant remembered Nico from the previous day. He escorted Nico into his office and bid him be seated. "I'm investigating Marco Ridolfi's murder, and I'm hoping you can help me," Nico said to explain the reason for his visit.

Cantore knew that Marco Ridolfi had died unexpectedly, yet he shuddered at the word murder and said in an uncertain voice, "You've determined that someone killed him? It wasn't an accident?"

Having no reason to withhold the truth, Nico said, "Marco Ridolfi was strangled."

Cantore crossed himself. "The poor soul was sent to the Lord before his time ... and on the day of his betrothal. How horrible. I can't believe anyone would do such a thing." Then Cantore's brow furrowed in puzzlement. "How do you believe I can help find his killer?"

"We are still gathering information about the guests. I was told that Marco's uncle, Berto Lenzi, is a member of your guild.

The guild welcomes men with a broad range of skills. Do you know the nature of Signor Lenzi's business?"

"He's a sugar merchant, like Antonio Ridolfi."

"Are the two competitors?"

"It would seem so, but I don't know for certain. Sugar is sold in apothecaries, so a pharmacist would be the one to answer that question."

"Pharmacists also belong to your guild. Can you name one I could speak with who might know both men?"

As he thought, Cantore said flatly, "There are so many pharmacies." He ran a hand through his hair as he searched for a name, then said, "The pharmacy in Piazza San Lorenzo does a thriving business and it's been selling sugar since I was a boy. Perhaps the owner of that shop can help you." As Nico turned to leave, Cantore wondered why Nico wanted information about Berto Lenzi. Did he believe Lenzi killed Marco Ridolfi?

Nico had already left the shop when Cantore rushed into the street and called to him. "I remember something." He paused, suddenly unsure whether he should repeat a story that was hardly more than a rumor. Nico retraced his steps and stood facing Cantore. "Last year, one of Lenzi's agents went missing." Cantore went silent for a minute, then said, "What I heard is that the man simply vanished." Cantore shrugged to show he had nothing further, turned, and went back to his shop, leaving Nico puzzled.

Nico found the pharmacy; although it wasn't in piazza San Lorenzo, it was on a small side street extending from the piazza toward the cathedral. A thin man wearing a smock spotted with dabs of colored paints was examining a selection of pigments arrayed on the counter when Nico entered the shop. The clerk, a young man with curly light brown hair, came to where Nico was standing, gestured toward the artist, and said, "He comes here nearly every week to buy pigments, and he is always slow to choose. May I help you while he is deciding?"

Nico judged the pharmacist to be about his own age, so he doubted that the man would have knowledge of Signor Lenzi's business practices; nonetheless, he introduced himself as a member of the Florentine Security Commission and asked, "Does your shop purchase sugar from Signor Berto Lenzi?"

Unsure, the young man shrugged and said, "I don't know. My father makes all the purchases. I'll ask him." He stepped through a doorway into an office behind the display room and returned moments later, trailed by an older man.

"You have a question about Berto Lenzi?" the older man asked.

Again, Nico introduced himself and asked whether the shop purchased sugar from Signor Lenzi. "Yes, we do," the man said without elaboration.

"Do you also purchase sugar from Signor Antonio Ridolfi?" The man nodded. "Since both are sugar merchants, why do you buy from both of them?" Nico asked.

"Their products are very different. Ridolfi imports the sugar from Egypt. His is the finest quality, but it is also expensive. Lenzi gets his sugar in Sicily; it's an inferior grade but lower in cost. My business caters to a wide variety of customers, each with their own preferences and financial means, so I sell both products."

Reflecting on the man's response, Nico said, almost to himself, "So, Lenzi and Ridolfi are not competitors."

"They may see themselves as competitors, even though I do not." The pharmacist raised a finger to emphasize his next statement. "When they began their business ventures many years ago, the two men worked together importing sugar from

Sicily. I don't know the details of that arrangement, but it ended when Antonio started importing from Egypt."

"Did their collaboration end amicably?"

"I didn't pry into their affairs, but now the two men never speak of each other. Maybe that's telling. Antonio has expanded his business and become one of Florence's most successful merchants, while Berto's business has stagnated. Who wouldn't be surprised if Berto were jealous?"

Jealousy, a motive that frequently drives people to commit murder, Nico thought as he left the apothecary shop. But why would a business split that occurred many years ago cause Lenzi to kill Marco Ridolfi now?

9

Nico found Massimo pacing across the Chancery meeting room when he entered. It was the same conference room where he had first met Massimo and Vittorio when Chancellor Scala invited the three men to join the newly conceived Florentine Security Commission. The assignment brought together Massimo, a decorated army officer, Vittorio, a renowned Guardia investigator, and young Nico only weeks after receiving his law degree from the University of Bologna. "We have chairs, my friend. You needn't wear out your boots by pacing the floor while you read," Nico teased.

"Soldiers need to be in motion," Massimo responded. "Were I to sit all the time, I'd grow pudgy like the Chancery clerks." He shot a sheepish glance at the doorway, hoping his remark hadn't been overheard by a clerk passing by in the hallway. Waving the collection of papers he had been reading, he said, "And were I to sit while reading these, I'd soon be asleep. These routine embassy reports rarely contain matters of substance."

Chancellor Scala caught Massimo's comment as he slipped

into the room and said, "Be thankful our ambassadors aren't burdened with serious matters, because their concerns become our problems to solve." He looked past Massimo's embarrassed expression and changed the subject, saying to Nico, "I commend you for taking control of the unruly crowd yesterday and starting the search for Marco Ridolfi's attacker ... and especially for your skillful handling of Signor Lenzi."

Looking at Nico and Vittorio, Scala asked, "Did you make any progress in finding the killer?"

Seeing Vittorio gesturing for him to begin, Nico said, "Vittorio determined Marco had been strangled by a leather belt, but we found no clues pointing to the killer."

Vittorio raised a hand to interrupt. "We can announce publicly that Signor Ridolfi had been strangled, but I suggest we not divulge that the killing was done with a leather belt. Often it proves useful to withhold details."

Nico continued, "Signor Ridolfi believes the murder was committed to thwart his business partnership with Signor Martone. Whether or not that's true doesn't help us find the killer. We decided our best course was to interview the men who attended the celebration, so Vittorio remained at the villa questioning the workers while I returned to Florence and began delving into Berto Lenzi's background." Nico related his conversation with the guild consul, who told him that one of Lenzi's agents had gone missing. "According to the consul, the agent simply vanished. It could be helpful to know whether Signor Lenzi had a role in the man's disappearance." Turning to Massino, he said, "I'd welcome your help in learning more about Signor Lenzi before we confront him." Massimo responded with a nod. Nico spread his hands to show he had nothing further to report.

Vittorio began, "Earlier, I paid a visit to Antonio Ridolfi to ask him questions that arose when I was questioning the villa workers. While we were meeting, Camello, the villa caretaker, came into Signor Ridolfi's office. His jittery movements and rapid speech showed he was upset. He reported that once the guests had left the villa, some servants consumed the wine that had been set out for dinner. They soon had stomach cramps so severe that he had to send for a doctor. By the time the doctor arrived, all the sick men were vomiting. The doctor's treatment may have saved one man who was having seizures. The chef discovered that the wine had been tainted. He found petals of *Scopa Fiori Giallo*, Yellow Broom Flower, in the jugs used for serving the wine."

Scala said, "I'm familiar with Scopa Fiori. Used in moderation, it is a medicinal, but taken in excess, it is poisonous. Assassins often chose it because the flower is easy to find. It grows wild in the hills."

Vittorio continued, "Camello said the man with seizures had consumed three glasses of wine. For those who drank only a single glass, the toxin wasn't strong enough to do more than induce sickness."

"What would drive someone to taint the wine and kill Marco?" Nico wondered aloud.

Massimo speculated, "Perhaps the killer had merely planned to pollute the wine, but his animosity grew while he waited for the wine to be served. Then, presented with an opportunity, he vented his hatred by killing Marco Ridolfi."

"That's one scenario," Vittorio agreed. "There are others, including the possibility that there are two guilty parties, one who wanted to ruin the celebration and another with a vendetta against Marco Ridolfi or the Ridolfi family."

After a minute of silence while the men considered Vittorio's hypothesis, he continued his report by summarizing his interviews with the workers at the villa. "They've all been employed at the villa for many years except for one man, a stable worker named Ugo Fornelli. He'd only been at the villa for a short time and he left on horseback, possibly headed for Florence, immediately after the killing. I've begun visiting stables in the city where he might keep a horse." He added confidently, "Someone must know him, so I'll find him eventually."

When Vittorio finished his account, Scala handed Nico a paper, saying, "This note for you was delivered to the Chancery." Nico unfolded the sheet and read,

> Nico,
>   I have information that may be pertinent to yesterday's incident.
>   F.

After reading the paper, Nico informed the others, "Yesterday at the villa, Francesca Pitti mentioned she had something to share with me, but the tragedy kept her from doing so at the time. This note says her information might help in the search for Marco Ridolfi's killer."

As he rose to leave, Scala said, "Francesca Pitti is a wonder … as is Giuliana Ridolfi. Her resilience following her brother's death is truly remarkable." To Nico, he said, "I noticed your initial reluctance sending the two women to Florence to fetch Signor Colombo." Rising to leave, he added, "I'm not sure I would have chosen to do it, but sending them proved to be a sage decision."

"They both volunteered forcefully, and none of the men vied for the chance," Nico noted.

After Scala left, Massimo pushed aside the embassy reports he'd been reading earlier and said, "A meeting with the devil would be preferable to reading these. I'll be happy to leave them and go with you to interrogate Signor Lenzi, but first I have something for you." He walked to a rear corner of the room, picked up a bag that was resting on the floor, and held it out to Nico. "Whenever we're on an assignment and I'm not with you, you manage to get yourself beaten by thugs. Your sister Alessa accuses me of being responsible for your injuries. She says I should protect you. Maybe this can let you defend yourself from wanton lowlifes when I'm not with you." Smiling, he added, "and shield me from Alessa's accusations."

Puzzled by Massimo's remarks, Nico opened the bag and withdrew a sheathed dagger. Massimo explained, "Only soldiers may bear swords in the city, but you may carry this dagger anywhere, and it's small enough to be hidden under your tunic."

Nico grasped the weapon, held it tentatively, looked down at its glistening blade, and chuckled. "I can tell the sharp end from the handle, but that's the extent of my knowledge. The university law school doesn't teach combat."

"That's a serious deficiency in your education, and one that could prove fatal if we continue to encounter thugs like the ones who attacked you in Milan and Pisa." Using his own weapon, Massimo demonstrated how to use a blade when being attacked. "Hold it low, at waist level, so you can slash from side to side while stepping back to keep your assailant at a distance. Don't hold it above your shoulder like a hammer."

Massimo observed Nico mimicking his example, then said, "Until you gain experience, you'll benefit from the other item." Nico reached into the bag and retrieved a small pouch. Massimo explained, "The pouch contains tiny stone chips I got from a sculptor friend. While menacing your opponent with the dagger, reach into the pouch with your free hand, grab a fistful of stone chips, and toss them at your assailant's face. Even a single chip lodged in an eye will incapacitate your attacker."

Massimo demonstrated with a slashing motion with one hand and a tossing motion with the other.

"And then?" Nico asked.

Massimo laughed. "You're an athlete, not a fighter. Your best chance for survival would be to run away."

Nico thanked Massimo for the gifts, although unsure whether he'd remember the instructions during an actual confrontation, and confident he'd be safer with Massimo at his side.

While fastening the sheath at his waist under his tunic, Nico said,

"After I learn Francesca's news, we can plan how to approach Signor Lenzi."

Massimo jested, "Ah, you call yourself my friend, yet you invited me to help you interrogate Berto Lenzi but not to accompany you in calling upon a woman whom you and Chancellor Scala consider impressive."

Returning Massimo's jibe, Nico said, "As you wish; come along. Now that I think on it, you and Francesca may deserve each other."

A guard at the entrance to Palazzo Pitti informed Nico that Francesca was in the garden at the rear of the house. Nico led Massimo around the side to the terrace at the rear of the building. From the elevated vantage point, they looked out into the spacious gardens where Francesca was nocking an arrow. They watched her pull the bowstring back smoothly, sight her target, and let the arrow fly. It traveled true the distance of a pallone field before it struck and split a clay disc. They continued observing her as she repeated the feat twice more. Massimo patted Nico on the shoulder and said,

"You may be right, lawyer. Maybe she and I do deserve each other."

They climbed down from the terrace and followed a curving path through a row of low bushes to where Francesca was pulling another arrow from her quiver. After being introduced by Nico as a friend and a member of the Security Commission, Massimo complimented Francesca, saying, "You're very skilled with the bow; you must practice often. You would excel in competitions."

Francesca cast an icy glance at Massimo and scoffed, "When have there ever been archery competitions for women? Women are never allowed a place in competitions; we're only permitted to watch and applaud the men."

Massimo raised both hands, palms spread apart defensively, and responded, "I meant no disrespect, only that I'm aware of men who see themselves as archers, yet lack your proficiency. Where did you learn the sport?"

"I have a cousin who competes in tournaments. I pestered him until he taught me." Francesca paused only a beat before adding, "In truth, he didn't require pestering. He's always been extremely indulgent of his unconventional cousin."

She offered the bow to Massimo, who accepted it, drew the bowstring, and found its draw weight to be substantially less than bows he had used in the army. He took an arrow from her quiver, and from its four-feathered shaft and hafting, Massimo recognized it as one crafted by the same fletcher who produced crossbow darts for the army. He sighted a piece of a disc that Francesca had split, released the arrow, and shattered the clay fragment.

To explain Massimo's proficiency, Nico said, "Before being named to the Security Commission, Massimo was in the army."

Massimo added modestly, "One of my duties was teaching archery to new recruits."

Francesca echoed his comment playfully, saying, "You must perform well in competitions." Massimo resisted the urge to reply to her jest by biting his lip.

Francesca set the bow aside and guided the men to a table on the terrace, where she offered them a drink of lemon water. Nico took a swig of the cool liquid, then said, "You have my gratitude for accompanying Giuliana to the Chancery yesterday. The men should feel ashamed that they didn't volunteer to ride to Florence. Before joining the Security Commission, Vittorio Colombo was the Guardia's most capable investigator, so I felt it important that he join the investigation as quickly as possible."

Francesca suggested, "Had Giuliana not come forward so quickly, one of the men might have taken the initiative, but once she spoke, decorum kept them from offering to accompany her."

Nico said, "Giuliana's impressive for one so young. After riding to Florence, she rode another eight miles back to the villa with Vittorio."

"I felt Giuliana would be safe with Signor Colombo, so I didn't return to the villa. What did he find?"

"As soon as he arrived, he examined the body carefully and determined that Marco had been strangled."

Francesca shook her head in disbelief. "At his betrothal. Who would do such a thing? Have you found the killer?"

"Unfortunately, there were no helpful clues in the bedchamber, so we've begun interviewing the workers and guests, hoping one of them will have information that can lead us to the killer. Vittorio has interviewed the workers. Massimo and I are going to begin with Berto Lenzi."

Francesca grimaced. "Once, Signor Lenzi asked my father to be his banker, but my father declined. He believes Berto Lenzi is unprincipled, and judging from Signor Lenzi's behavior yesterday, I share my father's assessment."

Nico nodded. "I've just begun asking about Signor Lenzi, and already I've heard questionable stories about him, so we're going to probe deeper before we confront him." Switching topics, Nico said, "Before leaving the villa, you mentioned you'd come across intriguing news."

Francesca refilled her glass, motioned for a servant to bring another jug of lemon water, then said, "I've known the wife of Signor Martone's banker for years. While I was chatting with her, I overheard her husband telling one of the other guests about the Martones' good fortune. He said their business profits had risen sharply and, in his experience, no merchant had ever enjoyed such rapid success. His words hinted at inappropriate conduct."

Nico said, "Antonio Ridolfi made a similar comment when I spoke with him. He told me that Marco was curious to know how the Martones achieved their unusual rise in income." Nico's attention was momentarily diverted by a bird flying low over the terrace. Upon refocusing, he said, "Those are interesting observations, but I don't understand how Martone's sudden wealth could relate to the killing of Marco Ridolfi."

Francesca's attention was diverted at seeing Massimo straighten and square his shoulders when the kitchen maid came out of the palazzo carrying a jug of lemon water. She introduced the young woman to the two men, then led Nico to the far end of the terrace to view a new statue, leaving Massimo alone with the comely servant.

After admiring the statue, a copy of Donatello's bronze of John the Baptist, Nico's thoughts returned to the murder. "My attention was fixed on Signor Lenzi. Perchance, did you notice any other guests behaving suspiciously?"

"Several guests and even some servants were acting

strangely, but I wouldn't characterize them as suspicious. I was amused by Angelo Lenzi leering at Daniela. She is, after all, a lovely woman who drew extended glances even from older men. But now when I think back on it, Angelo's lecherous look seemed almost sinister, as though he wanted Daniela for himself."

"*The Golden Ass*," Nico said.

Francesca raised an eyebrow in surprise and responded, "Nico, I'm awed to hear that you're familiar with that Roman folk tale. Surely you didn't learn it at the university law school. But yes, in that Roman story, Lady Charite was pursued by two suitors, one of whom kills the other out of love for her."

Nico shook his head. "I didn't hear the story at the university. Bianca introduced me to it. Her father has a copy of *The Golden Ass*. The tale of Charite's lover being killed is just one in the collection of stories ... as I'm sure you know." He stepped back to appraise Francesca. "Are you suggesting that lust might have driven Angelo to kill Marco? I doubt he has the status to claim Daniela's hand."

"True, he lacks Daniela's social standing," Francesca agreed, "but inflamed hearts can make men act like animals."

Massimo was still chatting with the maid when Nico and Francesca recrossed the terrace. Upon seeing her mistress coming, the maid picked up the empty jug from the table and scampered to the palazzo. Massimo's gaze followed her until she vanished into the building.

10

MARCO RIDOLFI'S FUNERAL

Nico and Vittorio left the Security Commission office together and approached Piazza di San Lorenzo where a crowd had gathered outside the basilica, awaiting Marco Ridolfi's funeral procession. Rather than join the others, they positioned themselves on Via dei Gori, the road the procession would take from the Ridolfis' home to the church, so they could study those attending the funeral.

Vittorio, who'd been researching Antonio Ridolfi's relatives and employees, pointed out several individuals to Nico. "The thin man with the beak-like nose is Marchionne, the warehouse manager. He gave me the names of men who've had disagreements with Antonio, competitors, past employees, and even former customers. While it's a lengthy list, only a few men had disputes serious enough that might provoke revenge. Marchionne said he'd let me know if he sees any of them at the funeral.

When I asked him about Marco, he said that, unlike his father, Marco had no enemies."

"I've heard the same," Nico agreed. "The two men shared a

common passion for their business, but in all other respects, they were very different. I wish I had known Marco."

Vittorio scanned the crowd. "I don't recognize the three men standing near the side of the church."

Nico said, "One of them is Cantore. He's a guild consul, so the other two are probably guild members." Even though Luigi Prizzi was a guild consul, Nico wasn't surprised that he hadn't come with the other guild members. "The young man standing with the older woman is Lazo, Marco's cousin. He was to be the groomsman at the wedding. The woman with him is his mother." Nico pointed out Daniela, who was standing off to the side with her parents. He noted her brother Polito was not with them.

Everyone's attention shifted to Via dei Gori as two men carrying a banner with the Ridolfi family crest came into view. The banner display was allowed by a recent change in sumptuary laws. Behind them, candle-carrying mourners in black robes flanked the casket bier that held Marco Ridolfi's body. Marco's family followed the mourners; his mother Simona, in a veiled black mourning dress was supported on one side by Antonio and on the other side by her sister Mena Lenzi. Berto and Angelo Lenzi were neither in the procession nor in the crowd at the piazza. Behind Simona was her daughter, Giuliana, accompanied by a young woman whom Nico did not recognize. A cortege of at least twenty robed mourners trailed behind the family.

Onlookers quieted as the procession crossed the piazza and entered the church. Inside, the two men carrying the banner attached it to an arched wooden frame set over the casket bier in front of the altar. The Ridolfi family stood to the side of the casket, with Antonio to his wife's right and her sister Mena to her left. Daniela's father brought her to the Baroncelli Chapel, a side chapel where she could view the service and not be disturbed by sympathizers. Nico and Vittorio took a position near the rear of the church, where they could observe the other attendees.

Out of respect for her sorrow, the men had postponed interrogating Daniela, but since she was fit enough to attend the service, Nico inferred it would be appropriate for Massimo to question her.

The bishop waited until everyone had entered the nave, then began the brief service with psalm twenty-seven as the first of the three readings. Simona held tight to her husband's hand throughout the service and twice she leaned against him for support. After the service ended, the procession reassembled outside the church and proceeded to the cemetery for Marco Ridolfi's burial.

The following day, Marco's parents hosted an *onoranza*, tribute, for their son at Casa Ridolfi. More people came to the lavish reception than had attended the funeral. As was the custom, everyone was welcome: relatives, friends, neighbors, and even casual acquaintances. Donato's Uccello restaurant provided trays of antipasti, elegant pastries, and casks of carefully selected wines from Tuscan vineyards.

Inside the casa, people paying their respects created a somber mood. Then, after savoring the delicious repast, they moved to the street, where a more cheerful atmosphere prevailed. Simona, who'd recovered enough that she could accept condolences without tearing, didn't see how false sympathizers quickly dropped their serious demeanor as soon as they left the house. Simona graciously accepted Nozzo Martone's apology for Daniela's absence. "Forgive her, but my daughter isn't ready to face everyone," he said. "Perhaps tomorrow she'll visit you when there is no crowd."

"I understand," Simona said warmly.

Nico joined the queue of those passing through the salon to pay his respects to Antonio and Simona. Antonio looked at Nico expectantly. Nico said, "My colleagues and I will not rest until we find justice for Marco," but even to him, the words sounded like an inadequate promise to a man whose only son had been killed. Justice was meager recompense for a life lost.

After leaving the house. Nico chose a spot away from the crowd where he could look for people who showed no signs of grief, or people who joined the throng outside, but didn't enter the house. He'd seen Mena Lenzi inside tending to details that would have otherwise fallen to her sister. Berto Lenzi did not accompany his wife. As expected, guild consul Luigi Prizzi did not attend the onoranza.

Nico had been watching the flow of people for nearly an hour when he spotted Lazo Ridolfi leaving the house. Rather than merging with the throng of people gathered outside, Lazo crossed the street and started walking away. Nico rushed to join him and said, "My associates and I have been interviewing people who were at Marco's betrothal. Can we talk now?"

Lazo motioned toward a nearby tavern; they bought mugs of ale and sat at a table. Lazo studied the person sitting opposite him, a man barely older than himself. "I imagine you're interviewing suspects who might have killed Marco. Surely you can't believe I killed him."

Nico replied flatly, "We've found no reason to consider you a suspect. But, besides suspects, we're talking with people who knew Marco well enough to identify his enemies."

Lazo snapped, "Marco had no enemies."

"Someone killed him," Nico protested.

Lazo held up a hand, signifying his objection to Nico's

reasoning. "His father, my Uncle Antonio, has enemies in abundance. You may find Marco's killer among them."

"So, to inflict pain on a man, attack his loved ones. Marco was killed to punish his father. Is that your premise?" Nico asked. Lazo nodded his agreement. Nico remained unconvinced and said, "You just told me that Marco was involved in the family business and your uncle said the same. He said even the partnership with the Martones was Marco's idea, so why do you believe Antonio has enemies yet Marco did not?"

Lazo shook his head. "Marco had a role, but he wasn't the decision-maker. You need to understand how their business operates. Uncle Antonio interacts with customers and suppliers. He's also the one who deals with the employees. Marco's domain was information. He scrutinized financial reports, not only those of his family's business but also whatever information he could learn about competitors and companies in similar businesses. It was one of his studies that led him to suggest a partnership with the Martones. He found the two companies could save by sharing resources, so he suggested the union to his father. But it was Antonio who made the decision to approach Nozzo Martone."

Nico asked, "Did Antonio also negotiate the betrothal?"

Lazo flashed a sour scowl that quickly turned to a grin. He replied, "Ah, you're being intentionally provocative. Have you heard the saying that two people in love share the same soul? If ever a man and a woman shared a soul, they were Marco and Daniela. Their betrothal was inevitable. I've known for years, perhaps even before either of them, that they would marry."

"You were close to Marco. Who were his other friends?"

"Marco had few friends. His devotion to the family business didn't afford him much time for other interests or friendships," Lazo said, then ran a finger along the top of his mug as he reflected on his departed friend. "It might be fair to say Marco had only two friends, and I was one."

"Who was the other?" Nico asked.

"Daniela."

They sat in silence drinking ale while Nico pondered what else to ask Lazo. "How did Marco learn about other companies?"

"He learned the value of businesses from the *catasto*, the tax records. For insights, he listened to braggarts. All businesses have at least one employee who can be induced to reveal company secrets, often for little more than a pitcher of ale."

Laughing inwardly, Nico thought, so Massimo isn't the only one who's perfected the skill of drawing information from indiscreet blowhards by frequenting taverns. He asked, "What businesses was Marco investigating?"

"I can't say. Marco rarely discussed business with me. He saw our time together as a rare chance to shift his mind away from business. We talked about other things, like the coming inter-guild fencing competition."

"Is there someone who might know what business opportunities Marco was exploring?"

"Possibly his father, although Marco explored many possibilities and only told his father about those that seemed promising." He paused a beat, then said tentatively, "Occasionally Marco had used a notary to help him with his research."

"Do you know the notary's name?"

Lazo shook his head. "No, but again, Signor Ridolfi might know."

Nico rubbed his chin, then took a swig of beer. It wouldn't have been unusual for Marco to employ a notary, but to be thorough, Nico made a mental note to ask Signor Ridolfi for the notary's name.

Lazo emptied his mug, leaned forward with one arm on the

table and said, "I tried to view Marco's body before I left the villa, but the goliath you appointed to guard the door wouldn't let me into the room. I've answered your questions, so, now, can you tell me how Marco was killed?"

"He was strangled."

Visualizing a scenario where Marco could be strangled, Lazo said, "Marco was no weakling. He would have fought off a lone attacker. Was there more than one assailant?"

"The attacker surprised him by coming at him from behind."

Still having difficulty believing Marco could have been subdued by a lone assailant, Lazo said, "The killer must have had powerful hands." Nico and Vittorio had agreed they wouldn't divulge that Marco had been strangled by a belt, so Nico refrained from commenting on Lazo's assumption.

"Have you made any progress in finding the killer?"

Nico replied vaguely, "We've narrowed the possibilities."

"I can help," Lazo volunteered enthusiastically. "Marco was my friend. I want to find his killer even more than you do. I'll talk to Daniela. When she and Marco discussed their betrothal celebration, he might have told her if something was troubling him."

"I appreciate your wanting to help, but there is no need for you to become involved. One of my colleagues is planning to interview Daniela."

"I've known Daniela for years. She'll tell me things she wouldn't say to a stranger."

Nico left the tavern disappointed that his discussion with Lazo hadn't been more productive. He'd hoped that Marco's closest friend might at least have been able to hint at a list of suspects and a motive. If Lazo were correct that the killer was an adversary of Antonio Ridolfi, the suspect list could expand significantly.

11

Nico, Massimo, and Vittorio agreed to meet early to discuss their findings and consider their next steps. Nico climbed to the Security Commission office on the upper level of the Palazzo della Signoria where he found Massimo reading the latest reports from Florentine envoys and Vittorio pinning notecards to the wall. High on the wall, Vittorio had fastened two cards side-by-side; one was labeled Berto Lenzi, and the other labeled Ugo Fornelli. Above the names and straddling both columns, he had placed a card reading "Suspects."

Below the Fornelli card, he had pinned other cards, each bearing a single fact about the stable worker. On one card in tiny print he had written, *Began working at Villa Ridolfi after villa chosen as betrothal announcement site.* The second card read, *Left villa and Calenzano immediately after murder.* On the last card he had penned, *Possibly in Florence.* The Berto Lenzi column held only a single fact card. It read, *Eager to leave villa after murder.* On a separate area of the wall, Vittorio had mounted three cards with information gleaned from his observations and interviews. The first read, *Marco Ridolfi strangled by a leather belt;*

the second, *Antonio Ridolfi believes killing to sabotage partnership with Martones;* and the third, *Unusual increase in Martone's profits.*

The basic technique of using cards arrayed on the wall to organize information had been adopted from Chancellor Scala, but Vittorio had improved on Scala's method by adding colored threads to connect related cards. As their investigations progressed, the wall evolved from an orderly array of cards into a complex maze of cards connected to each other by brightly colored threads. But at the outset, as was this investigation into Marco Ridolfi's murder, the nearly barren wall held only a few cards.

When Vittorio finished mounting the cards, Nico and Massimo gathered around him. They listened intently as he shared with them the discussions he had had with the priest at San Nicolo church in Calenzano and the woman at the Locanda Rustico inn summarized on the cards in the Ugo Fornelli column. All three men agreed it was highly suspicious that Fornelli had left the villa and the village of Calenzano immediately after Marco Ridolfi had been killed.

Massimo asked, "If Fornelli is in Florence, how will you find him, since the woman at the inn wasn't even sure of his family name?"

Vittorio said, "He left the inn on horseback, so if he came to Florence, it's likely that he left his horse at a stable in the city. I'll start by visiting each stable and asking whether someone named Ugo left a horse with them."

"Do you have a description of him?" Nico asked.

"None of the people I spoke with noticed any distinguishing features. They all gave similar descriptions: he is of average height, has brown hair, and is wearing a simple smock. None of them suggested anything that would set him apart from hundreds of other Florentine men."

When Vittorio finished his comments and sat, Nico went to

the wall and marked the card reading *Martone profits increased* with a symbol to show the statement had been confirmed by a second source. He explained, "At the villa, Francesca overheard Signor Martone's banker say he had never seen such a rapid rise in profits. He implied the Martones might be doing something illicit or unethical. It's an interesting opinion, but it doesn't really seem to relate to Marco Ridolfi's murder."

Nico recounted his conversations with guild consul Cantore and the pharmacist. "According to the pharmacist, Berto Lenzi and Antonio Ridolfi had once been partners, and the partnership did not end amicably, but the dissolution happened many years ago." He pinned a card in Berto Lenzi's column that read *Antonio Ridolfi dissolved partnership with Berto Lenzi. Lenzi still resentful?*

Next, Nico created a new column in the suspects area with a card labeled *Angelo Lenzi.* He and Massimo told Vittorio about Francesca's observation that Berto Lenzi's son had been leering at Daniela. In the new Angelo Lenzi column, Nico added a card reading *Excessive interest in Daniela. Jealousy?*

Massimo ambled slowly to the back of the room, scanned the cards to absorb the scant information they contained, and announced, "Thus far, we've only identified three suspects and the information we've gleaned about them is barely a starting point." Using his fingers to enumerate, he began, "First, if Marco Ridolfi was killed to block the business partnership, as his father suspects, it could have been done by anyone at the celebration, not just these few suspects." Raising a second finger, he continued, "If Ugo Fornelli is the killer, he could have been hired by someone who wasn't at the villa, someone with a vendetta against Marco or the Ridolfi family." He walked to the opposite corner of the room and continued, "It would have been easy for the killer to conceal a knife under a tunic, so why did he use his belt to strangle Ridolfi? And the question that puzzles me most: instead of the betrothal celebration where the list of suspects is known, why not commit the murder in a darkened street so the killer could escape unnoticed?"

Nico said, "The three men we identified aren't the only possible culprits." He held out a sheet of paper. "This is the list of names Donato compiled of everyone who was present at the celebration, both guests and workers. Even though the number is limited, there are about thirty people on the list. It will take a long time if we need to investigate them all."

While Nico and Massimo viewed the task ahead as daunting, Vittorio, who had extensive experience in conducting investigations, flashed a smile and in a rare show of levity said, "There are three of us, so each of us need be concerned with only ten suspects."

12

A fine mist had begun to fall as Nico headed toward Casa Argenti. A glance at the dark clouds gathering in the west made him regret he hadn't heeded Alessa's advice and taken his rain cloak. "Get in," a familiar woman's voice called to him from a carriage that had slowed to a stop next to him. Looking up, Nico hesitated momentarily in surprise at seeing Francesca Pitti and Giuliana Ridolfi together when the carriage door swung open. It seems adversity has brought them together, he reasoned.

He pulled himself up into the carriage and sat next to Francesca. Giuliana wore conservative dark clothes, but not a black mourning dress, and neither jewelry nor perfume. Without considering the propriety of his action, Nico reached across and took Giuliana's hand. "Everyone has the most loving words to say about your brother and bears his loss as a tragedy. He will forever be in our prayers."

Giuliana responded, "I appreciate your kind sentiment, Messer Argenti."

"Nico," he said softly.

"And I know you've been tireless in pursuing my brother's killer."

Francesca said, "As Giuliana said, we know you, Massimo, and Signor Colombo are relentless, but we also realize the lack of evidence makes finding Marco's killer an arduous task. You are impeded further because people have always been hesitant to speak openly with the Guardia, and now, by extension, some are reluctant to share information with members of the Security Commission."

Nico released Giuliana's hand, his attention drawn to Francesca, who continued, "Giuliana and I believe people will share their thoughts more freely with us." She held out a sheet of paper. "We've compiled a list of everyone who attended the betrothal celebration, and we intend to speak with each of them."

Nico sat speechless as he read the names. It matched closely the list that Donato had compiled at the villa in Calenzano. Nico knew that when Francesca set her mind, she couldn't be dissuaded, so he turned to Giuliana. "You should be with your family grieving for your loss."

She shook her head. "My mother grieves enough for both of us. Her grief frees me to seek justice for Marco."

Nico looked from one woman to the other. Francesca is molding this young woman to be her replica, he decided. If he couldn't discourage Giuliana, at least he could warn her. "If the killer learns you're hunting him, you could become a target. He's killed once. Nothing will prevent him from killing again." He glanced at Francesca. "Both of you could be in danger."

Francesca patted Nico's hand. "Nico, how sweet of you to worry about us."

Giuliana said, "If the person who killed Marco has a vendetta against our family, I may already be in danger. He might want my parents to suffer the loss of both of their children."

Her premise wasn't unreasonable. "That is an added reason for you to avoid provoking them," Nico said. He looked down at the list of names. "Do you know all these people?"

Francesca replied, "Together, Giuliana and I know most of them."

Looking at Giuliana, Nico said, "I was told Marco and Daniela decided who would be invited to the celebration?"

"They created an initial list, then my mother and father added to it."

"Which ones did your parents add?"

As Giuliana read names from the list, Nico marked them on the paper. When she finished, he said, "Can you limit your interviews to only those people your brother invited?"

Francesca said, "We can start with them."

Nico locked eyes with her. "You must be careful." He rapped on the side of the coach and called for the driver to stop the carriage. As he climbed down, he glanced up at Francesca. "If you learn anything, no matter how insignificant, tell me immediately."

As the women rode away, Nico scanned the nearby buildings to determine where the carriage had deposited him. The Santa Croce neighborhood. It would be a long walk to Casa Argenti. Thankfully, the mist had stopped, and the clouds were thinning.

13

PORTA SAN GALLO ENTRANCE TO FLORENCE

Polito Martone's driver waited patiently in a cart at the Porta San Gallo gate with his arms folded across his chest, his eyes closed and his head bent forward.

Polito climbed down from the cart and paced alongside the city wall, worried that his shipment had been delayed or robbed. Gazing at the road from the north, he squinted, hoping to spot wagons in the distance. Nearby, tax collectors inspected the cargo in the line of wagons awaiting entry into Florence. Most carried produce from farms in the valleys surrounding the city. Even though fruits and vegetables were not taxed, the law required that farm wagons be inspected to ensure they were not carrying contraband. The inspectors' slow pace made the line crawl, so to pass the time, the farmers climbed down from their wagons to chat with each other. For some, this was a welcome chance to talk with their neighbors.

Other wagons carried taxable goods from Africa, Asia, and the Levant that had passed through Venice en route to Florence. The tax collectors took their time and worked diligently while examining these wagons, but they rarely found anything that wasn't on the inventory list. Drivers paid the tax levy using letters of credit given to them by their employers.

Polito's shout of "I see them! They're coming!" jolted his driver awake. Three wagons came into view as they topped a small hill on Via degli Dei, the Road of the Gods. Even at a distance, Polito recognized his wagon drivers and his pacing quickened. When the wagons joined the queue awaiting inspection, Polito dashed to the first of his three wagons and asked, "Any difficulties?" His concern stemmed from knowing that bandits had been attacking wagons even in daylight, undeterred by the army units patrolling the road.

"None," the driver replied and pointed to the column of wagons behind him. "We traveled together all the way from Venice. There were too many of us for bandits to harass." Polito stood aside as the wagons crept forward.

When the first wagon reached the head of the queue, the tax inspector took the inventory sheet from the driver. His face brightened upon reading the name of the importer, Martone. The sheet listed the contents of the delivery as eighteen barrels of ginger from Alexandria, Egypt. The driver pulled aside the cloth that had been covering the barrels to let the inspector scan the contents of the wagon. He gestured toward the wagons behind his and said, "Two more wagons, each with six barrels." The inspector nodded his agreement that the inventory listed eighteen barrels. He pulled the lid to open one barrel, leaned down, sniffed the fragrant spice, and announced, "Ginger. The sheet says they are all ginger."

Polito smiled as the driver confirmed, "That's right. Eighteen barrels of ginger." The inspector went to a shed beside the road to consult the tax registers, returned, and announced the assessment amount. Unlike the other merchants who paid using letters of credit, Polito stepped forward, produced a pouch containing silver coins and handed it to the inspector, who accepted it without question. Whether that fee ever reached the Florentine treasury was not Polito's concern. Next, he handed the inspector a smaller pouch, and said, "In appreciation for your outstanding work." The inspector kept his face expressionless and waved the three wagons through the gate into the city.

Polito accompanied the wagons to the Martones' warehouse, where he supervised the unloading. He watched with little interest as his men carried barrels from the first wagon to the warehouse. When the barrels from the remaining wagons were secured, he removed their covers and smiled approvingly as he peered into the containers: four barrels of black peppercorns subject to a tax thirty percent greater than the tax on ginger, six barrels of cloves with a four times greater tax than ginger, and two barrels of saffron from Asia taxed at a rate fifteen times that of ginger. "This will be another profitable week," he gloated.

His driver asked, "Has your father become suspicious about the higher profit?"

"Not at all," Polito laughed. "He attributes the success to his effective business management. The only curious person was Marco Ridolfi. He questioned my sister repeatedly, but she knows nothing about the business."

14

CHANCERY ANNEX, FLORENCE

The Florentine Chancery was tasked with preserving agency proceedings, reports from diplomats, and all other significant government documents. While the Chancery offices, along with other government offices, were in the Palazzo della Signoria, the record repository was in a separate building known as the Chancery Annex. A century ago, when feuds between rivals were common, prominent families housed themselves in tall defensive structures that have become known as the tower houses. Even though the fashion had changed, those conspicuous buildings still adorned Florence's landscape. Some had been seized by the city when their owners had been exiled for a crime or failed to pay their taxes. The Signoria had designated one of the seized buildings as the home of the Chancery Annex. The gray stone structure, far from the city center on Via Gallo, lacked any government markings, so passersby might assume it to be a residence. Three of its five levels were occupied by the Annex; the two upper levels were reserved for expansion.

Nico passed through the small lobby and entered the

spacious room where clerks seated at desks around the periphery made copies of important documents. He paused to watch a clerk copying a new report from the Florentine envoy in Rome. After it was copied, the original report would be filed in the archive. One copy would be sent to the Signoria and a second copy to Chancellor Scala. In the center of the room, other clerks were adding indexing notations to documents spread out on a large table.

The wall to Nico's right displayed a fresco of Saint Francis in a field with white doves circling overhead. The first time Nico had come to the Annex, the image, which must have been painted when the exiled family still owned the building, had been obscured by a heavy layer of grime accumulated over a century or more. A recent cleaning revealed the painting's original colors, as vibrant as the day the artist applied his pigments to wet plaster.

A junior clerk looked up when he saw Nico's shadow cross his desk. He was about to greet the newcomer when Galetto, the senior notary, tapped him on the shoulder and said, "This is Messer Argenti, a member of the Security Commission." Galetto strode to where Nico was standing. "Greetings, Nico. I always welcome your visits because your queries are more challenging than the routine requests we get from our city's many bureaucrats." Expressing his exasperation, he recounted, "Just yesterday, an official of the Maritime Board sent his clerk to request a copy of notes from the latest Signoria meeting. He could have gotten those from the Signoria's secretary who is in a building two removed from his own; instead, he had his clerk waste time traipsing out to this remote part of the city." Feeling suddenly embarrassed at being garrulous, Galetto stopped speaking, straightened his tunic, then asked, "How can we be of service today?"

"I'm investigating a murder. You may have heard of it. The victim's name was Marco Ridolfi."

"Yes, I heard he was killed at his betrothal dinner. How tragic."

"Since there were no clues pointing to the killer, we have many suspects to investigate, so I may be returning here to the Annex often over the coming days." Or weeks, Nico thought.

Eager for the stimulation of aiding in a murder investigation, Galetto said earnestly, "I'm here to assist you in any way possible."

"Today I'm seeking information about two men. One of them is Berto Lenzi, a sugar merchant. One year past, an agent employed by Lenzi vanished and I'd like to know whether that incident is mentioned in any reports." Nico paused a moment before adding, "Or whether Signor Lenzi is mentioned in any other reports."

Galetto asked, "Do you have the name of the missing agent?"

"No."

Galleto nodded his understanding. "There are many ways to find information in our archive," he said with pride. "If the Guardia investigated the agent's disappearance, it will be mentioned in a Guardia report. If we need to search through all Guardia reports filed last year looking for one about a missing agent, it would be a time consuming, but not impossible, task. However, if the goddess Fortuna is kind to us, the report about the missing man will mention Signor Lenzi and, if so, his name will be listed in the index. Come with me."

Galetto lit two lanterns, handed one to Nico, and led him from the workroom to the index room, its four walls lined from floor to ceiling with shelves containing references to every document in the archive. He moved around the room until he spotted the shelf labeled LE. "Up there," he said, handed his lantern to Nico, set a ladder against the wall, and climbed to reach the shelf. He withdrew a folio from the shelf, opened it, and announced, "Three documents mention Berto Lenzi. There is also reference to a document for a person named Angelo Lenzi."

Nico said, "Angelo is Berto's son. I'd be interested in seeing the document that mentions him as well."

Galetto summoned a junior clerk, told him the document numbers he got from the index, and dispatched the clerk to the building's third level to retrieve the documents. While they waited for the clerk to return, Nico said, "The second man of interest might be named Ugo Fornelli. The person who identified him wasn't sure of his family name."

Gatello climbed the ladder to reach the shelf with the FO indexes; then called down to Nico, "There are no entries for Fornelli. There are entries for Forciano, Foretti, and Forzini, but none have the given name Ugo. Would you like to see the documents citing those men?"

Nico was about to dismiss the three names Galetto mentioned when he heard Vittorio's voice whisper to him: *Pull out every weed, lest the one you leave behind bites you.* Nico remembered laughing when he first heard the saying. He had grasped the sentiment but protested: Weeds don't bite. Vittorio had flashed a rare smile and assured Nico the non sequitur guaranteed the advice would never be forgotten. "Yes, I'd like those documents," he replied to Galetto, who sent a clerk to the Annex's second level to fetch them.

Galetto showed Nico to a vacant desk in the workroom where he could view the documents he had requested. The filing clerks spoke little, so except for the shuffling of papers, the room was quiet, making it easy for Nico to concentrate. Two of the documents citing Berto Lenzi were of little value as they had been originated by the Mercanzia, the administrators who set the regulations for international merchants. Those documents detailed claims Lenzi had made against shipping companies that transported his merchandise.

The third document contained the information Nico had hoped to find. It was the Guardia report of their investigation of Lenzi's agent. It belied the pharmacist's understanding that the agent had vanished. According to the Guardia's summary, the agent's body had been found in the woods north of the city by a hunter. The agent had suffered a skull-crushing blow from a heavy object, but searchers could not find the murder weapon. Guardia officers interviewed the agent's family, his known friends, and members of Lenzi's business, including Berto Lenzi, but the killer had not been found. Nico muttered to himself, "Without witnesses, the Guardia's investigations are rarely successful." When he reached the end of the report, he closed the folio, wondering why it said nothing about Berto Lenzi having discharged the agent.

Next, Nico read the document that referenced Angelo Lenzi, a Guardia report about a tavern brawl. Although the document mentioned that four men had been involved in the squabble, only Angelo and one other were charged with assault for brandishing knives. The reason for the altercation wasn't clear, although it had something to do with a woman. Was this merely an isolated event or testimony to Angelo Lenzi's violent behavior? Nico noted the name of the other person who had been arrested as someone who might have insight into Angelo's character.

Nico turned his attention to the second and larger stack of documents. The top folio on the stack held a minor government agency's announcement of Foretti's appointment to the road and bridge oversight commission. Next, he found a record of Forciano's bequest of a considerable sum to his parish church. The remaining six documents cited Checho Forzini, who, like Nico, was a lawyer. Each folio detailed tribunals in which Forzini had defended prominent citizens against corruption charges. A lucrative practice, but nothing to do with Ugo Fornelli, Nico concluded after poring through the six thick folios.

"Did you find what you were looking for?" Galetto asked when Nico returned the documents.

"Whenever I come here, I'm surprised to find more than I expected." He raised his hand, palm facing upward, in a gesture of resignation. "But not everything I could wish for."

Galetto responded, "Even with our extensive archive tracking people and events, some of our citizens remain invisible."

15

MARIA PAZZA TAVERN, FLORENCE

Berto Lenzi had rented an old wooden building on Via Gora in the Santa Maria Novella district as a warehouse to store his imported sugar. Midway between his warehouse and the docks, where sugar arrived on barges from Pisa, was a tavern called *Maria Pazza*, Crazy Maria.

Massimo entered the tavern feigning the stagger of one who appeared to have spent his entire afternoon sampling brews in the city's other taverns. He ordered a mug of beer from the barkeep, a woman whose bearing and demeanor were steadier than his. She can't be crazy Maria, he reasoned. As he made his way to a secluded table, he passed three men commiserating around a pitcher of beer. Earlier, he had spent an hour observing the same men as they loaded wagons at Lenzi's warehouse. From a hiding spot behind a nearby building, Massimo had watched the men until their day ended, then followed them to Crazy Maria.

Now, sitting at a table in a darkened corner of the room, he listened to them gripe about their wives. "She's becoming like her mother," one complained. She's never in the mood," a second man grumbled.

The third man listened to the familiar complaints, and once again gave thanks he wasn't married. "That's why God made brothels," he jested. "Women in brothels are always in the mood ... or at least they pretend to be."

After each of the married men downed a single mug, they left for home while their colleague stepped to the bar for a refill. Massimo followed and joined the man at the bar. "I couldn't help but overhear. Your friends sound wife weary."

"They just enjoy complaining. I've met both of their wives. The women are not painful to look at and they're decent cooks, although I can't testify to their other qualities. When the whining starts, though, I can only sit back and listen until they finish their rants."

Massimo began with a ploy he'd used before. "I was married once." Chuckling, he continued, "Truth be told, I'm still married, but thank the Lord my wife is far from here. She's in Naples. I hated to leave her because she really lit my fire, but her mother must have come straight from Hades. I swear, the devil must have sent her away because even he couldn't tolerate that witch ... and I couldn't get my wife away from her. The two were inseparable."

As Massimo's new acquaintance reached for his coin purse to pay for his beer, Massimo waved him away and handed a copper coin to the barkeep. He raised his mug and said, "When these are empty, my new friend and I will need a jug." They returned to the man's table, where they exchanged tales.

Massimo entertained his companion with anecdotes about his mother-in-law and life in Naples. The man reciprocated by recounting his past. He was raised on his uncle's pig farm in the Mugello Valley and had no memory of his father or mother. "Slopping pigs is the worst job in the world," he declared. "One day I just couldn't do it anymore, climbed up onto a plow horse, and rode to Florence. I had no saddle, so my ass was burning by the time I got to the city," he said, laughing. "A miller gave me a job sweeping floors at his mill along the river. It was wretched work, but better than slopping pigs."

Massimo waited until they had emptied the jug and the man's eyes glazed before shifting the conversation. "Have I seen you at the docks? Do you work there?" he asked.

"I don't work at the docks. I work at a warehouse here on Via Gora. If you saw me at the docks, it was when I was offloading a barge that brought sugar from Sicily."

"Is it good work? At the warehouse?"

"Better than sweeping floors or slopping pigs," the man said, his speech slurred.

"How long have you been at the warehouse?"

The man gazed into his beer as though hoping a memory might emerge from the foamy liquid. "Two years ... or maybe three." His faltering speech told Massimo it was time to make his point before the man became totally incoherent.

"Is Lenzi a good boss?" Massimo asked, confident that the man wouldn't realize that Lenzi's name hadn't been mentioned yet.

"He's tolerable when business is good, but when his profits sag, he finds fault with everything."

Massimo said, "I heard that one of his agents went missing last year. He must have been upset when that happened."

The man bit his lip as he tried to remember details of the event. "You must mean Iacopo. He didn't leave on his own, Lenzi turfed him."

Massimo wasn't sure what was meant by saying Iacopo had been turfed because the word had different connotations. Jousters used the word to describe someone who'd been unseated from his horse, while thugs use the word to mean someone had been killed.

The man leaned close to Massimo and tried to speak in a low voice to keep from being overheard, even though there were no others in the tavern. "Iacopo was Lenzi's agent in Sicily. He would buy sugar from the Sicilians and arrange for shipment. Lenzi found out that Iacopo was also working as an agent for a merchant in Genoa and Iacopo was getting better prices for the Genovese. The next time Iacopo came to the warehouse office, Lenzi rammed him against a wall, then punched him, like a bear swatting a fly. Iacopo dropped to the floor. Lenzi shouted at him and I'll never forget what he said. 'I gave you a job when you were nothing and you pay me back by giving deals to the wretched Genovese.' Before Lenzi could strike him again, Iacopo crawled to the door and slithered out of the office with Lenzi calling after him, 'Squirm like the snake that you are and never let me see you again.' That's the last time any of us saw Iacopo."

"Did you ever hear what became of Iacopo?"

The man shook his head. "Never heard a word about him again."

Massimo finished his drink, bid farewell to his companion, and left the tavern, appearing steadier on his feet than when he'd arrived.

16

CASA ARGENTI

Alessa trotted to the dining salon, singing a Neapolitan folk tune and carrying a jug of water in one hand and a jug of peach nectar in the other. She halted abruptly at the doorway. "What's that awful smell?" she exclaimed, her nose wrinkling as she tried to identify the powerful odor.

Nico, sitting at the dining table with the offensive source on a plate in front of him, replied, "Fish... and it tastes better than it smells. Donato brought it from the Uccello yesternight."

Grimacing, Alessa stepped tentatively into the room and set the jugs on the table. "Even in my village in Morocco, people refrained from eating fish at their morning meals, except for fishermen, and they were, for that cause, banished to eat alone."

Donato came into the room a few moments later, inhaled sharply, and addressed Nico. "I can tell you found the fish."

"Finding it was no challenge," Nico laughed. "The layer of salt covering it wasn't thick enough to contain its aroma."

"The markets don't normally have sea bream, and this one was big," — Donato held his hands out wider than shoulder width — "but not big enough to put on the menu at the Uccello. We served most of it to a group celebrating an anniversary in one of our private rooms, and I brought the rest here."

Alessa, who was only gradually becoming accustomed to the smell, said, "If you kind gentlemen will sit together at the far end of the table away from my nose, I'll share my peach nectar with you."

While cutting a piece of fish for himself, Donato addressed the serious matter. "There were many people at the betrothal celebration who could have killed Marco Ridolfi. Do you intend to interview all of them?"

Nico swallowed a mouthful of the pink fish. "It's been a while since I've had sea bream and this tastes even better than I remember. I wonder what herbs the chef uses." Then, returning his attention to Donato's query, he replied, "I hope we won't need to interview everyone. That would take months. Vittorio is looking for a suspect who'd been working at the villa for a short time and then disappeared right after the murder."

"That certainly seems suspicious," Donato agreed. "From what you've told me of Vittorio, if there's anyone who can locate fugitives, it's Vittorio."

"While Vittorio chases the missing person, Massimo and I have been concentrating on Berto Lenzi."

"That arrogant ass," Donato snapped.

"At the Chancery archives, a Guardia report mentioned that one year ago, hunters found the body of one of Lenzi's former employees. He'd been murdered, and his killer still hasn't been found. After I told Massimo about the report, he learned that shortly before the man was killed, he'd been discharged by Lenzi for giving preferential treatment to a competitor, a Genovese merchant."

"How did Massimo find that the man had been discharged?" Donato asked.

"He pried the information from one of Lenzi's warehouse workers."

Alessa, who'd been listening while eating raspberry torta and drinking watered peach nectar, said, "With his velvet tongue and a jug of beer to aid him, Massimo could pull information from a stone." Nico nodded his agreement.

Donato finished the last of the fish. As he went to the sideboard to cut a slice of raspberry torta, he asked, "Did the Guardia question Lenzi about the killing?"

"If they did, there was no mention of it in their report. Massimo believes Lenzi wasn't responsible for the agent's death, and we have no evidence to connect Lenzi to Marco Ridolfi's murder, but I want to confront him directly before we eliminate him as a suspect."

Chancery Office

While a student at the University of Bologna, Nico had taken a course in techniques for cross-examining witnesses at trials. The professor had shown that aggressive confrontation worked well with most people, whereas other methods were more effective with defiant witnesses. Students followed the professor's example and honed their skills in mock trials. Nico decided that a conciliatory approach might be best with Berto Lenzi. He penned a note —

Signor Lenzi,
     Please accept my apology for being brusque at the Ridolfi villa yesterday. I believe the investigation into Marco Ridolfi's

murder would benefit from your insights into the Ridolfi family. Accordingly, I request the opportunity to meet with you so I can gain your perspective regarding this tragedy.

Respectfully, Nico Argenti

Nico revised the note several times, aiming for a tone that appeared deferential and appealed to Lenzi's ego. He signed the note using only his name, not adding his title or his affiliation with the Security Commission. After he was satisfied with the composition, he sent a Chancery courier to deliver the note and went to the Security Commission office to study the notecards pinned to the wall while waiting for Lenzi's response. Massimo's conversation with Lenzi's warehouse worker and Nico's research at the Chancery annex resulted in a few more cards being added, but the number of suspects had not expanded, nor had any solid evidence been uncovered. And Vittorio's dogged search had, thus far, failed to find Ugo Fornelli.

Nico waited impatiently for the courier to return with Lenzi's response to his request. To him, it seemed hours had passed before he heard the returning courier's footsteps echoing through the hallway outside the commission office. "Signor Lenzi agreed to meet with you," the courier announced.

"Did he sound congenial or reluctant?"

The clerk hadn't observed Lenzi's attitude and struggled to recall the man's words. "Signor Lenzi said, 'Inform Signor Argenti that I am amenable to sharing my perceptions with him.' Those were his exact words."

"Hmmm," Nico muttered. He couldn't have constructed a more neutral response and wondered whether it came naturally to Lenzi or if he had labored to craft the phrasing. "Is Signor Lenzi at his home or his warehouse?"

"He was at his home when I delivered your message, but he was preparing to leave and said he would meet with you at his warehouse on Via Gora."

"Thank you," Nico said reflexively. Taking Nico's expression of gratitude as a dismissal, the courier spun around and left the office. Watching him leave, Nico sensed the young man to be no older than the altar boys at his church. They didn't expect to spend their entire lives as altar boys. Did the courier expect to spend his life as a courier, or did he have other aspirations? When he returned home at night, did he tell his family — his parents, because surely he was too young to have a wife — that he delivered messages, or did he claim he had helped a member of the Security Commission conduct a murder investigation?

When Nico was the courier's age, he'd already set himself the goal of becoming a lawyer. His father had secured exemplary tutors and provided the financial support needed to make Nico's dream possible. Then, after his father's passing, Uncle Nunzio guided him on the path to the University of Bologna law school. Upon graduation, Chancellor Scala had Nico appointed to the Security Commission. Nico was blessed with an encouraging family and an influential mentor. He wondered whether the courier enjoyed similar support.

17

LENZI WAREHOUSE

The warehouse seemed deserted when Nico arrived, with the only movement and sound coming from a flock of sparrows flitting through nearby trees. The main door, large enough to accommodate the wagons used for transporting commercial goods, was closed. Nico's rap on the small office door elicited a response from inside. Although it was too muffled to be understood, Nico took it as an invitation to enter. A single window high on one wall provided enough light to illuminate the building's owner, Berto Lenzi, who sat behind a desk across the room. Other than the desk, the only furniture in the sparse room were two chairs and a small table holding an oil lamp. A rain cloak hung from a hook on the otherwise plain walls. Lenzi's hands were clasped together and resting on the desktop. He didn't stand to welcome his visitor and only indicated a chair with a jerk of his head.

Nico walked slowly toward the chair, turned it to face Lenzi, and sat. Lenzi spoke first. "Are you here to arrest me?"

Seeing that Lenzi fought to suppress a smirk, Nico

responded in kind. "That wasn't my intention. Are there reasons you should be arrested?"

Lenzi continued the banter, saying, "On some days, possibly, but not today." Neither man chose to mention their dispute at the villa the previous day. Lenzi scratched his chin. "My wife cajoled me to attend that ... fiasco. She said we had to support her sister. I wouldn't have been there if my wife hadn't pressured me. From the time we arrived to when *you*" — he shot an icy glare at Nico — "allowed me to leave, I was with my family. I had no opportunity to kill the boy."

Lenzi shifted the conversation. "Since you are here speaking with me, I assume you haven't found Marco Ridolfi's killer."

"Perhaps you can help me do that," Nico replied. "Antonio Ridolfi believes his son was killed to prevent his business collaboration with the Martone family. Since you once had a relationship with Signor Ridolfi, I'd welcome your insights on his business practices."

Lenzi reached into a drawer, pulled out a bottle of wine, poured two glasses, and offered one to Nico. The friendly gesture contrasted with his sarcastic sneer. "You want to know whether I hold animosity toward Antonio Ridolfi. I have no reason to hide my feelings. Yes, I am bitter."

Lenzi took a large swig from his glass, leaned back, exhaled sharply, and began a story he'd apparently recited many times before. "As young men, Antonio and I began our careers importing sugar from Sicily. Our partnership flourished. It grew steadily, but not fast enough to satisfy Antonio. He was always dissatisfied and looking for new and bigger opportunities. He went to a lecture about printing machines where he heard machines were coming to Venice from the Holy Roman Empire, and, at the same lecture, he met someone who told him the Venetians were importing high-quality sugar from

Egypt. To Antonio, high quality meant higher prices and higher profits.

"He returned from the lecture convinced we should also import sugar from Egypt. I agreed we should explore the possibility and that Antonio should travel to Venice to meet with shipping companies. He wasted no time and departed for Venice the following day. Two weeks he was gone with no word from him. When he returned, instead of bringing information, the bastard had signed a contract with an agent who would import Egyptian sugar for him — not for the both of us, just for him. He devoted all his time and attention to expanding contacts in Venice and told me he no longer had an interest in importing from Sicily. He cast me aside like an aging mistress." Lenzi pounded his fist on the desk. "I have good reason to wish for the goddess Fortuna Mala to spit on him, but did I assault his son? No! If my dislike of Antonio could drive me to strike at his family, I would have done so long ago."

Lenzi folded his arms across his chest and looked down at the glass in front of Nico. "You haven't tasted the wine. Do you find my hospitality unacceptable?"

Nico ignored the question and shot Lenzi an icy stare. "I've heard your antipathy extends to more than just Antonio Ridolfi and that it can rise to violence. Last year, you assaulted an agent who disappointed you, an agent who was subsequently found murdered."

Lenzi gripped his desk tightly, turning his knuckles white. In a caustic voice, he seethed, "I wager even you would spew rage at one who deceived you. But anyone who says I murdered that untrustworthy scum is a liar. The snake was unharmed when he slithered from my office. I was glad to be rid of him. My workers heard our exchange. They are in the warehouse now. Go ask them."

Lenzi leaned forward, and reddened with anger, he declared, "Antonio Ridolfi has many enemies ... men like me, men he stepped on to build his empire. You want to know who killed his son? If I were you, I'd look to Luigi Prizzi. Prizzi's election as guild consul transformed our respected tradition into a fracas. He and Ridolfi nearly came to blows. I didn't witness the episode, but I'm told Prizzi punched Antonio repeatedly and slammed him against a wall. When guild members finally pulled Prizzi away, Antonio's tunic was stained with his blood."

"Signor Prizzi attended the betrothal celebration," Nico said as he puzzled over the incongruity.

"You're trying to understand why Antonio invited the man who recently beat him," Lenzi hissed. "And why did Luigi deign to attend?"

"You have answers to those questions?" Nico probed.

"I have my suspicions, but you're a clever lawyer. Ferret out your own conclusions." Lenzi picked up a folio from his desk. "Now, since you're not prepared to arrest me, I ask you to leave so I can return to my business."

Nico left Lenzi's warehouse and headed to the Security Commission's office. When he reached Piazza della Signoria, he spotted Massimo on the far side of the piazza talking with a woman. From her simple clothes, Nico guessed her to be a servant or the wife of a shopkeeper. She was older than most of Massimo's women friends, and not one whom Nico recognized. Curious, he stopped in front of the Palazzo della Signoria and leaned against the building to observe his colleague. Massimo maintained a proper distance from the woman and their behavior suggested they were casual acquaintances, not close friends. After several minutes, the woman turned away from

Massimo and entered a shop. Massimo crossed the piazza to where Nico was standing.

"She's the Martone's housemaid," Massimo explained as the two men entered the Palazzo della Signoria. Vittorio, who had been speaking with a Chancery office notary, joined them and the three men climbed to the Security Commission Office on the palazzo's upper level.

"Daniela sends the maid out with a variety of chores several times each day," Massimo explained.

"And how might you know that?" Nico asked.

"I've been observing the activities at Casa Martone."

"What reason did you give for stopping the maid in the street and questioning her?"

Massimo laughed. "Nico, my friend, your question implies I accosted her or subjected her to an inquisition. It was hardly that, merely a friendly chat. I inquired about Daniela's progress after the tragic incident, and she said Daniela spends most of her time in her room, coming out only for meals. She suggested we wait at least a day or two before interviewing Daniela."

"I suppose you should be the one to conduct the interview when she is fit," Nico quipped.

Massimo winked. "I could be persuaded to carry out that task."

Nico summarized his meeting with Berto Lenzi, including Lenzi's accusation of Luigi Prizzi. He fastened a new card with Prizzi's name to the wall beside the cards of other suspects. Vittorio said, "It's easy to cast aspersions on others, but did Lenzi convince you that he isn't the killer?"

"I'm inclined to believe him, even though he offered no proof of his innocence. He said he was with his family the entire time, so I plan to see if his wife confirms that claim."

"Instead of his wife, talk with the least resilient member of his family, his daughter." Maintaining his serious face, Vittorio added, "Or have Massimo talk with her." Massimo and Nico glanced at each other, unsure whether the remark was a rare bit of humor from the stoic investigator.

After weighing various ways to proceed, the men concluded Massimo should interview Berto Lenzi's daughter Tessa, Vittorio would interview his son, Angelo, and Nico would revisit guild consul Cantore to inquire about Luigi Prizzi.

18

Palazzo Tempi had gained a storybook reputation during the last century. One legend had it that a young man of the neighborhood fell in love with a young woman who lived in the palazzo. Their feuding families objected to the affair and somehow — the legend isn't clear on this — the man was condemned to death, only to be saved from the executioner's blade by the young woman's ardent pleadings.

When the Medicis acquired the venerable property, they granted a distinguished maestro of the performing arts permission to use the palazzo as a studio for giving dance instruction to girls and young women.

Massimo crossed the Arno to the city's Oltrarno neighborhood and walked along the riverfront until he reached a gray stone palazzo. A small sign beside the door confirmed it was Palazzo Tempi. He entered the building and climbed to its second level; there he expected to find the maestro instructing Berto Lenzi's daughter Tessa in the art of dance, one of the social skills valued by cultured Florentine women.

To the left of the second level landing, an archway opened

to a salon where Tessa and a dozen other girls her age were gracefully gliding across the floor in carefully choreographed steps. Their movements followed the rhythm of music from a flute played by a gangly youth standing in a far corner of the room. The maestro leading the girls bobbed his head and waved his arms in time with the music, giving himself the appearance of a stringed puppet.

Massimo glanced at the girls briefly, then turned right and entered the room occupied by the dancers' nursemaids, all women. Their conversations ceased upon seeing a man enter the room. He approached the closest woman, smiled warmly, and asked, "Who among you lovely ladies cares for Tessa Lenzi?"

The woman who was old enough to be Massimo's mother found the handsome man's attention had suddenly made her mouth too parched to speak. She lifted her hand and pointed to a pretty dark-haired woman. All eyes followed Massimo as he crossed the room and sat beside Tessa's nursemaid. In response to Massimo's query, she confirmed she was Tessa's caretaker, said her name was Agnese, and told him, "The girls are learning *Bassadanza*." The name meant nothing to Massimo. He responded with a smile and asked, "Is it a difficult dance to learn?"

"Bassadanza is the simplest of the dances Tessa will learn. She's been taking lessons for less than a month. When the maestro is satisfied with the girls' progress, he'll start teaching them the *Quadernaria,* a faster and more complex dance and when they become proficient at the Quadernaria, they'll learn two other dances."

"Have you learned all four dances?" Massimo asked.

Agnese's faced flushed. "I'm a nursemaid," she replied. Massimo swallowed and looked down, sorry that his question had embarrassed the woman.

They sat without speaking until the music stopped and the girls in the salon gathered around the maestro, eager to hear his final piece of advice for the day. The nursemaids moved as a group toward the salon to collect their charges, leaving Massimo and Agnese alone. Realizing that Massimo had come to the studio to question Tessa, Agnese tried to voice her concern, saying simply, "She's just a girl."

Massimo gave an understanding nod. "I'll try not to upset her."

Tessa grew anxious as the other girls and their nurses were leaving, and Agnese hadn't come for her. Glancing at the girls on the landing, Tessa finally saw Agnese in the room beyond and walked toward her. When she reached the landing, she spotted the stranger sitting with her nurse, and her pace instinctively slowed.

Agnese said, "Tessa, this is Signor Leoni. He's a member of the Florentine Security Commission investigating the death of Marco Ridolfi, and he'd like to ask you some questions."

Massimo flashed his most disarming smile, one that never failed to win over women. He could only hope it would soothe a twelve-year-old girl. Tessa stood beside Agnese, reached down, took her hand, and looked apprehensively at Massimo, who said, "You went to Marco Ridolfi's betrothal ceremony with your family. Marco was your cousin. Did you know him well?"

"I'd only seen him twice."

"Your family isn't close to his," Massimo said, hoping to elicit a reaction from the girl, but she said nothing. Realizing he needed to be direct to prompt a response, he asked, "What did you do when you arrived at the villa?"

She looked down at her shoes, remembering that the shoes she'd worn to the villa had become soiled with mud. "We went to the terrace."

"Did you speak with any of the other guests?"

"I didn't know any of them. My mother spoke with some of the women."

"Did your father talk with the men?"

"No. My father wasn't happy to be there."

"Were you all together on the terrace the entire time until you were called to dinner?"

Tessa's nose wrinkled as she considered whether to mention her brother, then decided not to shield him. "Angelo didn't stay with us."

"Where did Angelo go?"

"I don't know. Maybe to look for Daniela. He's taken with her. He kept saying Marco didn't deserve her." With a sarcastic tone, she added, "He actually believes he might attract her interest."

Massimo repeated his earlier question. "Did you stay with your father the whole time, from when you arrived at the villa until dinner in the peristyle?"

Tessa nodded. "Yes, he was with me and my mother."

Again Massimo flashed his best smile and said, "Thank you for answering my questions." As the three descended to the street, Massimo said, "I saw you dancing earlier. My knowledge of dance is limited, but I thought you all looked lovely." That triggered a shy grin from the girl. He helped Tessa and Agnese into their waiting coach and watched them drive away toward the bridge that would take them from the Oltrarno district to the city center. When he returned to the Security Commission office, Massimo added a card to the wall: *Daughter Tessa confirms Berto Lenzi was never away from his family.* He added another card to the Angelo Lenzi column: *Was not with his family the entire time.*

Guild consul Cantore registered surprise at seeing Nico return to his shop. "Have you come this time to purchase one of my exquisite glassware items? Last time you were here, you were enticed by the animal collection." He lifted a sparkling figurine of a rearing stallion from the shelf behind him. "This piece just arrived from Venice." He twirled the piece slowly in his hand. "See how it shimmers in the light."

"It is lovely," Nico admitted, "and I know someone who would be delighted to have it."

Returning the statuette to the shelf, Cantore said, "Perhaps another time, but now, your tempered tone tells me you are here for a different purpose."

"Be assured I will come again for that piece or another, but you are correct; I am again in need of information. I was told of an altercation at the recent guild meeting between Antonio Ridolfi and Luigi Prizzi when both were vying for election as guild consul. The report was hearsay because my source didn't witness the incident himself, but he claims Prizzi attacked Ridolfi and the encounter ended with Ridolfi being bloodied."

Cantore shook his head vigorously. "No. No. That's not what happened, not at all. The confrontation began a verbal exchange with both men hurling invectives at each other. It turned physical when Ridolfi grabbed Prizzi's arm, a foolish move. Prizzi isn't a big man, but he's been in brawls before and he handles himself well. Guild members, and I was one of them, separated the two men before they could injure each other. There was no bloodshed."

Troubled by the memory, Cantore ran his hand through his hair and stared into the distance. "The quarrel ended with Prizzi shaking a fist and swearing he would destroy Ridolfi. His words were said in anger, so none of us gave credence to his threat at the time."

Nico probed, "But now? Now that Marco Ridolfi has been murdered?"

Cantore shrugged and spread his hands. "I'm loath to think Luigi would do such a thing, but ..."

Nico asked, "What prompted the clash?"

"I don't know what sparked the tangle this time. It wasn't their first squabble. A week earlier, Antonio became incensed when Luigi announced he would seek the position of guild consul. Antonio felt his business success made him deserving of the position. He isn't sensitive to the attitudes of others. If he were, he'd have known how many men resent his shabby treatment of the guild's shopkeeper members."

"Shopkeepers like you?"

Cantore nodded. "Not only me, but also pharmacists, barbers, and funeral arrangers like Prizzi." He pointed to a table and chairs in a corner of the shop. He sat and Nico joined him. "The animosity between Prizzi and Ridolfi is not new," Cantore explained. "It began two years ago when Antonio's mother passed. At that time, the men were cordial to each other. Antonio had called upon Luigi to arrange for the archbishop to say a mass at the cathedral for her. Another funeral mass was already slated at the cathedral on the day Antonio had selected, so Luigi moved the mass for Signora Ridolfi to the following day.

"Antonio was livid. He insisted that the mass for the other woman should have been moved. He argued that the woman was merely the wife of a butcher, so her mass should be in a parish church, not the cathedral. That was the episode that started their feud. Luigi told everyone that Antonio was being unreasonable, and since then, Antonio has been making derogatory remarks about Luigi whenever he can.

"The feud grew more intense last year when the owner of a stable in the San Niccolò neighborhood inherited a farm in the Chiana Valley; he decided to sell the stable and become a farmer. Luigi Prizzi opted to buy the stable, intending to use the building to house his wagons and other materials."

"Coffins?" Nico speculated.

Cantore shrugged. "I suppose so. Prizzi saw the acquisition as a step toward expanding his business. Antonio heard about the transaction from the notary, who was preparing the transition contract. He contacted the seller, outbid Prizzi, and bought the stable. That happened a year ago and the building still stands empty."

Nico mused, "Antonio bought the property solely to undermine Luigi?"

Cantore bit his lip. "It seems there can be no other explanation."

Blending all the incidents Cantore had described, Nico reasoned, "Their ire has been intensifying over the past two years."

Cantore said wistfully, "I can imagine Luigi seeking revenge, but I can't fathom him murdering Antonio's son."

"Luigi may not have planned for murder, but harnessing

hatred is not always easy. Once set free, it can cause more misery than intended. Did you arrive at the villa with Prizzi and were you with him the entire time?"

Cantore's face lit up. He said buoyantly, "Yes, we rode in the same carriage, and we were never apart, so I'm certain he couldn't have killed Marco."

Walking from the glassware shop to the city center, Nico pondered whether to discount Prizzi as a suspect, or to gather more information. According to Signor Cantore, Prizzi couldn't have killed Marco Ridolfi himself, but given the animosity between him and Ridolfi, might he have hired an assassin?

At the Security Commission office, Nico found Vittorio studying the wall of notecards. Pointing to a new card Massimo had added, Vittorio said, "Massimo added this after his interview with Tessa Lenzi. She said her father was with her during the entire time they were at the villa. Massimo is confident she was being truthful, making it unlikely that Berto Lenzi is the killer."

Nico said, "I agree. When I spoke with Berto Lenzi he admitted that he still resents Angelo Ridolfi, but their feud dates from an old dispute. If Lenzi wanted revenge, he would have taken it years ago."

He told Vittorio about his conversation with the guild consul. "Signor Cantore didn't have any kind words for Antonio Ridolfi. According to Cantore, Ridolfi's lack of respect for others has gained him many adversaries, but none motivated to commit murder. He told me how the antagonism between Prizzi and Ridolfi began and its latest incident. If there wasn't a murder involved, I'd say the two men were behaving like spoiled children. Cantore said that Prizzi was with him the entire time at the villa, so Prizzi couldn't have killed Marco Ridolfi or tainted the wine."

Vittorio said, "It's premature to dismiss Prizzi as a suspect. Men like him like keeping their hands clean. If he is the instigator, he might have hired someone to commit the crimes."

Nico stared at the cards tacked to the wall. After a long moment, he puzzled, "Is it possible there were two perpetrators? One who contaminated the wine, and another who killed Marco Ridolfi?"

"That's a passable assumption," Vittorio agreed.

Nico shook his head. "We've made little progress finding the killer. The prospect of hunting two men is unsettling."

Sensing his colleague needed encouragement, Vittorio said, "Since both crimes targeted the same victim on the same occasion, finding the two criminals might not be as difficult as you imagine."

Unlike Marco Ridolfi and Polito Martone, Berto Lenzi's son Angelo had no part in his family's business. He spent his days playing cards with a disreputable crowd at a seedy tavern in the Santa Maria Novella district. He'd developed a fair level of skill for the game and a shrewdness at wagering that let him win as often as he lost. On those occasions when fortune went against him and he suffered a string of losses, he fawned on his mother until she lent him the florins needed to return to the games.

After surveilling Angelo to discover his daily routine, Vittorio targeted one of his inept card playing associates. By plying the man with a jug of ale, Vittorio learned of Berto's failed attempts to bring Angelo into the family business. The man told Vittorio that Berto had lost several customers because Angelo had muddled orders and billing. When Berto finally accepted that his son had no business skill, Angelo, freed of all responsibility, became content to pass his time gambling and taking pleasure at the nearby brothel when his winnings allowed.

Vittorio decided that the most straightforward approach to getting information from Angelo was through gambling. He waited outside until Angelo exited his favorite tavern. He held out a gold florin to get Angelo's attention, introduced himself as a member of the Florentine Security Commission, and proposed a wager. "A game of *freccetta*. If you win, this florin is yours. If I win, you answer my questions."

Intrigued by the idea, Angelo accepted the challenge. In his hand, Vittorio held two short arrows. He gave one to Angelo, and pointed to a tree a distance away. "The knobby growth protruding from that tree trunk is our target. We will each throw one frecetta and whoever sticks his closest to the knob is the winner. You may throw first if you wish."

The sun had fled, and darkness had overtaken the eastern sky. The dim light would hinder both men, but Angelo had an additional handicap; he'd spent his afternoon drinking. The effect of his indulgence showed in his unsteadiness. He fingered the miniature arrow to gauge its weight and balance; then he reached out, took the second projectile from Vittorio, and judged its qualities. Grinning, he said, "I'll throw this one." Keeping one arrow, he passed the other back to Vittorio.

Although not his favorite game, Angelo had some experience with freccetta. He squinted to sharpen his focus then raised his arm and moved his hand back until the arrow's feathers nearly grazed his cheek. He stepped forward with one foot, and then, with his full body in motion, he let the missile fly. The arrow pierced the rough tree bark barely a hand's width below the knob. Angelo jumped into the air and cried out, "Ah, no need to waste your effort, commissioner. You can save your pride and just hand me your gold."

Showing no emotion, Vittorio moved to the place Angelo had stood, cocked his arm, and released his arrow. It whistled through the air and struck the soft wood of the knob, but rather than sticking, it peeled away a strip of bark and dangled, wiggling as though it might work itself free. Angelo inhaled sharply, expecting the arrow to fall; instead, it steadied and held fast, with its shaft leaning against the knob. "Damn!" Angelo exclaimed; then, resigned, he dropped onto a nearby stone bench and said, "Ask your questions."

Vittorio began, "Your father seemed to resent being at his nephew's betrothal celebration."

Before Vittorio could frame a question to follow his statement, Angelo snorted, "Yah. My mother is the only one in our family who wanted to be there. Our families haven't been close since Antonio abandoned my father for the chance to import sugar from Egypt. He didn't have the decency to ask my father to join him in his new business, and my father never forgave him for that." Angelo leaned back, looked hard at Vittorio, and said, "But I'm sure you know that because your colleague already talked with my father."

Angelo let a moment pass, then said, "Are you asking me whether my father was angry enough to kill Marco Ridolfi? He already told your associate that he didn't."

"Was your family together the whole time you were at the villa?"

"I don't know. I didn't stay with them because I tired of listening to my mother and father bickering. A servant girl entertained me in a salon until we were called for dinner. And if you want proof, the girl's name is Ginerva. You can ask her. She's a short, busty girl with wavy hair." Adopting a lecherous smirk, Angelo added, "She's a bit plump for my liking, but very friendly."

To disrupt Angelo's impudence, Vittorio declared, "You and your friend were arrested by the Guardia for cutting someone with a knife in a brawl at a tavern."

Surprised by the accusation, Angelo's mouth dropped open. "I didn't cut anybody. Some troublemakers came into the tavern and started harassing my friend. All I did was wave my knife. That convinced them to leave us alone. They were backing away when two Guardia officers came into the tavern and misinterpreted the situation."

"Is your default to cut someone when you have a disagreement?"

Angelo glowered, but said nothing. Once again, Vittorio diverted the conversation to keep Angelo off guard. "Are you wearing a belt?" he asked.

Angelo pulled up on his tunic to reveal a plain leather belt devoid of metal studs or other decorations. "Of course I'm wearing a belt." He hesitated a moment. "Oh, you want to know whether I'm wearing a knife." He raised another section of his tunic to display his knife in a scabbard hanging from the belt. "Yes, as you can see, I'm wearing a knife."

Vittorio said, "At the villa, when you were seated in the peristyle, your attention was locked on Daniela."

Angelo recovered quickly. He rubbed his hands together. "Yes, Daniela gets my juices flowing. She always has. Do you find that surprising? Maybe now that ..." He stopped mid-sentence, completing the thought in his head, but realizing it was best not to express it aloud, then pushed himself up from the bench and faced Vittorio. "Uncle Antonio clawed his way to success by taking advantage of my father and other men. I have no respect for him. None in my family would weep if his business failed." Angelo turned and walked away.

Vittorio watched Angelo until he disappeared around a corner, then he entered the tavern and approached the barkeep. "I'm looking for someone named Dario. Might you know him?"

The barkeep gesture toward a bony man with a square jaw who was leaning against the bar a distance away. Vittorio moved down the bar, introduced himself as a member of the Security Commission, and said, "You and your friend Angelo were arrested for assaulting someone with a knife."

"Mother of God," Dario seethed. "All I was doing was defending myself. Ever since, the Guardia won't leave me alone, and now the Security Commission is harassing me. Don't you have real criminals to hassle?"

"I'm not here to hassle you. I want to ask you about Angelo Lenzi."

Dario motioned toward the door. "Angelo just left."

Vittorio ignored Dario's comment and said, "When you were arrested, Angelo was there. He was also arrested. The Guardia report says he cut someone with a knife, but he denies it. He also claims he was just defending himself."

Dario took a swig of beer. "Someone came at him. He might have cut the buck, but I didn't see it. I think the report is wrong. We found out later the lout who came at Angelo is the son of a rich mill owner. His father probably told the Guardia what to write in their report."

"Has Angelo drawn his knife before to threaten someone?"

"He can get upset when he's pushed and when he's been drinking. Everybody's got their limit."

"Have you ever seen him violent? Violent enough to commit murder?"

"Murder?" Dario echoed, then the realization struck him. "Angelo told me there was a murder. You think he did it?"

"What did he tell you?"

"Just that he was at a betrothal celebration and someone was killed."

"Did he seem happy when he told you?"

"You mean happy that someone was murdered?" Rather than respond, Vittorio waited for Dario to continue. "I don't remember his expression, but I don't know why he would be happy."

"Do you think Angelo could commit murder?"

"I don't know. Maybe. But why would he do that?"

"Did he mention a woman named Daniela?"

Dario's eyes narrowed. "Yes, he kept blathering about her, saying she was spicy and how he might chase after her now that she's available."

"Did he mention a woman named Ginerva?"

"The servant girl. Yes, he bragged about having her in a salon." Dario took a swig of beer, then chuckled. "I never know when to believe Angelo's stories."

Without a single word of farewell, Vittorio turned and left the tavern, having found no proof that Angelo was the killer or any evidence to exonerate him. He would need to locate Ginerva.

20

The Martones lived in a three-level stone building in an affluent neighborhood of the San Lorenzo district, close to the central market. The housemaid whom Massimo had met previously answered his knock. Not certain whether she remembered him from their brief meeting in a piazza, he introduced himself. "I'm Massimo Leoni of the Florentine Security Commission."

The maid smiled sweetly. "Yes, I remember."

"Has Signorina Martone recovered enough for me to speak with her?"

"I believe so. Wait here and I'll ask if she's able to receive you."

While he waited outside the house for the maid to return, a line of carriages moving along Via Larga toward Palazzo Medici caught Massimo's attention. He recognized only one passenger, Signor Mozzi, First Chair of the Ten of War and overseer of the Florentine Security Commission. Mozzi's carriage followed one that displayed the banner of the Duchy of Milan. The last carriage in the procession was approaching when, behind him, the door opened, and the maid called, "I'm sorry to have kept you, Signor Leoni. Come with me." Etiquette prevented her from introducing herself and him from inquiring about her name.

Vases filled with flowers brought the fragrance of a springtime meadow to the house, in contrast to the musty smell of antiques that filled the homes of many wealthy Florentines. Massimo followed the maid to the second level, where he was intercepted in an anteroom by Daniela Martone's mother Lavinia. Her appearance gave no indication she was grieving. She wore an ankle-length blue *giornea* with a silver brooch on her left sleeve. Her hair had been braided and styled into a coil on her head and topped with a clove-scented netting. She noticed Massimo glance at a partially finished painting on an easel of a couple walking through a garden. In a simpering voice, Lavinia said, "That's Daniela's work. I'm not sure she'll ever finish it now. She's still recovering from the tragedy. It would be best if you could speak with me instead of her."

Massimo responded, "I'd be happy to talk with you, Signora." He flashed a disarming smile to shatter Lavinia's resolve. "But Daniela knew Marco better than anyone, so I will need to speak with her. If she is not well today, I can return another time."

Lavinia pressed her hands together and turned slightly, signaling for Massimo to join her. "Since you're already here, you might as well speak with her now, but please be mindful of her condition."

She led Massimo to a reception salon where Daniela was seated on a couch. Lavinia sat next to her daughter and rested a hand protectively on Daniela's arm. Unlike her mother, Daniela wore neither jewelry nor perfume. Her hair had been brushed, probably by a maid, but it had not been styled.

Massimo sat on a nearby chair and introduced himself. Looking at Daniela, he said, "I am truly sorry for your loss. Before being appointed to the Security Commission, I served with the Florentine Army. Two of my close friends died in the conflict with the troops of Alfonso of Aragon at Maremma. I still miss them and think of them often, but I'm sure my loss doesn't compare with the pain you are suffering."

Daniela stayed silent while Lavinia said, "Daniela is thankful for your condolences at this tragic time."

Lavinia's response to a comment aimed at her daughter made Massimo doubt Daniela's readiness for the interview. Nonetheless, he continued, still addressing Daniela. "I appreciate your agreeing to speak with me. We're interviewing everyone who might help us identify the culprit. Any piece of information could be significant. I understand you met frequently with Marco to plan the dinner."

This time it was Daniela who responded. In a voice soft enough that Massimo had to lean forward to hear, she said, "Marco and I created the guest list, but his mother did all the planning."

"When you last met with Marco, did he seem troubled?"

"He wasn't upset any more than usual. Business uncertainties always troubled Marco."

"I've been told that he was always searching for ways to improve his family's business. Do you know what new ideas he was considering?"

Daniela's voice grew louder when she realized Massimo's questions were not related to the murder. She said, "He wanted to expand beyond Florence into other cities in Tuscany and to the Republic of Siena. He met with consuls of the Arte della Mercanzia, the guild of merchants, in Siena."

That statement surprised Massimo. "Marco's father had said nothing about him traveling to Siena."

"Marco might not have told his father. Marco always said his father got overly enthusiastic whenever he mentioned a new prospect, so he didn't divulge his ideas until he felt confident they had promise."

"Was he encouraged by the visit ... encouraged to expand into Siena?"

"The consuls told him the Ridolfis could sell sugar to apothecaries in Siena, provided they joined the guild. Marco took that as encouragement, but a week later, a merchant from Siena came to see him and told him Florentine merchants weren't welcome in Siena. He said he'd make sure the Ridolfis could never do business in Siena."

Massimo stiffened. "That sounds like a threat. Did Marco take it seriously?"

Daniela coughed, a dry raspy cough. Lavinia fetched a glass of water for her daughter from a pitcher on a nearby table. Daniela took a sip, cleared her throat, and said, "Marco didn't see the man's caution as hostile. He said rivals always resist competition."

"Perhaps he should have taken the warning seriously," Lavinia said curtly, without shifting her gaze to make eye contact with either Daniela or Massimo.

"Did Marco mention the merchant's name?"

Daniela said, "No, Marco didn't say a name. He only mentioned the incident in passing."

Massimo looked at Lavinia hoping she might comment, but she remained silent.

Changing the topic, Massimo asked, "Are you aware that Marco used a notary to help with his research?"

"There is a notary who had worked for the tax office. Marco said the notary was familiar with tax records, so he could do research on other companies efficiently."

"Did he ever tell you the name of the notary?"

Daniela stared into the distance for a long moment, trying to refresh her memory. "I remember Marco mentioning the name Bernardo but I can't recall him saying the man's family name."

While Massimo framed his next question, Daniela whispered almost as though speaking to herself, "I saw Marco at the celebration. He was speaking to the chef and when he saw me, he smiled. Whenever I close my eyes, I can see his smile, like a ghost haunting me. A ghost who doesn't know the terrible fate that awaits him." She leaned over and rested her head against her mother's shoulder, prompting her mother to request that Massimo end the interview so Daniela could rest. As he rose to leave, Massimo said, "I have one last question. Were there any other matters capturing Marco's attention?"

Regaining her strength, Daniela said, "He was very interested in knowing how our family business profits rose suddenly. He asked me the reason, but I couldn't tell him anything because I'm not involved in the business. Afterward, when I asked my brother Polito that question, he became furious. He said Marco should stay out of our business." Daniela shot a sideways glance at her mother and chose her words carefully. "Sometimes my brother can be difficult."

Massimo thanked Daniela for agreeing to meet with him. Lavinia summoned the housemaid, who escorted Massimo to the door, where he flashed a charming smile and said, "I don't expect to contact Signorina Martone again, but I hope we'll have the chance to meet in the future." The maid returned Massimo's smile. Massimo said, "I'm sure Signora Martone mentioned your name, but I didn't hear it."

"Octavia," she responded. As Massimo turned to leave, guilt washed over him, but only for an instant. Was it inappropriate for him to dally with the maid while the household was in mourning? Some might think so, but Massimo had seen soldiers consumed by grief after their cohorts were killed. Those experiences had convinced him that sorrow needed to be balanced by hope.

21

The three commissioners gathered at the Security Commission office to hear about Massimo's discussion with Daniela. "I'm grateful Daniela agreed to meet with me because Marco's death still weighs heavily on her. When I asked about Marco's plans for the business, she mentioned that he'd gone to Siena to inquire about selling spices in that city."

Vittorio bristled. "When I spoke with Antonio, he never mentioned that Marco had gone to Siena."

Massimo continued, "Shortly after Marco returned from Siena, a Sienese merchant came to Florence to tell Marco that his guild would never allow Ridolfi Imports to sell goods in Siena. Marco dismissed the incident, but from the way he described the episode to his business associates and family members, they viewed it as a threat."

Nico said, "From what you've told us, I agree with them. It's difficult to believe that the merchant traveled all the way from Siena just to give a friendly caution."

"I had the same reaction," Massimo agreed. "As did Signora Martone. She felt Marco erred in not taking the coercion seriously. Unfortunately, neither Daniela nor her mother knew the merchant's name."

Vittorio said caustically, "I find it revealing that Antonio neglected to mention the merchant's visit. He's not been forthcoming in sharing information that could help us find his son's killer. He failed to acknowledge his strained relationships with fellow guild members and he didn't mention his quarrel with Prizzi."

Massimo said, "Antonio may not be the only person with secrets. Daniela said her brother got extremely defensive when she asked him about the family business. It's possible that Polito feels intimidated by his sister because Daniela is an intelligent woman. He may see the business as his refuge and view any interest by Daniela as an intrusion.

"Daniela also confirmed that Marco had employed a notary to help him research other companies. She remembered the notary had previously worked in the tax office and his given name is Bernardo, but neither she nor her mother recalled the man's family name."

Massimo added note cards to the wall, summarizing the information he'd gotten from his conversation with Daniela. When Massimo stepped away from the wall, Vittorio pointed to a notecard in the Angelo Lenzi column and looked at Nico. "Angelo Lenzi claims he couldn't have killed Marco Ridolfi because he was dallying with a serving girl named Ginerva. I want to verify his claim by speaking with the girl. Does she work for your cousin Donato at the Uccello?"

Nico thought for a moment. "I don't recall her name, but Donato is at the Uccello now. You can ask him." Nico turned to Massimo. "We shouldn't dismiss the possible threat from the Sienese merchant. Marco went to Siena to meet with the guild consuls. They might know which of their members objected so strenuously to Ridolfi Imports expanding into Siena that he went to Florence to confront Marco."

After further discussion, Nico and Massimo decided to journey to Siena to meet with the consuls of the Sienese guild.

Workers at the Uccello were busy even during the mid-afternoon lull, readying the restaurant for its dinner service. Aromas of grilled meat and sounds of vegetables being chopped emanated from the kitchen. Men with brooms of bundled straw moved systematically through the dining room to clear away the roadway dirt that had been tracked in by mid-day diners. Members of a government commission responsible for maintaining the city's roads sat at the only occupied table in the restaurant. Rather than hold meetings in their staid conference rooms, senior government officials preferred to convene at Florence's quality restaurants, where they could savor exquisite dishes and have the cost paid for by the Florentine treasury. The Uccello, regarded as the finest restaurant in the city, was their favorite.

Donato was sampling a new vintage of wine when he saw Vittorio enter the dining room. Vittorio had been to the Uccello before, but always accompanied by Nico. Donato motioned for Vittorio to join him. Believing Vittorio was looking for Nico, he said, "Nico isn't here," and held out a glass of shimmering crimson wine. "Taste this. It's called Valetellina. The importer says it comes from grapes grown for more than a thousand years in a region in Lombardy beyond Milan near the Swiss cantons."

Vittorio accepted the glass and took a sip. "I'm no expert, so discount my opinion, but it seems lighter and less robust than our local Tuscan wines."

Donato smiled. "Ah, a good observation. That's my opinion as well. I'm eager to hear the impressions of our regular dinner guests. I think they'll enjoy this one because they like to sample different vintages." Donato set his glass down. "As I said, Nico isn't here. I haven't seen him since we left the house this morning."

"I was just with Nico, but he's not why I've come. At the Ridolfi betrothal celebration, there was a serving girl named Ginerva. Is she one of yours?"

"Ginerva is too young to be on the staff at the Uccello. She's only twelve years old, from a wonderful family of five sisters. Her father is a carder at a woolen factory, so money is always scarce with them. I hire Ginerva for special events like the betrothal celebration. Is there a problem? Did she do something wrong?"

"No, nothing wrong. Angelo Lenzi claims she can verify that he couldn't have killed Marco Ridolfi. I want to know whether she can corroborate Lenzi's story."

Donato gave Vittorio directions to a small house crowded close to others near the river in the Santa Maria Novella district. A woman with tired eyes and tousled hair answered Vittorio's knock. She pulled the door open enough to see her caller. She wore an apron over a frayed smock. A girl about six years old sheltered behind her mother and looked up curiously at the stranger.

"I'm Vittorio Colombo of the Security Commission. Do you have a daughter, Ginerva?" The woman stiffened, as people usually did when Vittorio mentioned the Security Commission. Sensing the woman's apprehension, Vittorio said, "Don't be afraid. I only want to ask her about someone who was at the Ridolfi betrothal celebration in Calenzano."

Without turning or opening the door further, the woman said to the youngster behind her, "Go get your sister."

Moments later Ginerva squeezed beside her mother so she could look out at the stranger. Her mother put a protective hand on Ginerva's shoulder. Vittorio looked down at the girl's pretty, innocent face and thought, by what right can a brute like Angelo Lenzi make advances to this child? He introduced himself to Ginerva and said, "Angelo Lenzi said he was with you while food was being prepared for the dinner. Is that true?"

She said, with more confidence than he had expected, "I was in the kitchen setting lemon custard tarts onto serving trays. The tarts were to be served as the dessert. Signor Lenzi entered the kitchen and came near me. I had trouble filling the trays because he was standing so close to me. He told me I was pretty and ran his fingers along my cheek. He said we should get together after the dinner." The distasteful remembrance made Ginerva squirm. "I wanted him to leave, but I couldn't say anything because he was a guest, and I was just a servant."

"How long was he with you?"

"I can't remember. It seemed like a long time before someone came into the kitchen and announced that the guests were being seated, so we should get ready to bring out the food. When Signor Lenzi heard the announcement, he left."

Vittorio almost wished Ginerva's account hadn't substantiated Angelo Lenzi's claim that he was with her during the time Marco Ridolfi was killed. He would have welcomed an excuse to shackle the reprobate who had accosted the poor girl. He thanked the girl and her mother for their cooperation and said, "If you are ever in that situation again, Ginerva, go to Signor Donato Argenti and tell him what is happening. You can trust him. He will understand and shield you from men like Angelo Lenzi."

22

TO SIENA

The following morning, shortly after dawn, Nico and Massimo set out on horseback for Siena. Of the several roads connecting Florence to Siena, they chose the Via Cassia at Nico's suggestion. Even at the early hour, the road was filled with a steady stream of wagons bringing wine and olives from the Chianti Hills to Florence. No wagons were headed in the opposite direction, away from the city. Massimo said, "I haven't been to Siena in almost two years and I've never gone there on this road. In the army, when going south to Siena and beyond, we always went first to Lucca and from there took the Via Francigena."

Nico said, "Ah, the Roman road used by religious pilgrims. Have you traveled its entire length from Rome to the town of Canterbury in *Inghilterra*?"

"Twice on military assignments, my unit went south to Rome, but in the opposite direction, I've only been as far north as Piacenza, and that was far enough. Pilgrims must have great devotion to walk the entire distance from Inghilterra to Rome."

"Devotion, stamina, and time," Nico said. "It must take

them nearly half a year to walk the entire distance. A section of this road, the Via Cassia, was also built by the Romans. Their original road went from Florence to Arezzo before turning south to Siena, but about seven hundred years ago, the route was changed to make the journey shorter. The new road kept the same name, but it no longer goes through Arezzo."

"Surely you didn't learn that bit of information at the university," Massimo quipped.

"No, I learned it from my cousin Donato. He buys produce from farms in the Chiana Valley near Arezzo, and farmers there still cling to the name Via Cassia. Tradition remains deeply ingrained, even after seven hundred years."

Having missed his morning meal, Massimo convinced Nico to stop midway between Florence and Siena for something to eat. At a farm in the Chiana Valley, they bought slices of dried Chianina beef, a chunk of bread, and pecorino cheese. Carrying the food in a sack, they rode a short distance to a hill-side vineyard, where they purchased a jug of Chianti wine, and enjoyed the repast sitting under the warm sun near a grove of olive trees.

In early afternoon, they passed through the Siena city wall at the Porta Ovile gate and headed to the Loggia della Mercanzia where the offices of the Merchants' Guild were located. The only desk in the reception hall was occupied by a clerk who had moved all his documents aside, so he had space to play a card game. Upon seeing the visitors, his face flushed with embarrassment. Quickly, he gathered the cards and hid them from view except for a single card that fell to the floor. "May I help you?" he asked feebly, while reaching out with his foot to shield the wayward card.

Hearing no sounds from elsewhere in the building, Nico grew concerned that their visit to the office might be a waste of time. "Are the consuls available?"

With his leg extended out to the side, the clerk awkwardly slid the stubborn card under the desk. "They are in the consul office, but they're occupied." Looking up at Nico with a smug expression, he added, "They've been asked to host a Roman envoy who will arrive next week. It's a great honor, so they're working hard to prepare an agenda that will make a favorable impression."

Nico introduced himself and Massimo as members of the Florentine Security Commission and said, "Kindly inform the Consuls that we've come from Florence to discuss a pressing matter with them."

The clerk sat momentarily befuddled, as though no one had ever asked him to interrupt the Consuls. Annoyed by the clerk's inaction, Nico pressed, "Or show us where they are meeting and we'll tell them ourselves."

The clerk jumped up from his desk and headed toward the hallway. "Wait here. I'll tell them." Without bothering to knock, he vanished into a room midway along the hallway for a mere moment before reappearing. He returned to his desk, walking cautiously like a dog with its tail tucked between its legs. "I told them."

"Will they see us?"

"They will if you can wait. They need to finish an important matter."

Massimo asked, "How long before they're finished?" The clerk merely shrugged.

Nico and Massimo explored the reception area while they waited for the Consuls. Portraits of two distinguished looking men hung on one wall, either the current guild consuls or the guild's founders. A smaller painting of the guild's insignia hung between the portraits. Daylight streaming in through windows high on the opposite wall illuminated footprints on the dusty floor. Nico and Massimo grew increasingly impatient as they examined a miniature replica of the Siena Cathedral when footsteps caught their attention. A man with a broad chest and short legs marched up to them and said brusquely,

"We are busy with crucial work. What is the purpose of your visit?"

Nico said, "A Florentine sugar merchant named Marco Ridolfi came to Siena and inquired of the consuls whether his company might be allowed to import sugar to Siena."

With disinterest, the consul said only, "That may be so."

Nico continued, "A short time later, a merchant from Siena went to Florence to dissuade Signor Ridolfi from expanding his business to Siena. We would like to speak with that merchant."

"Why did you come here? The consuls can't possibly know the actions of all our members."

"A few days ago, Signor Ridolfi was murdered."

The consul bristled, "Are you accusing a member of our guild of murder?"

"We're making no accusations. We are simply gathering information. Anyone who spoke with Signor Ridolfi may know something that could help us find his killer."

"You are wasting your time ... and mine. As I said, I can't possibly know whom you are seeking. But I assure you no member of our guild has information about a murderer. Now you must excuse me." The consul turned and stomped away.

The clerk came to where Nico and Massimo were standing. Displaying a sheepish expression, he said, "He isn't always so unsupportive. The pressure of arranging the Roman envoy's visit must be weighing on him. Our city council believes the envoy's visit could be prelude to a major trade treaty."

The clerk wandered slowly to his desk, leaned against it, and said, "I remember a Florentine merchant meeting with the consuls to inquire about doing business in Siena." He paused, thinking. "Marco ... I don't recall his family name." Suddenly, the clerk's head jerked back. "Oh, Mother of God. You said someone was murdered. Was it him?"

Nico replied, "Yes, it was. His name was Marco Ridolfi." Encouraged by the clerk's concern, Nico repeated, "Shortly after Signor Ridolfi came here, a merchant from Siena went to Florence to dissuade him from expanding his sugar importing business to Siena. We would like to speak with that merchant."

The clerk shrugged. "I don't know who that might be, but it could be helpful for you to have the names of all the merchants in our guild. There are too many for anyone to remember all their names, but they are listed in the register." The clerk stepped away and, hurrying toward a nearby hallway, called back over his shoulder, "Wait here while I get the register."

Moments later he returned, cradling in his arms a weighty volume that he dropped onto the desk, opened, and began searching through its entries. After several moments muttering to himself, he announced, "There are twenty merchants." He pointed to five entries. "I'm certain these five trade in sugar, although others may as well."

Nico made note of the names and directions to their businesses. Outside the building, with a combination of determination and exasperation, Massimo said, "I suppose we should start by visiting the five known sugar merchants."

Nico grinned. "There may be another possibility ... the connector."

"Connector?" Massimo echoed.

As he led Massimo toward one of the Chancery's outlying buildings, Nico explained, "The connector is a member of the Chancery who brings together people who need to interact with others. He's also skilled at linking people with the information they require."

Still puzzled, Massimo said, "I've never heard of a position called a connector. Does the Florentine Chancery have a connector?"

"Yes, Florence has a connector, but you probably haven't encountered him because connectors shun attention. I crossed paths with the Sienese connector while tracking down an assassin who was targeting Luca Pitti." They turned onto a narrow street and Nico pointed to a gray stone building with Siena's coat of arms displayed above the doorway. "That's it."

A clerk sitting at a lone desk in the loggia looked up when the two men entered. Nico announced, "I need to speak with the connector."

Before the clerk could respond, a man with chiseled features and streaks of gray in his hair emerged from a nearby hallway. "Nico Argenti," he proclaimed. "Are you chasing another assassin?"

Nico recoiled in surprise that the connector remembered his name. "Not an assassin, but a killer." He introduced Massimo, explained their purpose, and showed the connector the list of names he had gotten at the guild office.

After eyeing the five names of known sugar merchants, the connector pointed to two names and said, "This one's in Sicily and this one injured himself last month and still walks with a cane, so these can be dismissed." He skipped over the next two names and declared, "Signor Costa is most likely the man you're seeking. He's an agitator who has a record of being arrested for getting into altercations with other patrons in a tavern. At one time, other guild members tried to have him expelled."

Nico and Massimo followed the connector's directions toward the Porta Tuffi city gate, where Signor Costa rented a building to store his merchandise. The wooden structure was in worse condition than the connector had described. Its warped boards and missing roof tiles showed neglect.

The harsh words of someone being rebuked reached them when they pulled open the door. The man berating his minion had a compact torso with short legs. A large round nose jutted from his flat face, and he huffed when he moved, reminding Nico of a wild boar. Upon seeing the two visitors, the brute shoved his underling toward the door and barked, "Get out! Go make it right!"

Massimo and Nico threaded through a cluster of barrels, possibly filled with sugar, as they entered the space. Nico detected an earthy, almost musky scent and questioned whether the odor was coming from the building or from Signor Costa. Tired from having spent hours on horseback riding from Florence to Siena and dispirited by the unpleasant surroundings, Nico bypassed introductions and asked directly, "Did you visit Signor Marco Ridolfi in Florence to warn him against expanding his business to Siena?" Amused by Nico's bluntness, Massimo smiled, knowing that his friend was usually more tactful. It felt good to see Nico adapt to the situation.

Costa bellowed, "You have no right to come here and question me!"

Continuing Nico's aggressive approach, Massimo grabbed Costa's arms, pushed him down onto a chair, and said, "The man you threatened was murdered, so we do have reason to question you."

The loud exchanges attracted a man who charged in from an adjacent room. Believing Massimo was assaulting Costa, the man pulled a knife and charged at Massimo from behind. Nico stepped in front of the man, reached into the pouch at his waist for a handful of stone chips, and hurled the chips at the man. The man shrieked when the shards lacerated his cheeks. He dropped his knife, jumped back, and raised his hands to shield his face, but too late. His eyes stung and filled with tears. Baffled, having seen only that Nico expelled a cloud of dust from his hand, the man froze, fearing Nico to be a wizard who had cast a spell on him. Costa, who was also unsure what had happened, dismissed his minion, saying, "We're just talking. Go. I'll call you if I need you."

Barely able to see through his narrowed eyes, the man staggered toward the door. After the man left, Costa returned his attention to Massimo and asked, "The Florentine merchant was murdered?"

"Yes," Massimo fumed. "He was murdered after you threatened him."

"I didn't threaten him!" Costa bellowed. "He wanted to sell sugar in the Republic of Siena. Only merchants who are guild members can sell products in our republic. I told our members about him; that a Florentine merchant wanted to steal our business. I convinced them they would be ruined if they allowed this foreigner to sell his goods in Siena. They all agreed and voted to ban any Florentine merchant from joining our guild. After I got the support of our guild members, I went to Florence and told the Florentine to forget about expanding his business into Siena. I persuaded him by letting him know he would never get approval from the guild to sell in Siena. He was angry at first. We exchanged bitter words, but in the end he acknowledged the reality of the situation. He had no choice and said if he couldn't sell in Siena, he would expand into Lucca. I had achieved my goal, so I had no reason to kill him."

Nico and Massimo exchanged glances. Daniela had said Marco was considering expanding to Siena, but she'd said nothing about Lucca. Had Marco not told her about Lucca or was Costa's story a fabrication? Sensing he wasn't being believed, Costa spit out three names. "Talk to them. They'll vouch for me."

Nico recognized the names as those given to him by the guild clerk. As they walked back to the center of the city,

Massimo placed a hand on Nico's shoulder. "I'm grateful beyond measure for your bravery, my friend. If you hadn't foiled my attacker with the stone chips, I'd be in pain right now because I didn't see him coming."

Nico flashed a smile. "I've been thinking about that episode as well, contemplating the best way to tell Alessa how I seized the opportunity to protect you for once."

In a stern voice, Massimo said, "Ah, but if you were a staunch friend, you wouldn't tarnish my reputation by recounting the tale. And you must know Alessa would not be keen to learn that you put yourself at risk by stepping in front of a bruiser's blade."

Adopting a mischievous tone, Massimo playfully added, "Moreover, you failed to execute the maneuver correctly. You should have thrown the chips after you fended off the attacker with your knife."

"I'll try to do better next time," Nico laughed.

Along Via dei Pispini they came to a low building with a sign reading, *Zucchero più pregiato*, Finest Sugar. Inside they found two men measuring sugar into small sacks. Signor Petrucci?" Nico inquired.

"Si, I am Petrucci," the smaller man replied.

Nico introduced himself and Massimo, explained their reason for being in Siena, and related what Signor Costa had told them. Petrucci threw his hands into the air. "Ah, that Costa is a *rompicazzo*, a pain in the ass. He's always causing trouble, but this time he tells the truth. He berated us until we all agreed not to let the Florentine join the guild, so he couldn't sell his sugar in Siena." Petrucci reflected a moment, then added, "At least this time maybe he did something good for us."

"Would you call Signor Costa a violent man?" Massimo asked.

"Violent? No, I wouldn't call him violent. He's always

complaining and arguing, but I've never seen him raise a fist against anyone. As I said, he's just a rompicazzo."

Nico asked, "Did Signor Costa say that he went to Florence to speak with the Florentine merchant?"

"Yes, he wanted everyone to know that he went to challenge the Florentine face-to-face. He said that he left the swine in tears and that we'd never have to worry about Florentines invading our territory again." Petrucci shrugged. "I don't know if any of that is true. Costa says many things and they're not all true. Maybe he went to Florence because he has a woman there."

Upon leaving Petrucci's warehouse, Massimo said, "After listening to Costa and Petrucci, I don't feel a need to visit the other two men Costa mentioned."

"I agree," Nico said. "Costa is a loudmouth who tries to impress people, but it seems unlikely that he went to Calenzano or hired someone to kill Marco Ridolfi."

As they headed toward Piazza del Campo, Siena's main public square, Massimo asked, "Is Bianca expecting you?"

"No, we decided to come to Siena so quickly I didn't have a chance to let her know I'd be here." He gestured toward a street heading toward the Loggia del Papa. "It's likely I'll find her still working in her loft at this time of day."

Massimo made a slight bow. "Convey my warmest regards to your beloved partner."

Nico asked, "And you, Massimo, are you going directly back to Florence?"

Massimo flashed a mischievous smile. "The last time I was in Siena, I made the acquaintance of a charming young widow. Perhaps today the goddess Fortuna will grant me renewed pleasure in the lady's company ... if she hasn't again been drawn into marriage."

The men separated, Massimo seeking an old flame and

Nico heading to the loft where Bianca had her dressmaking business. As Nico walked along, the surrounding city faded, replaced by his earliest memory of Bianca. He'd seen her first at Palazzo Pitti, where he'd gone to share information with Francesca. A servant at the palazzo had escorted Nico to the salon where Bianca was adjusting the dress she had made for Francesca. Bianca stood in front of a window where streaming sunlight lit her golden hair like an angel's halo. As he moved closer, the sight of her lovely face, soft skin, and blue eyes stirred Nico's heart, a sensation that recurs whenever he's in her presence or merely thinking of her. When Francesca left the room, Bianca asked him about his work. Her questions reflected a keen awareness of the issues facing the Florentine Republic, and they laughed together at the foolishness often displayed by government officials. As they spoke, Nico found himself fascinated by Bianca's intelligence and wit. From that moment, he was captivated.

Nico set the memory aside, climbed to the second level above the candlemaker's shop, and pushed open the door to Bianca's loft. She saw Nico's reflection in a window glass, spun around, and floated across the floor to him. He ran a hand along her cheek, down the curve of her chin; then without a word, they enveloped each other in a warm embrace. The world disappeared as they held onto each other and pressed their lips together. Nico's heart raced as he felt her body tight against his.

When they finally pulled away and their eyes met, Bianca said, "What a wonderful surprise having you here. I didn't know you were coming to Siena."

Nico took hold of Bianca's hands, looked into her eyes, and in a serious tone, said, "Marco Ridolfi was killed at his betrothal celebration. I was there at his villa when it happened."

"Oh, no. How awful. I can't imagine ..." Bianca shuddered and leaned her head against Nico's chest.

"That tragedy made me realize life is fragile and I can't envision a future without you by my side. Since first we met, my heart beats fast whenever I see your smile and feel your touch. I love you and I've hesitated asking you to be my wife only because of the guilt I would feel uprooting you from your home, your family, and the thriving business you've built here in Siena. But I can wait no longer. My beloved Bianca, will you marry me?"

Bianca looked up with tears glistening in her eyes. "Yes, Nico. Yes, I will marry you. And Florence is not so distant from Siena that I will be torn from my family." They kissed again, a lingering, passionate kiss.

Nico brushed a droplet from her cheek. "Now I must secure your father's blessing. As a surgeon at Santa Maria della Scala hospital, your father surely knows other esteemed physicians; he may have identified one of them as a worthy match for his daughter's hand."

Bianca laughed. "My father's approval will be no obstacle. He sees how my spirit brightens in your company. I'm certain he entertains no thought of offering me to another. I'll be having supper with my parents this evening. Join us so my mother can share in hearing our news when you speak with my father ... unless your return to Florence is urgent."

When Nico didn't respond immediately, Bianca said, "Something troubles you?"

Nico kissed her forehead. "No, nothing troubles me, but I'm suddenly overwhelmed thinking of all the tasks ahead. We must plan a wedding and find a place in Florence to live and a loft for your business."

A sweet smile graced Bianca's face. "Fret not my champion.

Doing those tasks together, we will make them be pleasures, not chores."

The sun had dipped low in the western sky, casting Siena's Gallo district into shadow as Nico walked along Via della Fonte toward the home of Bianca's parents, Manzio and Dorena Cellini. He'd taken a room at an inn where he could wash and brush his hair, but he still wore the same tunic that he'd worn on his early morning journey from Florence. He was sure Bianca's parents would understand that he hadn't brought extra clothes.

Bianca answered Nico's knock. He noticed her bite her lip, a behavior she only did when she was tense. At a pastry shop owned by a talented Neapolitan chef, Nico had purchased cream-filled Zeppole, favorites of Bianca's mother. He held out the sack. "These are for dessert."

Bianca peeked into the sack, turned, carried it to her mother, and announced, "Nico brought Zeppole, your favorites, the ones with the cherries."

From the kitchen where she was preparing dinner, Dorena called, "Nico, how thoughtful of you."

Manzio poured a glass of wine, handed it to Nico and said, "Bianca told us you are investigating a murder, and you came to Siena to interrogate a suspect."

"That is so," Nico replied, set his glass down and said, "But there is something more important for us to discuss." His gaze darted to Bianca for an instant, then returned to Manzio. He straightened his shoulders and took a deep breath. "The first time I saw Bianca, I knew she was a special woman. As time passed and we've gotten to know each other, my feelings for her have deepened. I love her and I want to spend the rest of my life caring for her and making her happy. I humbly seek your blessing and consent for us to wed."

Bianca moved to stand beside Nico and took his hand. Nico's words drew Dorena from the kitchen. Manzio crossed the room to his wife, put an arm around her, pulled her close, and said, "Dorena and I have watched love blossom between you and Bianca. We've seen how you cherish her and we could want nothing more for our daughter than for her to spend her life with one who honors and respects her as you do." He glanced at his wife, then back at Nico. "You have our blessing."

Smiling through her tears, Dorena dashed to Bianca and hugged her. She reached out one hand to Nico and embraced him. Manzio handed wine glasses to his wife, his daughter, and Nico. He raised his own glass and said, "May the future bring you enduring happiness and may your love grow stronger every day you are together."

23

FLORENCE

Alessa and Joanna were in a sitting room mending clothes for children at the orphanage when Nico arrived at Casa Argenti. Donato, who had been sorting clothes for the two women, poured glasses of wine for himself and Nico, and said as he refilled his wife's glass, "Welcome back, Nico. Was your trek to Siena successful? Did you find the merchant who'd threatened Marco Ridolfi?"

"We did find the merchant." With a childish grin, Nico added, "And my time in Siena was more successful than I'd expected."

Alessa said, "Turn this way so I can see your face, and let me see your hands."

Nico spread his fingers apart and wiggled them in front of her. He bent and touched his nose to hers. Laughing, she said, "I don't see any wounds or bandages. This must be the first time you've ventured away from Florence without being injured."

"I not only kept myself from harm, but I prevented Massimo from being attacked."

At the mention of Massimo's name, Alessa straightened her

dress, brushed a hand through her hair, and glanced quickly at the doorway. "Did Massimo return with you?"

"We returned to Florence together, but he had to stop at the Chancery. I invited him to join us, so he should be here shortly."

Donato said, "I'd like to hear about the man who attacked Massimo."

Nico's speech quickened. "Do you remember me saying that Massimo had given me a dagger and a pouch of stone dust to defend myself?" He glanced at Alessa, "because you blamed him whenever I got injured." Returning his attention to Donato, he said, "Massimo was interrogating the merchant, and when Massimo questions people, he can be intimidating. A man who works for the merchant came into the warehouse and thought his boss was in danger, so he pulled out his knife and came at Massimo from behind. I stepped in front of the man and threw a handful of stone dust at his face. The dust blinded him momentarily, just as Massimo said it would."

Alessa scolded, "A man came forward brandishing a knife, and you jumped in front of him?"

"It may sound foolish now, but there was no other option. If I hadn't acted, he would have stabbed Massimo. When the merchant saw what had happened, he told the man to put the knife aside."

Massimo's hands clapping loudly drew everyone's attention to the doorway where he stood, having just entered the room and heard Nico's retelling of the incident in Siena. "Nico would have been more menacing if he'd have drawn his own knife; nonetheless, I'm thankful for his quick action because it may have saved me from yet another knife wound."

Alessa asked, "Did you convince the merchant to confess that he threatened Marco Ridolfi?"

Massimo flashed a smile at Alessa and replied, "No, he

claimed to have told Marco that only guild members could do business in Siena and Florentine merchants weren't allowed to join the guild."

Nico added, "We spoke with another guild member who confirmed the story, so we're convinced he's not the killer."

Donato poured a glass of wine for Massimo, leaned against a side table in thought for a moment, then said, "A thing that's been puzzling me is why Antonio invited people who dislike him to the betrothal celebration."

Massimo explained, "During my interview with Daniela, she mentioned that she and Marco decided on the guests for the dinner. Mostly, they chose relatives, business associates, and guild members. Marco may have been unaware of the animosity between his father and certain guests."

Donato asked, "Have you narrowed the number of suspects?"

Nico nodded slowly. "We've made some progress. We've eliminated Berto Lenzi from the list." He opted not to name those who were still under investigation.

Joanna waited until the conversation ebbed, before asking, "What did you mean earlier when you said that your time in Siena was more successful than you expected?"

With one large swallow, Nico emptied his wineglass, refilled it, and with a broad smile, said, "I asked Bianca to marry me; she said yes, and her parents gave us their blessing."

Surprise silenced the room for an instant. Alessa jumped up, ran to Nico, and wrapped her arms around him. "I'm so happy for you."

"It's about time," Massimo teased. "Bianca is truly an exceptional woman. You're fortunate she hasn't been courted by someone else."

"Had you been planning to ask her, or was it a sudden decision?" Joanna asked.

"I believe I've loved Bianca and wanted to marry her since the first moment I saw her, but I've been afraid of disrupting her life in Siena with her family and her business. Lately though, I've been haunted by Marco Ridolfi's murder. He and Daniela wanted a life together, but that possibility was stolen from them. Thinking about them made me realize that happiness can be fragile."

With a joyous voice, Joanna gushed a stream of questions. "Have you and Bianca begun making plans? Have you picked a wedding date? Will the wedding be held in Siena at Bianca's parish church?"

Nico raised a hand defensively. "We haven't had time to discuss any of those issues. Bianca intends to come to Florence soon, perhaps next week, to deliver a dress to a client. When she does, we'll look for a place for us to live and space for her dress business."

Donato offered, "One of my regular customers at the Uccello rents buildings in the Santa Croce neighborhood. Other men speak well of him. He may be able to help you find rooms. Come to the Uccello tomorrow and I'll introduce you to him."

Carlo, the house servant, came into the sala and handed a note to Nico. All eyes fixed on Nico as he unfolded and read the paper. "It's from the Officials Over Orphans," he announced. "They're inviting me to become a member of the Officials. Several weeks ago, I had a chance encounter with the convener of the Officials. He reminded me again how pleased their members are that I exposed the corrupt superintendent of the orphanage and he mentioned that one of their members was at the end of his term. I found his behavior odd, as if he were concealing something. Now I know what he was hiding; they were planning to invite me to join the Officials." Nico looked up from the paper and looked at Alessa. "They should be inviting you to join the commission. You're the one who first noticed that something was amiss at the orphanage."

Joanna said sarcastically, "The bureaucrats in this city wouldn't dream of asking a woman to serve on one of their commissions."

Donato placed a hand on her arm. "Easy, my dear. I share your sentiment, but there's no value in becoming upset over something you can't change."

Massimo asked, "Our Security Commission assignments keep you occupied, and now you'll need to plan a wedding. How will you find time to serve on the orphans' commission?"

"That commission isn't very demanding. Their sole purpose is to ensure the orphanage operates smoothly."

While Nico, Joanna, and Donato resumed the discussion about Nico's upcoming wedding, Alessa turned to Massimo and said, "Nico told me that Daniela was distressed when you met with her. I've developed a deep appreciation for Italian culture, but it lacks a healing way to cope with the loss of a loved one. I believe the practices of my childhood village in Morocco could help her. Can you introduce me to her?"

"I can take you to meet her, but you will find that Daniela's mother is very protective of her daughter. You might not be able to speak with Daniela without her mother being present."

Alessa said, "I'm certain her mother won't find my words offensive."

24

Rain fell constantly from early morning. By evening, a wet greasy film coated the cobblestone surfaces of Florence's main roads. The few people out in the dismal weather trod cautiously over the slick stones, taking short and deliberate steps. Those brave enough to venture through the city's dirt roads faced a mosaic of mud and puddles. Anyone who had a choice opted to stay in a warm dry house or a friendly local tavern. It was a night hated by Guardia officers who patrolled the streets and alleys. They could only curse their assignments and pray the rain would stop before dampness soaked through their rain cloaks.

Far from the central district, within sight of the city wall near the Porta San Gallo gate, a line of storage buildings held imported goods being readied for distribution to shops throughout the city. Rainy nights, when people stayed indoors, were perfect for the city's derelicts to explore the buildings, searching for one with an unlocked door. Overindulgence in beer and wine set one pauper's hands shaking, slurred his speech, and made him unfit for any meaningful work. He survived by begging during the day and pilfering at night.

From experience, he knew the wide doors through which wagons loaded and unloaded merchandise were always locked. If there were an unlocked portal, it would be a small door at the side or rear of a building. He'd tested doors at three storage buildings without finding one unlocked. Undeterred, he proceeded to the next structure, the warehouse of Antonio Ridolfi. Sheltered from the rain by the roof overhang, he grasped the latch of the building's side door, hoping it would release when a gruff voice commanded, "Stop!"

Guardia officers patrolled in pairs, typically a seasoned veteran mated with a recent recruit. The veteran, with the recruit close behind, splashed through puddles as he dashed across the street and grabbed the derelict's arm. "I was just looking to get out of the rain," the man protested.

The veteran officer pushed the man against a wall and fumed, "I don't need your lies. My feet are swimming in my boots and I'm so wet that if I were to piss myself, I wouldn't even know it." The officer took a step back, away from his captive. "Even the rain hasn't washed the stink off you. What you need is a couple of nights in a prison cell to sober up."

Light coming through a window from inside the building caught the young recruit's attention. He continued watching and when a shadow swept across the window, he announced, "Someone's inside."

The senior officer looked up at the window. "No one works at this hour. This bastard must have a partner who's in there looting the place. Stay with him while I go after the other one."

The officer pressed the latch. It wasn't locked. He pushed the door open and crept quietly into the warehouse. In the dim lantern light, he could make out two barrels upturned with sugar spilled out onto the floor. A small man with a thin face had removed the top from another barrel and was pushing it onto its side. "Stop what you're doing!" the officer commanded.

The man froze momentarily, then scanned the space, looking for a way to escape, but there was no other exit. The officer raised his truncheon, advanced toward the vandal, and announced, "I'm a *birro*, a Guardia officer. You're under arrest."

The following morning, a young Guardia officer rapped on the open door of the Security Commission office. "Signor Colombo?" he queried.

Vittorio eyed the visitor. "I'm Vittorio Colombo."

"Last night, one of our patrols apprehended a vandal destroying property in a warehouse. Sergeant Grimaldi thought you would be interested in knowing about this" — Grimaldi had been a colleague when Vittorio was a Guardia investigator — "because the warehouse is owned by Antonio Ridolfi, and the man who broke into the warehouse is Ugo Fornelli."

Vittorio's face brightened. "I certainly am interested. Where is Fornelli being held?"

"At the Stinche."

Vittorio set down the papers he had been reading, stood, and said, "I'd like to speak with him right now."

The young officer accompanied Vittorio to the Stinche, although his help wasn't necessary because Vittorio knew how to find the prison. He'd committed dozens of criminals to Florence's infamous prison during his tenure as a Guardia investigator. As the young officer left Vittorio and headed back to Guardia headquarters, Vittorio said, "Extend my appreciation to Sergeant Grimaldi for remembering my interest in Fornelli, and tell him I'm in his debt."

Vittorio ignored the sour smell of dried sweat and urine as a prison guard escorted him through the dingy corridors to the cell where Fornelli was being held. The din of prisoners whining, complaining, and squabbling with each other kept Fornelli from hearing Vittorio approach. When Vittorio called his name, Fornelli came to the front of the cell, grasped the bars, and asked, "Are you a lawyer?"

Vittorio ignored the question, informed the prisoner that he was a member of the Security Commission, and said acidly, "Wasn't murder enough for you? After you killed Antonio Ridolfi's son, you vandalized his warehouse."

Fornelli raised a hand in protest. "What are you saying? I didn't kill anybody."

Vittorio scoffed, "You took a job at Ridolfi's stable before the betrothal dinner, and you disappeared right after Marco Ridolfi was assassinated. What had Antonio Ridolfi done to you that drove you to kill his son and then break into his warehouse?"

"I have no issue with Ridolfi. I was paid to ruin the store of sugar in his warehouse. Some men lack the courage to take on certain tasks themselves, so they hire a *Solitario* like me to do jobs for them. The warehouse stint was just a job."

"Who hired you to break into the warehouse?" Fornelli refused to answer and simply glared at Vittorio. "Was it the same person who hired you to murder Marco Ridolfi?"

"I already told you, I didn't kill anyone."

"You're a fool if you expect me to believe you took a job in the stable at the villa because you enjoy shoveling horse shit. If you don't give me a good reason for being at the villa, I'll have your trial delayed, so you'll never get out of this stinking hole."

"All I did at the villa was to put Scopa Fiori in the wine so the guests would get sick and the celebration would be ruined." Again, Fornelli repeated, "I didn't kill anybody."

"Was the person who hired you to poison the wine the same one who hired you to ruin the sugar?"

"I didn't poison the wine. Scopa Fiori isn't a poison; it just makes people sick. No one was to die. If Marco Ridolfi died, it wasn't from the wine."

"Don't say Scopa Fiori isn't a poison. One villa worker who drank the wine would have died if a doctor hadn't treated him. Who hired you to poison the wine?" Vittorio demanded.

Fornelli stepped back from the bars and brushed his hair away from his eyes. With a smirk he said, "If you want to know who hired me, get me out of this rat hole."

"You're here because the Guardia charged you with a crime. I can't have you released without their consent, but if you're willing to help them prosecute the person who hired you, I'm confident the Guardia will eliminate the charges against you, and if you're willing to testify against the man who hired you to taint the wine at the villa, I won't file charges against you for attempted murder."

Fornelli slammed his fist against the cell bars, gritted his teeth, and growled. "Get me out of here and I'll tell you."

Vittorio said, "I'll be back after I speak with Sergeant Grimaldi."

25

Nico and Vittorio were already seated in the Chancery conference room when a clerk brought Fornelli and Sergeant Grimaldi into the room. Fornelli, a smirk on his face, took a seat without invitation, leaned back, and clasped his hands together on his lap. Grimaldi gave a quick nod of recognition to Vittorio, then turned his gaze towards Nico, assuming that he was the person who had requested the meeting. "Bringing the prisoner here is highly unusual. We usually go to the Stinche to meet with them," he declared and waited for Nico to justify the situation.

"Yes, it is unusual," Nico agreed. "And I appreciate your willingness to accommodate us. I understand you are the person who apprehended Signor Fornelli when he was vandalizing the Ridolfi warehouse."

Grimaldi responded with a quick nod. "My men apprehended him."

Nico continued, "Vittorio and I believe the warehouse incident may be related to the murder of Signor Ridolfi's son."

Fornelli tensed, preparing to defend his innocence against the murder accusation, but he said nothing. "You believe he committed murder?" Grimaldi asked, with uncertainty in his voice.

"The murder happened during a betrothal celebration in a villa near the village of Calenzano. Fornelli was at the villa. He admits to having contaminated the wine so guests would become sick, but claims he didn't commit the murder."

"Do you believe him?" Grimaldi asked.

Vittorio replied, "I searched his room and didn't find the murder weapon, so it's possible he's being truthful."

"He could have disposed of the weapon," Grimaldi suggested, wondering why Vittorio had disregarded that option.

"It's possible," Vittorio agreed, "but the weapon is a personal item, and the killer would have little reason to discard it." Grimaldi could tell Vittorio chose not to describe the weapon, so he didn't press further.

Nico said, "Signor Fornelli claims that the person who hired him to taint the wine is the same one who hired him to vandalize the warehouse. He agrees to reveal the name of the person who hired him if the charges against him are dismissed."

Grimaldi glared at Fornelli. "Ah, so that's what this meeting is about. You want me to dismiss the charges against him?"

Nico said, "Our aim is to apprehend the person who incited the crimes. He may also be the person responsible for the murder. But I don't propose dismissing the charges simply in exchange for a name. Fornelli will have to do more than that. He'll have to help us get enough evidence to convict the person who hired him."

Grimaldi rubbed his ear as he considered Nico's proposal.

He inhaled deeply. Exhaled. "Can I be the one to charge the person who hired him?"

Nico nodded.

"Both crimes?"

Again, Nico nodded.

"What about the murder?"

Vittorio said, "Fornelli says he doesn't know about the murder, so we'll have to continue our investigation."

Grimaldi leaned forward and looked across the table at Nico. "I'll release him if he leads us to the one who hired him."

Nico turned to Fornelli. "You must help us gather proof to gain convictions. Do you understand? Otherwise, you will be charged with both crimes."

"I understand," Fornelli grunted.

"Give us the name," Nico directed.

"Prizzi. Luigi Prizzi."

"Signor Prizzi, the funeral director?" Grimaldi echoed skeptically. Fornelli nodded.

Nico explained, "We've heard several reports of an ongoing feud between Luigi Prizzi and Antonio Ridolfi. Prizzi's a funeral director and Ridolfi's a merchant, but they both belong to the same guild, and they've had repeated altercations at guild meetings."

Fornelli grumbled, "I can't let it be known that I gave his name to the Guardia. It would be bad for business if people find out I betrayed my clients."

"He's a respected businessman and you're a criminal. To get a conviction, we'll need more than just your word against his. How did he find you to offer you these jobs?" Nico asked.

"This time?" Fornelli said with a smirk.

An incredulous Grimaldi responded, "You've done jobs for him before?"

"Just once. He was swindled by the owner of an apothecary, or so he said, and he recruited me to make the man suffer."

With barbed words, Grimaldi said, "I remember that incident. Someone broke into the shop and dumped the medications into a bucket, all mixed together. We never found out who did it." The sergeant's consternation caused Fornelli's smirk to widen. Grimaldi continued, "Last week a stable was entered during the night and all the horses were released. Was that you too?"

"Not me. One of my competitors."

Nico refocused the conversation to the matter at hand, asking, "How are you getting paid? Will you meet with Prizzi?"

Fornelli nodded. "We'll meet at the *Il Buon Amico*, the Good Friend."

Vittorio said, "I know it. It's a tavern on Via del Giglio in the Santa Maria Novella neighborhood." Without seeking Grimaldi's agreement, Vittorio locked eyes with Fornelli and said, "When you meet with him, I'll be sitting close enough to hear your exchanges. You must make him admit he hired you to sabotage the betrothal celebration and vandalize Ridolfi's warehouse."

"I can do that." Fornelli said confidently.

"Get him to talk about the killing. Ask him why he retained someone other than you to kill Marco Ridolfi. From his reaction, I'll know whether he ordered the killing."

"When I do that, the charges against me will be erased?" Fornelli asked.

Before answering, Grimaldi turned to Nico. "Are you confident Luigi Prizzi can be convicted solely on Signor Colombo's testimony?"

"I am," Nico replied. "Magistrates have consistently placed great trust in Vittorio's testimony, and we'll also have Prizzi's payment to Fornelli as evidence." Fornelli grimaced upon realizing that Nico intended to seize his fee.

"And I'll be the one to charge Prizzi with the crimes?" Grimaldi asked. Nico responded with a nod. To Fornelli, Grimaldi said, "Then yes, when Prizzi is convicted, the charges against you will be erased."

The meeting ended with Fornelli penning a note to Prizzi requesting that they meet at Il Buon Amico the following morning so Fornelli could receive his payment. By that time, word would have reached Prizzi about the destruction of Ridolfi's warehouse, but Fornelli's capture would be kept secret. Grimaldi returned Fornelli to his prison cell, where he would remain until he was brought to the tavern the following morning.

Vittorio went directly to the tavern to determine whether his plan to eavesdrop on the conversation between Fornelli and Prizzi was feasible. The tavern had a bar along one side wall and two long tables along the opposite wall. At the rear, a thin curtain hanging in a doorway separated the bar room from a storage room. Vittorio walked through the room and stood near the curtain. Three men chatting with each other at the bar were speaking at a moderate level, a level that would not prevent him from overhearing Fornelli and Prizzi. But the four men playing cards at one of the tables were speaking loudly and punctuating their conversation with even louder raucous outbursts. He couldn't risk the possibility of that group being in the tavern while he was eavesdropping on his marks. He needed a better plan.

The following morning, three Guardia recruits stood at the bar in Il Buon Amico, drinking beer and engaging in quiet conversation while other officers sat on wooden benches at the front table. The rear-most table, the one Fornelli would choose when he arrived, had been pushed against the back wall close to the curtain divider, behind which Vittorio waited. Outside, Grimaldi diverted anyone who attempted to enter the tavern.

Fornelli walked along Via del Giglio observed from behind at a discreet distance by a Guardia minder. He entered the tavern and took a seat at the designated table, unaware that all the other patrons were members of the Guardia. A short time later, Luigi Prizzi entered, stopped at the bar to get a mug of beer from the barkeep, who'd been apprised of the ruse by Vittorio, then walked to the rear table and sat across from Fornelli.

"I understand Ridolfi suffered a sizeable loss." Prizzi said and slid a coin purse across the table to Fornelli.

"That's what you wanted, isn't it?"

"Yes, that's what I wanted. You did well," Prizzi admitted, thereby implicating himself as the person who instigated the destruction at the warehouse.

"Is it all there?" Fornelli asked. "Payment for both jobs? I did the job at Ridolfi's villa, spoiling the wine. If young Ridolfi hadn't been killed, the guests would have gotten sick and the celebration would have been ruined as you wished."

"Payment is there for both jobs, as we agreed. You couldn't have foreseen that the event would be disrupted by the killing of Antonio's offspring." Laughing, Prizzi said, "I heard the servants at the villa are the ones who got sick."

"I heard the same," Fornelli agreed.

Prizzi's admission of responsibility for the crime at the villa satisfied Vittorio, who stayed hidden behind the curtain, waiting patiently for Fornelli to finish the scenario they'd prepared. Finally, as Vittorio had prepped him, Fornelli asked,

"Why did you hire someone else to kill Marco Ridolfi instead of giving me the job?"

Prizzi grinned. "That bastard Antonio has many enemies. Any of them could have hired the assassin." Turning serious, Prizzi seethed, "Think twice before blaming me without evidence." Fornelli, intimidated by Prizzi's words and glare, leaned away and remained silent.

Vittorio, concluding he would learn nothing further, stepped out from behind the curtain and signaled Grimaldi's men, who moved from the bar to Prizzi's table to arrest him. Prizzi slammed a fist on the table. "You bastard!" he raged at Fornelli. "You betrayed me!"

Fornelli raised his hands wide apart and said as a feeble defense, "I didn't ..."

Prizzi charged at the arresting officer, his arms flailing frantically. Two burly recruits seized him and dragged him out of the tavern. After Grimaldi watched his officers take Prizzi away, he entered the tavern. Seeing him, Fornelli, still shaken by Prizzi's outburst, asked, "Am I free to go?"

Grimaldi eyed Vittorio, who said, "He did well. He got Prizzi to admit hiring him for crimes at the warehouse and the villa, although Prizzi didn't admit that he arranged Marco Ridolfi's murder."

To Fornelli, Grimaldi said, "You will need to testify at Prizzi's trial, but for now, you may go."

Vittorio grabbed Fornelli by his collar. "I found you once. If you try to flee, I'll find you again and you'll have no reprieve from prison." Fornelli walked out into the street, sighed, and, beaming, he walked away.

"Men like him never change," Grimaldi said to Vittorio. "He may go free this time, but every time there's a robbery or a break in, my team will question him."

Vittorio agreed. "He'll continue his life of crime and

inevitably make mistakes, so I'm sure you'll apprehend him eventually."

From the tavern, Vittorio headed to the notorious Stinche prison, the windowless brown stone building on Via Ghibellina. The warden directed a guard to escort Vittorio to the cell where Luigi Prizzi had been incarcerated only minutes before. At the tavern, Prizzi's attention had been fixed on the Guardia officers who were restraining him, so he hadn't noticed Vittorio behind him. When Vittorio peered into his cell, Prizzi stopped pacing across the small space, eyed the investigator, and snapped, "Are you a lawyer? If you're a lawyer, get me out of this stinking hole."

Vittorio didn't respond to Prizzi's question, nor did he identify himself. In a calm voice, he said, "You didn't deny hiring the killer when Fornelli questioned you about Marco Ridolfi's murder."

Prizzi stepped forward in the cell and locked eyes with Vittorio. "Who are you and why are you asking me about Ridolfi?"

"I'm a member of the Security Commission. Did you hire Marco Ridolfi's killer?" Vittorio wasn't expecting Prizzi to answer honestly, but he wanted to observe Prizzi's reaction.

Prizzi bellowed, "Antonio Ridolfi is an abomination. If I were going to kill someone, it would be him, not his son!"

Prizzi's anger and defiance, his hands waving in the air and his erratic blinking prevented Vittorio from assessing Prizzi's truthfulness. Vittorio said, "I'm going to search your house and your business. I'm going to question everyone who knows you. If I find proof you had anything to do with Marco Ridolfi's murder, you'll leave this rat hole, but only to meet the executioner."

As Vittorio walked away from the cell, Prizzi shouted after him. "I want a lawyer! Get me a lawyer!"

Vittorio joined Grimaldi, who was chatting with the warden. "Did he confess to the killing?" Grimaldi asked.

"No, he claims he didn't hire a killer."

"Do you believe him?"

"He didn't give me a reason to believe him," Vittorio said, and as he turned to leave, he added, "I'm not finished with him."

26

Showers began early and gained intensity throughout the day. By late afternoon, steady rain prompted people to seek refuge in their homes. Shops closed early and streets were deserted. Notary Bernardo Vernacci had spent a long day at his office preparing inheritance documents for a client. He reviewed the documents a final time and, satisfied the materials were complete, inserted them into a folio, ready for presentation at a tribunal in the morning.

Vernacci donned his hooded rain cloak. To avoid having to return to his office in the morning to retrieve the folio, he tucked it into his cloak and left his office. Wind driven drops lashed his face as he moved slowly along the slick cobblestones. He passed a derelict taking cover in a butcher shop doorway and two Guardia members sheltering under a portico fronting a jewelry shop. When he reached the church of Saint Egidio, he turned right onto a narrow dirt street. The blackness was broken only by the feeble lantern light seeping out of a shop window in the distance. Rain pelting against the church to his left and storefronts to his right masked the sound of footsteps approaching from behind.

A hand reached out and grabbed Vernacci's shoulder, interrupting his gait, causing him to stumble and almost fall. He felt surprise rather than pain as the attacker's knife sliced through his sinewy back muscles. The assailant pulled the knife free, tensed his arm, readying for a second cut, and jabbed just when Vernacci turned. The folio, pressed against Vernacci's chest, deflected the blade, changing a potentially deadly attack into a grazing hit that stuck the knife tip in a rib. Vernacci's knees buckled; he slid to the ground. There he lay on his back with rain washing his face.

His attacker spun around, scanning for any onlookers; however, the darkness concealed everything, making it unlikely that anyone could see him. For a minute, he observed the motionless figure at his feet. Believing that life had fled the body, he drifted away into the night.

A short time later, a pause in the rainfall encouraged the two Guardia officers to resume their patrol. At the corner, after passing Saint Egidio church, the senior officer glanced into the side street, spotted a break in the otherwise unbroken blackness, and said, "There's something in the road."

"A dead animal?" the recruit speculated. He trailed his superior only a short distance before blurting out, "Mother of God, is he ..."

The senior officer leaned down over the body. Vernacci wheezed, barely above a whisper, "I was attacked from behind."

The comment puzzled the officer, since the knife was protruding from Vernacci's chest. He contemplated removing it, but decided that doing so might worsen the injury. "We need to take him to a hospital. Get some men to help us," he commanded.

Guardia headquarters was halfway across the city, so rather

than go there, the recruit enlisted men at a local tavern. The tavern owner directed them to the nearby house of a mason who had a cart that he used for transporting stone blocks. The senior officer stood aside, giving instructions and criticism as four men lifted Vernacci onto the borrowed cart and wheeled him to Santa Maria Nuova hospital.

The men lifted Vernacci from the cart and carried him into the hospital. "This way," a medico said and led them to a ward, where they deposited Vernacci on an empty bed. The medico held up a hand signaling for quiet, leaned his ear close to Vernacci's mouth and listened. "He's breathing, but weakly." To the nun who had joined him, he said, "We must act quickly."

The medico wiggled the knife free, and handed it to the Guardia officer, who said, "It's a stilleto. Mercenaries prefer these because the thin double-edged blades can pass easily through chain mail and penetrate deep enough to kill their enemies." He examined the blade just below the guard, looking for the insignia of the foundry that made the knife. "A backward letter P. I don't recognize that marking." Looking further, he said, "Brass guard and bone handle. A quality dagger, but nothing unique that could lead us to the attacker."

While the Guardia officer focused on the weapon, the medico opened Vernacci's rain cloak, removed a coin purse and the folio Vernacci had been carrying, and set the two items aside. He lifted the tunic to study the wound. Puzzled, he said, "This cut is deep, but it is off to his side. A wound like this one usually isn't serious." Looking closely, he noticed other blood-stains on the cloak and tunic; he rotated the body and exposed the more severe wound.

"When we found him, he said he'd been attacked from behind," the Guardia officer stated. "After he fell, the assailant must have stabbed him again, this time in front."

"A cautery!" the medico demanded. The nun rushed away.

Shortly, she returned with a cauterizing knife, its tip heated to red hot, followed by a second nun who carried bandages and a flask of honey. Vernacci shrieked then fell unconscious when the medico pressed the burning tip against the wound in his back to stem the blood flow. The acrid smell of burning flesh drove the onlookers back.

"Another cautery?" the nun asked.

"No, the wound in front is not bleeding badly," the medico replied. He applied a dab of honey to each puncture to prevent infection, then directed the nuns to bandage the wounds. To the Guardia officer, he said, "He has lost much blood, but I believe he will recover."

"When can I question him?"

"Not tonight. Maybe tomorrow."

"We can trust Saint Peter will note in his book that we've done a good service for our fellow man. Now let's get back to our beer," one of the tavern goers appealed to his comrades.

At Guardia headquarters, the junior officer questioned, "The knife tip was embedded in a rib, but the medico could wiggle it free. Why did the attacker leave it?"

"Perhaps someone came along and he feared being caught," the Sergeant speculated.

"Why do you suppose he was attacked?"

Lifting the coin purse the medico had removed from Vernacci's belt, the sergeant replied, "This is hefty, so robbery wasn't the motive." He set the coin purse down, opened the folio, and thumbed through the papers. "These are filings for an inheritance claim. He was a notary. Why would someone want to kill a notary?" Then, noting the signature on one page, he said, "His name is Bernardo Vernacci."

Later that evening, two Guardia officers visited Bernardo Vernacci's house. The junior officer stood aside while his superior, Sergeant Belloza, a Guardia investigator, rapped on the door. It opened a crack and a pair of close-set gray eyes peered out. "Are you Signora Vernacci?" the sergeant asked. The woman nodded slowly. "I'm here about Bernardo, your husband."

"He's working late, but he should be here soon."

Delivering grim news was part of Belloza's job, so he knew no words could make this moment less painful for the poor woman. "I'm sorry to tell you, your husband was attacked. He's at Santa Maria Nuova."

"That can't be. He's working late," she repeated. When the shock of the investigator's words registered, the door swung open as she staggered backward, gripping the door tightly to keep from falling, her knuckles turning white.

Belloza helped her across the room to a chair. On the table in front of her sat the bowl for the stew that was to be her husband's dinner. She bent forward, her head in her hands, her stringy hair masking her face, and sobbed. He gave her time. At length, she asked, "Why?"

"I'm hoping you can help me answer that question, signora. It wasn't robbery." He set Vernacci's coin purse on the table. "He was attacked while walking on a darkened street. A Guardia patrol found him. He had been stabbed."

She crossed herself. "Mother of God, my Bernardo is a good man. Why would anyone do that? I must go to him. Where is he?"

"He's at Santa Maria Nuova, but the hospital won't let you see him now. He's sleeping. You can go to him in the morning."

Belloza waited until her whimpering stopped, then set

Vernacci's folio on the table and opened it. "He had been preparing papers for a tribunal. Do you know anything about this?" She shook her head. He pointed to the page showing the client's name. "Do you know this man?"

Again, she shook her head. "Bernardo is a notary, so he's always writing papers. He never tells me about them."

Belloza sat at the table facing her. "Do you know anyone who would want to harm him? A client who might have been unhappy with his work?"

She shuddered. "I don't know. He said nothing. Why would anyone do this?"

"Does Bernardo work with someone? A partner or a clerk who would know about his business?"

"He works for many people, but always alone."

"Is the Badia your parish church?" Surprised by the question, Signoria Vernacci nodded slowly. Belloza directed his subordinate, "Go to the church. Tell the priest what has happened and ask him to send a nun to stay with Signora Vernacci tonight."

27

Nico and Vittorio stopped at a small grassy area midway along Via dei Pandolfini in the Santa Croce neighborhood and gazed across the cobblestone street at a two-level building with a slate roof. Nico said, "According to the guild clerk's description, that is where guild consul Prizzi lives. He rents rooms on the upper level and the owner lives on the lower level. The owner's wife is Prizzi's housemaid. Shall we have the owner let us into Prizzi's rooms?"

Vittorio held up a key. "We needn't trouble the owner. Sergeant Grimaldi let me borrow the key they took from Prizzi at the prison."

They climbed stone steps to the second level. Vittorio unlocked the door and stepped into a spacious salon, with Nico close behind. Directly ahead, a painting of a woman, curly brown hair, dimpled cheeks, and a pleasant smile, hung on the wall. "She's too young to be Prizzi's mother," Nico noted. "Could that be his wife or daughter?"

"We didn't discuss casual pleasantries, so he never mentioned a family," Vittorio replied. He scanned the room, and added, "This room is well kept, but that's probably because of the housekeeper. There are no signs that a woman lives here."

To their right was a table with two chairs and an opening to the kitchen area beyond. To the left, a jug rested on a low table in front of a couch, and just beyond them was a doorway leading to the bedchamber. Unlike the sitting salon, the bedchamber showed no signs of the housekeeper's touch. A pair of purple hose stretched across the bed and hung down over the side. At the foot of the bed, wrinkled clothes piled atop a wooden chest spilled over onto the floor. Hooks next to the doorway held a cloak and a soiled tunic. Papers strewn haphazardly covered a desk set under the room's only window.

Nico wrinkled his nose. "It stinks in here." He pulled back the linen cloth covering the window enough to let stale air escape without inviting a breeze that might scatter the papers on the desk. While Vittorio searched through the clothes, Nico examined the papers. "These are contracts pertaining to Prizzi's funeral business," Nico said. "One document describes arrangements for a burial tomorrow."

Vittorio looked up from the heap of dirty clothes in front of him. "They'd better have a plan for the funeral to proceed without Prizzi because he'll be spending tomorrow in the Stinche."

A belt looped over a chair alongside the desk caught Nico's attention. "Here is Prizzi's belt."

Vittorio stretched the belt across the desk and removed a slip of paper from his coin purse. He unfolded the sheet and pointed to two lines. "I marked this paper when I examined Marco Ridolfi's body at the villa. These lines correspond to the distance between the metal disks on the belt used to strangle him. He held the paper against the designs on Prizzi's belt.

"They match," Nico said, excitement in his voice.

"And the designs on this belt are diamond shaped similar to the impressions on Signor Ridolfi's neck," Vittorio observed. He rotated the paper, pointed to another pair of lines, and said, "These lines fit the width of the bruising on Ridolfi's neck." He set the paper on the belt. "This belt appears to be narrower ... although it's possible the belt shifted slightly when Marco grabbed at it, trying to free himself. That could have made the mark on his neck wider than the belt itself." Unable to draw a firm conclusion, Vittorio returned to the wooden chest and continued ferreting through the clothes.

"Was Prizzi wearing a belt when he was arrested?" Nico asked.

"He was, but it was a plain leather strap, with no embellishments." It was unlikely that Prizzi had more than two belts, but Vittorio wanted to be certain. A noise in the sitting salon distracted the men. Heavy footsteps crossing the salon announced the plump woman who appeared in the doorway wearing a clean white apron, holding a broom in one hand. Her mouth dropped open at seeing two strangers in Signor Prizzi's bedchamber. Nico introduced himself and Vittorio and informed her that Signor Prizzi had been arrested. "We're looking for evidence in a criminal trial." He gestured to the clothes piled in front of Vittorio. "Are these all of Signor Prizzi's clothes?"

"I can't say. He told me I should never enter his bedchamber." She watched Vittorio meticulously sorting through the clothes in the chest and searching under the bed as she absorbed what was happening. "Signor Prizzi was arrested," she said, more to convince herself than to expect a response from the men. "I came here to clean. Should I ..."

Nico said, "All we can tell you is that Signor Prizzi won't be returning soon."

She cleaned plates that Prizzi had left on the table, tidied the kitchen area, then left. After searching the bedchamber, Nico and Vittorio moved on to scour the other rooms. When they finished, Nico suggested, "Even if Prizzi didn't kill Marco himself, he might have hired an assassin."

"Possibly," Vittorio agreed, "but I've never known an assassin to strangle his victim with a belt. Those who kill by garroting typically use rope or wire because a thin ligature takes less force." He glanced again at the leather belt. Disappointed by the uncertainty, Vittorio said, "This belt could have been used to kill Signor Ridolfi, but it's hardly solid evidence."

28

Luigi Prizzi's funeral service business was located a short distance outside the Porta al Prato gate in a building that was formerly owned by a grain merchant. As Nico and Vittorio approached, horses grazing in a nearby field glanced up only momentarily at the strangers and then returned to nibbling the tall grass at the field's edge. From a distance, the men spotted two figures loading a large object into a wagon. One figure had a bushy white beard and hunched slightly when he walked. The tunic stretched tightly across his midsection wasn't soiled, but neither had it been freshly laundered when he donned it. The second figure was an apprentice. His gangly frame and flapping arms gave him the appearance of a giant insect. Despite his age, the man showed little difficulty hefting the coffin onto the wagon, but the boy was still panting from the exertion when Nico and Vittorio reached the building.

"What?" the man called brusquely while securing the coffin.

Nico introduced himself and Vittorio and declared, "Signor Prizzi has been arrested!"

The announcement elicited no reaction from the man. When he finished fixing another rope to the coffin, he asked, "Are you the ones who arrested him?"

Nico replied, "He was arrested by Guardia officers. You don't seem surprised to hear that he was apprehended." The man grunted.

Vittorio said, "He's been charged with inciting two crimes. He hired someone to sabotage Antonio Ridolfi's importing business and disrupt his son's betrothal celebration."

The man placed his hands on his hips and poked his lip out onto his beard and spit onto the ground. "Their feud isn't new. They've been caviling as long as I can remember. After Signor Prizzi bested Ridolfi in the guild election, Ridolfi tried to disparage him. Ridolfi said the election had been stolen, that Signor Prizzi paid guild members to vote for him. If Ridolfi weren't mindless, he'd realize that Signor Prizzi isn't the only one who mocks him. He's a bully who believes his business success grants him sainthood."

Nico asked, "Did Signor Prizzi say how he planned to get revenge?"

"I don't remember," the man grumbled.

Vittorio stepped forward. "We're concerned about a different crime, a more serious crime. Antonio Ridolfi's son Marco was murdered. Did Prizzi ever mention Marco Ridolfi?"

The man's response came instantly, before Vittorio's words had faded from the air. "I know nothing about that." Climbing aboard the wagon, he said, "This coffin needs to be delivered." He turned abruptly, held out a coin purse to the apprentice, and instructed, "When you finish cleaning here, go to the graveyard behind the church and pay the diggers, four denari each. They should be finished by the time you get there. When they leave, stay by the hole and make sure it is not disturbed."

Without glancing back at the commissioners, he eased the wagon forward and headed toward the city.

Nico, wondering how to proceed, looked at Vittorio, who said, "He's being obstinate to protect his boss. If these were the days before Cosimo de Medici came to power, we could have tortured him. That always made criminals and witnesses tell the truth, but it's more difficult to get people to talk now that Cosimo has outlawed torture."

Vittorio watched the apprentice sweeping up fallen sprigs of thyme and lemon balm that had been used to sweeten the fragrance of the coffin for the funeral service. To encourage the apprentice to speak freely, Vittorio began a friendly conversation by asking, "What's your name?"

While continuing his task and without facing the questioner, the apprentice said softly, "Taddeo."

"How long have you worked for Signor Prizzi?"

"Less than a year."

"Are you a relative?"

"No. Signor Prizzi lives in my uncle's building. My uncle arranged for me to be Signor Prizzi's apprentice."

"Ah," Vittorio said earnestly. "I may have met your aunt. Is she Signor Prizzi's housekeeper?"

"Yes, she is."

The youngster's movements slowed as he became invested in the banter. Vittorio took the behavior as a signal to focus the conversation. "You heard me say that we're investigating a murder. An innocent man was killed on the day his betrothal was to be announced." Vittorio paused a moment to let the boy absorb the seriousness of the situation, then said, "Signor Prizzi enjoyed boasting about how he would get revenge on Signor Ridolfi, and we know you heard some of his rants."

Taddeo shifted uncomfortably and swept the broom over the same area repeatedly. "I ... I don't know."

"Think of the man who was killed. The lives of his family and his fiancée have been shattered. Their grieving can't end until the killer is caught. They deserve justice. Don't you agree?"

"But what if Signor Prizzi finds out that I talked to you? My father wouldn't forgive me if I lost this job."

Vittorio walked to where Taddeo was standing, faced him squarely, and placed his hands on the youngster's shoulders. "I know this is difficult for you, but I can promise that whatever you say will remain between us; Signor Prizzi won't learn of it. Help us understand what happened."

Nico recoiled. If the apprentice had heard Prizzi admit to killing Marco Ridolfi, he would have to be called as a witness at Prizzi's trial, so how could Vittorio assure the youngster that his words would remain private?

Taddeo's fear dissolved, and words flowed. "I was harnessing the horse when I heard Signor Prizzi talking with the foreman ... he's the man who just left. They were talking normally, then suddenly Signor Prizzi got louder. He was almost yelling, accusing Signor Ridolfi of something ... I'm not sure what. He shouted, 'Someone's going to kill that bastard.' When I finished with the horse and came into the building, I heard him say, 'I'll make him pay. When I'm finished with him, his life won't be the same.' That's what I heard."

"Did he say what he had planned?"

Taddeo clenched his fists as he tried to recall. "He said he was going to hire someone."

Nico asked, "Was he going to hire just one person, or more than one?"

Trembling, Taddeo said, "One maybe. I don't know. That's all I can tell you."

Vittorio patted the youngster's shoulder. "Thank you. We appreciate your help."

Nico said, "If Prizzi said 'someone's going to kill that bastard,' it doesn't sound like Prizzi was planning the killing. And the comment referred to Antonio, not Marco."

Vittorio shrugged. "I suspect everything the apprentice just told us is meaningless. If Prizzi believed that someone else intended to kill Antonio, he would have had no reason to hire Fornelli."

Following Vittorio's reasoning, Nico said, "And if Prizzi intended to hire an assassin himself, he wouldn't have also hired Fornelli."

Vittorio nodded.

29

Octavia, the housemaid, responded when Massimo and Alessa knocked on the door at Casa Martone. "Massimo, I'm surprised ... and pleased to see you again," she said with a beaming smile.

"I didn't expect to be calling again, but I'm happy to see you as well." Gesturing toward Alessa, he said, "I brought someone who would like to speak with Signorina Daniela if she's able to receive guests."

"I believe she is. Come inside and let me ask her."

Octavia escorted Alessa and Massimo to the anteroom. As she turned to leave the room, Massimo asked, "Is Signora Martone with her?"

Glancing over her shoulder, Octavia replied, "No, Signora Martone is visiting a sick friend."

To Alessa, Massimo said, "We're fortunate Signora Martone is away. She's a good woman and a caring mother, but she's set in her ways."

A minute later, Octavia reappeared in the doorway. "Come with me." She led the visitors to the second level, through the grand sala, to a salon where Daniela was seated at a desk writing. She put down her pen and smiled. Upon seeing Alessa accompanying Massimo, she glanced around the room, and noting its small size, said, "Let's move to the sala. It will be more comfortable. My mother and brother are away, so we'll not be disturbed."

The grand sala, decorated as lavishly as Florence's most elegant palazzos, had its entire ceiling covered with a fresco of angels frolicking in a garden. Stucco walls embellished with delicate floral patterns held large paintings depicting Biblical scenes. Floor-to-ceiling windows along an entire wall filled the space with light. Daniela led her guests to a seating area in a corner of the room.

Eschewing formality, Massimo said, "Daniela, I'd like you to meet Alessa, Nico Argenti's sister."

Alessa's curry-brown skin tone brought a look of surprise to Daniela's face. Alessa responded with a smile, saying, "Yours is a typical reaction. I'm Nico's adopted sister." Seeing Daniela intrigued by the explanation, she elaborated. "I was born in a village in Morocco. As a young girl, I was abducted and sold at a slave market to a sea captain." Daniela shuddered. "Eventually, Nico's cousin bought me from the captain, took me to Florence, gave me my freedom, and welcomed me as a member of his family."

"You poor dear. How awful to be taken from your family."

"That was a terrible time. Some nights I awakened suddenly from a horrid dream where I see another child being auctioned and I'm with other children, each of us waiting our turn. Always it was the same dream, but that was long ago. I was blessed that Nico's cousin found me and took me here to this wonderful city."

"Have you ever gone back to Morocco to find your family?"

"In Morocco, small villages like mine scattered throughout the hills don't have names like the cities here. I wonder what became of my mother and my brother, but I wouldn't know where to look for them."

Alessa clasped Daniela's hand. "But I didn't come here to talk about my story. I came to express my sorrow at your loss."

"Do you still have the dream?" Daniela asked.

"No. Thankfully, the dream and the horror have faded over time."

Daniela clasped her hands together. "I, too, have been having a dream or a vision. Every time I try to sleep. It's a vision from the past when I was seven or eight years old. Our family owns a villa on a lake south of Florence. It was hot in the city that year, so my father hired a carriage to let us escape the heat by going to the villa. It must have been August because I remember being upset that we would miss the Ferragosto celebration. My mother and Marco's mother were working on a church project, so she, Marco, and Marco's sister Giuliana came with us."

Daniela shifted uneasily. "Marco, Giuliana, Polito and I were playing foolishly and recklessly as children do, running along a rock outcropping above the lake shore. Without warning, Polito pushed Marco; I'm not sure why, perhaps to impress Giuliana. Marco tumbled off the ledge. I screamed, fearing that he would be dashed on the rocks below. Every night now I have that vision and I wake up shivering, afraid to close my eyes again."

"What happened to Marco at the villa?" Alessa asked gently.

"He missed the rocks and landed in the water. He paddled along the shore to a place where the bank wasn't steep and climbed out. My brother thought his escapade was funny. He didn't realize Marco could have been hurt. I was furious with him." A moment later, she added, "I don't know why I'm seeing that incident again every night in dreams."

Alessa chose not to mention how Daniela's current loss related to her past anxiety about Marco's safety. Instead, she focused on easing Daniela's pain. "During my time in Florence, I've adopted many traits of Italian culture, but I find some to be misdirected. One is the way Italians grieve the loss of a loved one. The custom is for people to mourn for a set time during which they wear dark colors and are kept isolated by well-meaning family and friends. Then, after the mourning period ends, the bereaved person is expected to return abruptly to her routine. But people cannot do that. We can't turn grief off like the flame of a lantern."

From a small pouch, Alessa removed a multi-strand woven bracelet and a collection of beads. "My birth-culture believes the grief of losing a loved one needs to unfold gradually." She slipped the bracelet onto Daniela's wrist and held up a bead. "Every day, focus on one quality of your beloved. Fasten the bead to the bracelet and let it represent that quality. Eventually, the bracelet will come to symbolize the one you lost. When you look at it, you will see all the reasons you loved him. There will no longer be any need to mourn, because wearing the bracelet will give you a spiritual connection to that person."

Daniela ran a finger over the bracelet. "How many beads…"

"For each person, it is different. Some bracelets may want a cluster of beads, for others, three may be enough. You will know."

Daniela reached across and embraced Alessa. "You're right about being isolated by family and friends. More than anything, I've been feeling lonely. It's wonderful having you here."

Massimo left the two women when Daniela commented on Alessa's dress and their discussion shifted to fashion. They continued talking for a time, and when Alessa eventually departed, she promised to return in a few days.

Two days later, Alessa called at Casa Martone carrying a basket of traditional Moroccan sweets. Octavia led her to a salon where Daniela, pretty again with glowing skin and bright eyes, was sitting alone reading. Her veil of sorrow now removed, or at least thinned, Daniela raised her arm to display her bracelet adorned with beads. She seemed more alert than she had been days before. Alessa had told Daniela that making the bracelet was a deeply personal experience, so neither woman discussed the significance of the beads Daniela had added. Daniela said only, "I feel my connection to Marco has deepened."

Signora Martone came into the salon just as Alessa was uncovering her basket. "These are called Sellou; they're a traditional Moroccan treat."

Biting into the morsel Alessa offered to her, Lavinia said, "Mmm. I can taste almonds and something else. Another nut, perhaps?"

"You're probably tasting sesame, although there are spices that also add flavor."

"Did you learn to make these when you were a girl?" Daniela asked.

"I didn't learn how to make them then, but I do remember my mother making them for special occasions. At the Uccello restaurant, I described them to a merchant who travels to Africa on business. He found the recipe for me during his travels. These don't taste exactly the same as the ones my mother made." Chuckling, Alessa added, "But maybe my memory has faded over the years."

Polito poked his head into the room. Upon spotting Alessa,

he spun away and walked off. Lavinia called out to him; when he didn't return, she followed him.

"That was my brother, Polito," Daniela explained. "He's never been sociable, but lately he's become almost rude. Our family business imports spices from the Middle East and sells them to apothecaries in Florence. Father has given Polito responsibility for managing the imports and Polito is desperate to prove himself a success by raising profits. The pressure may be too much for him. Father tolerates Polito's haughty behavior, but it infuriates mother."

Alessa elected not to comment on Martone family matters. She let a minute of silence pass, then changed the topic. "When I came here last, I noticed an easel with a partially finished painting. Are you the artist?"

Daniela laughed lightly. "It would be an injustice to label me an artist. I'm barely a neophyte."

"Last time, I had only a brief glimpse of the painting. Would it be possible to see it again?"

"If you wish," Daniela replied, her tone a mix of reluctance and enthusiasm. She led Alessa to the nearby salon, where the painting stood unchanged from the last time Alessa had seen it. Daniela said, "I have a cousin who dreamed of becoming an artist. He began by sketching and painting in his free time; now he's apprenticed to an artist in Prato. Before he left Florence, he taught me some basic techniques and instructed me as I painted this. I haven't worked on it since he went to Prato." Daniela turned away from the painting. "It's not very good," she said modestly. "The colors don't blend together smoothly."

Alessa, still looking at the painting, said, "Nico has an artist friend, Sandro Botticelli, who apprenticed to maestro Lippi. Sandro is now a master member in the guild and enjoys helping others improve their technique. If you're interested, I could speak to him on your behalf and see if he'd be willing to tutor you."

Daniela reflected for a moment before responding. "I'd like that. I need activities to occupy my time and my thoughts. My mother enjoys playing cards with her friends, but I find those games boring. I need more creative outlets."

Alessa laughed. "If painting isn't enough to occupy your time, I could teach you to mix spices to make fragrances."

30

Nico entered Palazzo del Podestà through a seldom-used door on the narrow street behind the imposing building.

He chose that entrance rather than the palazzo's main entrance because it gave the most direct access to the dingy room at the rear of the building where Luigi Prizzi's trial was about to begin. The trial drew the drab chamber room because the charges against Prizzi, befouling wine and sabotaging the sugar warehouse, were deemed minor offenses. Accordingly, an inexperienced, low-ranking magistrate had been assigned to preside over the tribunal.

Nico's friend, prosecutor Luca Sasso, always arrived at court early. When Nico entered the chamber, Luca was at the prosecution table conferring with his notary. The court clerk, the only other person in the room, was lighting lanterns set on stands at the front of the windowless room.

Luca looked up when he saw Nico approach. "Will you be winning the favor of Lady Justice today?" Nico asked.

"As you well know, my friend, magistrates can be unpredictable, especially unseasoned ones, so I never assume an outcome." Luca displayed a thin smile and added, "Although the testimony of my witnesses seems indisputable."

"Do you have confidence in what Fornelli will say?"

"I met with him yesterday to review his testimony and to assure him that if he says anything different to the magistrate, I'll see that he occupies a prison cell alongside Prizzi. He took my warning seriously because he'd spent time in the Stinche in the past for other crimes and doesn't want to return."

Sasso's notary stepped away from the table to talk to the court clerk, giving Nico the opportunity to sit next to his colleague. Sasso said, "I'm confident that Signor Colombo will be a powerful witness."

"Yes," Nico agreed. "Vittorio is always a convincing witness. He testified at countless tribunals when he was a member of the Guardia and more since becoming a member of the Security Commission. He has a reputation among magistrates for being honest and forthcoming. They value his word."

"I also have a third witness," Sasso declared. "He's a member of the Guardia who was in the tavern when Prizzi was apprehended. He sat close enough to overhear the conversation between Prizzi and Fornelli, so he can support Signor Colombo's testimony."

A creaking of the door at the rear of the chamber drew Nico's and Luca's attention. Luigi Prizzi entered the room, accompanied by his lawyer. Prizzi's head bent forward, his gaze downward. He lacked the haughty defiance often displayed by accused criminals. The lawyer walked stiffly as though his knees couldn't bend. His combination of prominent forehead and long chin gave the impression his face had been squashed together. Prizzi and his lawyer headed for the defense table. Neither one glanced across the room to Sasso at the prosecution table. The chamber had no gallery for seating onlookers, so the Guardia officers took positions standing at the rear of the room.

Eyeing Prizzi's lawyer, Sasso said, "That's Garo Contadini. He's competent, but he's not among Florence's best defense lawyers. Prizzi certainly could have afforded better. Contadini's peers call him the Bird, in part for his appearance and in part for his behavior in the courtroom. He never develops a strategy. Instead, he begins his defense with one approach, and if that doesn't win favor with the magistrate, he switches to a different one. Contadini changes tactics like a bird who nibbles at one plant and if it doesn't yield a tasty morsel, he quickly jumps to another. His technique rarely gains acquittals for his clients, but it is effective in winning reduced sentences. Since most of his clients are guilty, perhaps short sentences are the best they can hope for."

"Have you faced Contadini before?" Nico asked.

"Twice. I prevailed easily the first time. The second involved a man charged with brawling in public. After the magistrate accepted my proof of guilt, the Bird worked his magic. Contadini convinced the magistrate that the man's wife and two children would suffer if the man was imprisoned, so the magistrate found the man guilty but waived his sentence."

Nico said, "Sometimes it's best when compassion prevails, but not today. Prizzi needs to be held to account for his actions."

Sasso fixed on Nico. "The intensity of your words suggests you believe Prizzi guilty of more than these crimes alone. Do you hold him responsible for Marco Ridolfi's murder?"

"I don't know. He's been too careful to admit any involvement, so thus far, we haven't found evidence to implicate him, but we're still looking." Nico stood when he saw Sasso's notary end his conversation with the court clerk and move toward the prosecution table. "I'm sure you'll earn another conviction today, but I can't stay to watch the trial. There's another person I must speak with who may have information relevant to Marco Ridolfi's murder." The two friends clasped hands and Nico gazed again at Prizzi and his lawyer before turning to leave the courtroom.

From the Palazzo del Podestà, Nico walked across the city to the building that held the offices of the Magistrates' and Notaries' Guild. As Nico caught sight of the Guild's coat of arms, a gold star on a blue field, displayed proudly above the doorway, he recalled the first time he came to that office to apply for membership in the Guild shortly after receiving his Doctorus Juris degree from the University of Bologna. Without realizing it, Nico twisted on his finger the silver ring bearing the university insignia. In the few years since joining the Guild, his life had transformed dramatically: he'd been appointed to a vital commission, put himself at risk several times to defend the Florentine Republic, and he'd met a wonderful woman who would soon become his bride. If only his parents could have lived long enough to celebrate those achievements with him.

A senior magistrate, identifiable by the wide red stripes on his black robe, came out of the building and held the door for Nico to enter. Nico had never appeared before that magistrate but recalled seeing him presiding over a tribunal in the court of justice. Nico climbed to the reception room on the second level, where the clerk assigned to greet visitors chatted with a colleague. Both men quieted when Nico entered the room and approached the desk. "May I help you?" the seated clerk asked.

"I am Messer Nico Argenti. I need to find a notary and I know only that his given name is Bernardo."

"Do you know his family name?"

"No, I do not."

The two clerks looked at each other, then the seated clerk said, "We'll have to search the register."

His associate volunteered, "I'll take him," and to Nico, "Come with me."

They passed through a short corridor and entered a darkened room where dust hung in the air. The clerk pulled the linen window covering aside, revealing a desk in front of the window and shelves filled with books and document folios. "This is the records room," the clerk announced. He gestured toward three volumes. "These are the registers of current guild members." Tapping one book, he said, "This contains listings of magistrates." Pointing to a green covered book, he said, "This one lists the lawyers." He lifted a blue covered volume. "This one has information about the notaries."

He handed the register to Nico. "You can sit at the desk to search through it. I suspect you'll find several notaries named Bernardo. The register contains information besides names that may help you find the notary you're looking for."

The clerk turned to leave, and when he reached the doorway, he paused. "It's a coincidence that you're looking for a man named Bernardo. A notary with that name was brought to Santa Maria Nuova hospital two nights ago. I don't know exactly what happened, but I heard he was attacked while walking home from his office." The clerk shook his head. "I lived in Pistoia before coming to Florence. People can walk the streets of Pistoia at any time without fear, even women. But there are neighborhoods in Florence where I would not venture even during the day."

Nico agreed it likely was just a coincidence, then wiped a thin layer of dust from the register's cover, opened the book, and leafed through every page. He found three with entries for men named Bernardo. On a separate sheet, he recorded their names, home locations, and business office locations. Two men had their own businesses preparing contracts, bequests, property transfers, and other documents. The third man served on a city government commission. Although he worked for the city, Nico thought he might also have private clients, so Nico recorded that man's information as well.

Sheets in the register had been prepared by the guild secretary who prided himself on his handwriting. His own embellishments added to a lettering style known as Carolingian Minuscule, a decorative technique devised six centuries earlier in the court of Charlemagne. No one dared tell the secretary that his fanciful lettering made documents nearly illegible, and clerks joked that several times even the secretary had been seen struggling to read papers he had written himself.

To be certain he hadn't missed an entry, Nico sifted through the pages a second time and noticed an entry for a notary named Bernaba. Nico recorded information for that man in the event that Daniela or Massimo had made a mistake remembering the name of the notary consulted by Marco Ridolfi. Scanning the listings of office locations, Nico pictured the optimum route that would let him visit the offices of all four men. He decided to start with Bernardo Spotsi, whose office was closest to the guild hall.

31

A short distance from the guild hall above a storefront doorway, Nico found a sign, gold lettering on a blue background, announcing Bernardo Spotsi Notary Services. A woman with sparkling eyes and a pleasant smile flitted like a butterfly into the reception room from an interior room when Nico entered the office.

Before Nico could speak, the woman said, "Ser Spotsi is unavailable at the moment. He is filing documents with the Tribunale della Mercanzia." Nico smiled inwardly, wondering whether the notary was truly conducting business at the prestigious tribunal or whether the woman merely used the name to impress her visitor.

The woman continued, "I am Ser Spotsi's assistant. Do you wish to make an appointment?"

The gold ring on her hand suggested she was probably Spotsi's wife and possibly his confidant with knowledge of his clients. Nico said, "Perhaps you can help me. Has Ser Spotsi ever done work for a man named Marco Ridolfi?"

She adopted a sheepish expression. "I'm sorry, but I can't

help you because Ser Sposti keeps the names of his clients confidential."

Nico introduced himself as a member of the Security Commission and explained, "Marco Ridolfi was murdered, and the notary who worked with him may have information that could let us find his killer. So, I ask you again, has Ser Sposti ever done work for Marco Ridolfi?"

The woman's practiced smile morphed into a pensive expression. Not wanting to upset a member of the Security Commission, she said pleasantly, "I don't know that name." She turned; said, "One moment," and trod to the interior room, this time with footsteps sounding more like those of a domesticated animal rather than the lightness of a butterfly. She returned a minute later carrying a folio, placed it open on a desk, and gesturing toward it, said, "There's no record of anyone named Ridolfi being a client of Ser Sposti."

Nico thanked her, left the office, and consulted the sheet he had prepared listing the locations of the notaries' offices. The second Bernardo, the one who worked for the city, shared office space with several other notaries in a loft near the center of the city, close to the cathedral. Nico made the short walk to that building and climbed to its upper level, where he heard murmurs of conversation even before entering the office. Inside, at desks spaced throughout the large open area, notaries were intently discussing projects with low-level bureaucrats, men contracted by the city to repair roads, build bridges, expand offices, and perform other tasks to keep the city prospering. Shrill words voiced by a man complaining that the city failed to pay him for work he had done repairing a road caught Nico's attention. Other men discounted that man's plea as if complaints by unhappy tradesmen were nothing unusual. The office did not have a person charged with greeting visitors, so Nico waited until one of the notaries was free, then approached him and asked about Bernardo. The man pointed to an empty desk across the room. "That's his station. He works alone, so I've no idea where he's gone or when he might return."

Rather than wait, Nico opted to visit the next man on his list. The third Bernardo's office was a distance away in the San Marco district. As Nico gazed at his notes, he recalled the guild clerk saying that a notary named Bernardo had been taken to Santa Maria Nuova hospital. Since the hospital was only a short distance away, Nico decided to go there rather than make the longer trek to San Marco.

Hoofbeats reverberating through the narrow street alerted Nico to the approaching wagon. He flattened himself against a storefront to avoid being struck as the wagon sped past him. It stopped a short distance ahead in the piazza fronting Santa Maria Nuova hospital. Two men jumped from the vehicle, raced to the rear, and lifted a man who had been lying prone in the wagon bed. With one man on each side, they shouldered him toward the hospital entrance. The patient appeared to be conscious, but he couldn't walk. His feet bounced along the cobblestones as he was dragged across the piazza.

Nico trotted ahead intending to open the door, but a nurse came out and held the door before Nico reached the building. He followed the men guiding their patient into the lobby, expecting to witness a hectic scene with doctors and nurses ready to minister to the newly arrived patient. Instead, he saw only one nurse, the one who had held the door. She calmly gave directions to the new arrival. Following her directions, the two men guided the patient along a corridor and into a ward. The nurse watched until the men were out of sight, then turned to Nico and said, "You don't seem to be injured. How may I help you?"

"I'm looking for a notary named Bernardo Vernacci."

"This hospital serves the poor and indigent. Names mean little to us. Some who are brought to us cannot speak. Others remember neither their names nor little else."

"He was brought here two nights ago by the Guardia. They found him in a street where he'd been attacked."

"I'm here only during the day. If you come back later, you can ask the nurse who is here at night. She might remember him." Seeing Nico's shoulders slump in disappointment, she pointed to a corridor. "The men's wards are that way. You are welcome to look for him."

Nico had never seen Bernardo Vernucci, so there was little chance he could identify him. He was about to decline the offer when he heard Vittorio's voice: "Never dismiss a possibility, no matter how unlikely it might seem."

Nico entered the first ward, a long narrow room with twenty or more beds lining the walls on each side of him. He froze momentarily, overcome by the smell of sickness and death. A chorus of moans punctuated by shrieks assailed his ears. He moved forward through the rows of beds, glancing side-to-side at men wrapped in bandages and covered with thin sheets. Nurses tending the sick paid him no heed. He couldn't possibly hope to spot Bernardo. When he neared the far end of the room, a priest with a cherubic face asked, "Are you looking for someone, my son?"

"Yes, but they all look the same."

"You are seeing them only as a gathering of unfortunates, but if you speak to them and get to know them as individuals as I have, you'll appreciate their differences. I've come to know most of these souls. Which one do you seek?"

"His name is Bernardo Vernucci."

"Ah, Bernardo. He is not in this ward. I can take you to him, but first, there is one more here," the priest gestured toward the bed at the end of the row, "who needs our prayers. Come with me and we can pray together."

"I... I don't know..."

The priest took Nico's hand. "The words are not important. Say whatever fills your heart." He bent low and whispered into the ear of a man who could do no more than shift his eyes to look up at God's messenger.

Nico recited softly a verse he recalled from psalm forty-one: "The Lord will sustain you on your sickbed and restore you from your bed of illness."

When the priest stood and moved beyond the man's hearing, in a trembling voice, Nico asked, "Will he recover?"

"A doctor may have an answer to that question, but I never inquire about the prospects of patients, but to my untrained eye, this one seems to be improving."

As they walked down the corridor to a nearby ward, the priest said, "The one you seek, Bernardo, was brought here two days ago. He suffered a head wound that made him senseless. His wife came to see him after the Guardia told her about his injury. She found him unable to speak or open his eyes. He couldn't respond when she spoke to him. The poor woman was mortified. When I visited him earlier today, he had regained his senses. I promised to send word to his wife that his wits have returned. It will be a while before I can leave the hospital. Would it be possible for you to deliver that message to her?"

"Yes, I can do that."

The second ward they entered was like the first, with beds lining both walls, but lacking the sour smell and the din of painful moaning. Some men were sitting up talking to those in the next bed. The man in one bed looked expectantly at the priest as he approached. "This is Bernardo," the priest announced to Nico.

"Have you told my wife?" Bernardo asked. "Does she know I am conscious?"

Nico replied, "I'll go see her and tell her you're recovering as soon as I leave here." He thanked the priest and introduced himself to Bernardo. "Do you know what happened to you?"

"A doctor told me I was brought here by the Guardia. He said they found me in a street and that I'd been stabbed." He shook his head. "But I don't remember any of that. I only remember walking home from my office and then waking up here two days later."

"Can you think of a reason you were attacked? Or who might have done it?"

"There can be no reason. I'm just a notary who prepares documents. The man who attacked me must have been a thief." Staring into the distance, he added, "There was a time when it was safe to walk about in this city... but no more."

Nico clenched his teeth together. "I don't believe the one who attacked you was a thief. Thieves rarely stab their prey. Whoever assaulted you intended to incapacitate or kill you."

"Why would anyone do that? I have no enemies."

"If the assault was not directed at you, it might have been intended to cause harm to one of your employers."

Bernardo responded quickly, "I'm doing work for several men, but nothing unusual. Nothing that would provoke violence." He went silent, reflecting for a moment, then said, "It could be the testament. I'm revising the testament of a banker to change his bequests. Upon his passing, his current testament calls for dividing his estate between his two sons. He hired me to create a new testament in which each son would receive only a small sum and the rest of his wealth would go to the church. The two sons were livid when he told them of his intention, and they swore they would stop him from making the change. Could one of them...?"

"Possibly. You should tell this to the Guardia so they can investigate." Nico paused a moment, then asked. "Did you ever do work for Marco Ridolfi?"

"Marco... Oh, the poor man who was killed. How awful. He was a good man." "Yes, I did work for him." Seeing Nico's curious expression, Bernardo felt the need to explain further. "Marco had been approached by a shipping company that transports goods from the Levant to Venice. The company was eager to become the carrier for Ridolfi's sugar imports, so Marco hired me to assess the company's capabilities."

Nico understood that investigating such matters was a common task for notaries." Was that the only work you were doing for Marco Ridolfi?"

Bernardo winced as he ran a hand over the bandage wrapping his head. "He mentioned another company that drew his interest, one that imports spices. He believed their profits had increased by an unreasonable margin and wanted me to examine their tax records."

"What is the name of that company?"

"I don't know. Marco said we would discuss that job after I finished my report on the shipping company." Nico knew immediately Martone Spice Importers was the company that had piqued Marco's interest. Bernardo looked intently at Nico and asked, "Why are you asking me questions about Marco Ridolfi?"

"I'm a member of the Security Commission investigating his killing. Any information we learn about Signor Ridolfi might help us find his killer."

As Nico rose to leave, he said, "I'll go directly to see your wife. I'm sure she'll be delighted to learn that you're now lucid."

From Santa Maria Nuova hospital, Nico crossed the city to the Vernacci home, three rented rooms above an apothecary shop on a quiet street near the university. Nico judged the elderly woman who answered his knock to be too old to be Bernardo's wife. "Signora Vernacci?" he asked with doubt in his voice.

"I am her neighbor. She's resting."

"I've come from Santa Maria Nuova hospital with news about her husband."

The neighbor stepped aside, allowing Nico to enter the modestly furnished room. The wall directly in front of him held a portrait of a young woman, too young to be Bernardo's wife, perhaps his daughter. He caught a whiff of something cooking in another room. Chicken soup, he assumed. "Signor Vernacci is conscious and eager to see his wife," Nico announced.

Signora Vernucci, curious to know the caller's purpose, had been listening attentively in an adjoining room. She stepped into the doorway. "I was at the hospital this morning. Bernardo couldn't hear me talking to him. He said nothing, like he was under a spell."

Nico looked at the woman. "Yes, suddenly he came alert, as though he cast the spell aside. He's worried about you and would like to see you."

Tears welled up in the woman's eyes. "My cloak!" she exclaimed, turned, then, while offering a prayer to the Holy Mother, she disappeared into the other room. Moments later, she returned and hurried out the door, leaving Nico and the neighbor behind.

After leaving the building, Nico wandered past the apothecary shop, while his thoughts replayed the tidbits of information from Bernardo Vernucci. Both Daniela and Marco's cousin Lazo had mentioned Marco's interest in the rapidly rising profits of Martone Imports, but Bernardo said that Marco's interest went beyond curiosity; he had intended to hire the notary to delve into the company's tax filings. Although Nico knew nothing about records kept at the tax office, he was aware of another document repository that might hold information about the workings of Martone Imports. He wended his way through the city streets to the Chancery Annex.

Galetto, the highest-ranking notary, appeared to be berating a junior clerk when Nico entered the annex. While he waited for Galetto to finish with the clerk, Nico stood to the side, watching the bustling activity of men organizing and filing the plethora of newly arrived documents. Even from a considerable distance away, Nico could see the young clerk flush with the shame of his foolish error. After duly reprimanding the neophyte, Galetto put a reassuring hand on the young man's shoulder, delivered soothing words of encouragement, then left the man to continue his duties.

"Ah, Nico. When you were here last, you thought you might

be returning to gather more information. Are you still investigating the Ridolfi murder?"

"Yes, we're still searching for Marco Ridolfi's killer, but it's a different matter that brings me here today... a different matter, but one somewhat related."

Galetto raised an eyebrow at Nico's enigmatic response. Nico continued, "Some people we've questioned about the murder have mentioned a rapid rise in the profits of the Martone Imports company. They describe the rise as being sudden enough to be suspicious."

"We have financial summaries here at the annex, but the detailed filings are at the tax office."

"I understand, but I've always been fortunate in finding the information I need here at the annex. If Fortuna doesn't favor me this time, then I'll go to the tax office."

Galetto led Nico to the room holding the document indexes and pulled a thick folio from a shelf. "This index references the summaries of goods declared by all importing companies." He opened the folio, scanned several pages, muttering, "Martone Imports," then declared, "We have records of goods declared by Martone Imports for the past eleven years. Would you like to see all the documents?"

"If something changed in their business, it happened recently. Records from the past three years... four years should be sufficient to show the change."

Noting the filing key, Galetto dispatched a clerk to the building's third level, where the documents were stored. When the clerk returned, he handed Nico a folio containing the sheets he had retrieved; four sheets, one for each of the past four years. As Galetto had said, the sheets contained only minimal information; they specified the type of goods imported, but not the quantities. If the Martones' profits had increased recently, it was likely they were importing a larger quantity of spices.

Nico began with the oldest record, reading, "peppercorns, cloves, and ginger." The next sheet noted the same three spices. Last year's sheet added saffron to the list. Since saffron was much more valuable than the other spices, that might explain why the Martones' profitability was increasing. Finally, Nico examined the sheet listing goods imported this year. It mentioned only one item: ginger, the most common and there-fore least valuable spice. "There must be an error," Nico said to himself. "Why would the Martones stop importing valuable spices in favor of ginger?" A notation at the bottom of the page stated that the summary had been prepared by the republic's tax office.

Nico left the Chancery Annex and headed to the tax office, only to discover that tax records were also stored in an outlying building in the San Lorenzo district. He retraced his steps along Via San Gallo past the Chancery Annex to a building that had once been a grain store used during hard times to feed the city's indigent. The century-old wooden building consisted of a single voluminous room containing rows of shelves filled with tax documents. The sound of the door opening reverberated through the space when Nico entered.

Unlike the Chancery Annex, with its complex archiving system and large clerical staff, the tax repository had only two clerks. Tax documents were rarely requested by anyone after being sent to the repository, so the clerks were elated to help their visitor, especially upon learning he was a member of the Security Commission. Both men interrupted their mundane filing task, gathered around Nico, and explained that the docu-ments were sorted chronologically on the shelves. Records could be retrieved only if the requester knew the original filing date.

Fortunately, Nico had noted the dates on the summary pages he'd seen at the Chancery Annex. Immediately after he recited the four dates, the clerks scurried into the aisles of shelves.

In contrast to the brief summaries at the Chancery Annex, the tax records contained details about each shipment received by Martone Imports. Nico studied the most recent filings and found ginger listed as the sole spice in shipments for the past six months. Shipments in prior years always contained quantities of peppercorns, ginger, and cloves, as well as a variety of other spices, including turmeric, nutmeg, saffron, cinnamon, and cumin.

The clerks clustered around Nico, eager to know whether the documents they'd given him provided the information he required or whether he needed additional help. They pointed out notations on the filings that showed all the shipments were inspected at the Porta San Gallo gate, suggesting that the goods had come to Venice by ship and then overland to Florence.

Nico and the clerks found it odd that in recent months, shipments had always passed through the Porta San Gallo gate on Thursdays or Fridays, since sea transport from the Levant to Venice was subject to the vagaries of weather and not always predictable. Was there a reason the Martones made sure their shipments always arrived on those days? The clerks also pointed out that the shipments always reached Florence in mid-morning. It wasn't possible to leave Venice at daybreak and reach Florence by mid-morning, and the risk of encountering thieves was too great for wagons to travel at night, so the wagons must have spent the previous night at an inn somewhere along the Via degli Dei road. Why incur the expense of an inn when they could have left Venice at dawn and arrived in Florence by evening? Nico's examination of the tax records left him with more questions than answers.

33

Early the following morning, a Thursday, Nico headed to a field outside the Porta San Gallo gate to join Massimo. From that vantage, they planned to view the tax inspectors examining wagons entering the city. Clouds hid the sun, still low in the eastern sky, and glistening droplets of morning dew clung to the tall grasses. Nico groaned as he felt the squelch of the wet greenery seeping into his shoes. He found Massimo sitting on a dry patch of ground, leaning back against a tree. Massimo offered his colleague a sweet roll he'd bought at a *pasticceria*. "Get comfortable," Massimo urged. "We could be here until noon."

Nico gestured toward his wet shoes, groaned, then took the sweet roll and sat beside his friend.

Most wagons in the stream that flowed through the gate every day carried non-taxable produce from farms in the nearby river valleys. Tax collectors examined only those vehicles bringing goods other than fruit and vegetables.

"How will we recognize the Martones' wagons?" Massimo asked.

"That will take some ingenuity," Nico replied. He pointed to a wagon in the line awaiting inspection. "Some will be easy to dismiss just by noting what they are carrying, like that one loaded with glassware, most likely from Venice. The tax records showed that Martones' spices are carried in barrels. When we see wagons with barrels, we'll have to wander close enough to hear the conversation between the wagon master and the tax inspector."

They watched as the tax inspectors assessed goods in the parade of wagons bringing furs, salt, wine, leather, wax, and even coral from North Africa. Two wagons carrying salt in barrels were the only ones that demanded Nico and Massimo draw close enough to hear the tax collector mention the contents of the barrels.

Clouds had dissipated, and the sun glowed high in the sky when Nico's attention shifted to a wagon coming out of the city through the Porta San Gallo gate. For a long moment, Nico studied the men in the wagon, then exclaimed, "That's Polito Martone! I'm sure the one riding in the wagon is Polito Martone."

Polito's wagon turned away from the gate and came to a stop alongside the city wall. Polito and his driver remained seated, eyeing the line of wagons moving slowly toward the inspectors. Nico and Massimo crept forward out of the grassy field and toward the city gate, taking care to remain out of Polito's field of view. Massimo leaned toward Nico and said softly so his voice would not carry, "I can see barrels in the three wagons at the end of the line."

When the three wagons reached the front of the line, Polito climbed down from his wagon and walked to where an inspector was counting the number of barrels. His driver remained behind, watching Polito walking toward the inspector until two young women coming through the city gate captured his attention.

Nico remained shrouded behind a shrub hidden from Polito's view while Massimo moved closer, close enough to hear the exchanges between Polito and the inspector. "Sixteen barrels," the inspector declared. Polito grunted his agreement. "Ginger?" the inspector posited.

"Ginger," Polito repeated. The inspector announced the tax amount and recorded it in a register. Polito echoed the amount and placed a coin purse in the inspector's hand. The three wagons, laden with barrels of spices, followed by Polito's wagon, passed through the gate into the city.

"The inspector didn't examine the contents of a single barrel," Nico said incredulously.

"At least he counted the number of barrels," Massimo quipped. "What do you suppose is in the barrels?"

"They're certainly not all filled with ginger," Nico responded. Massimo concurred. "This explains how the Martones increased their profits. No matter what spices they import, they pay only the low assessment for ginger. Plus a few denari to line the pockets of the tax collectors."

Nico said, "This also explains why the Martones' shipments always arrive on Thursdays or Fridays. The tax collectors rotate posts during the week. These" — Nico searched for a word — "reprobates must be stationed at Porta San Gallo only on those two days."

"An interesting situation," Massimo observed. "We know the inspectors were derelict in not examining the contents of the barrels, but we can't say for certain that Polito Martone committed a crime. It's possible that all the barrels are filled with ginger."

Nico gave Massimo a piercing glare. "You don't believe that, do you?"

"No more than you do, my friend."

"But you're correct. What we've witnessed doesn't prove the Martones are evading taxes. To expose their deception, we need to catch them selling spices other than ginger, since they claim that's all they are importing. We'll have to follow them when they distribute the spices to their customers."

Nico and Massimo took positions behind a wood pile alongside a horse barn, a vantage that gave them a view of men processing spices in the Martones' warehouse. The barn's roof overhang afforded little protection from the light drizzle that had begun falling, so now it wasn't only Nico's shoes that were becoming waterlogged. He and Massimo stepped cautiously around the puddles formed by rivulets streaming down from the barn roof.

Although Polito hadn't accompanied the wagons to the warehouse, his men worked efficiently, filling earthenware crocks of various sizes from the barrels and loading the crocks onto a cart for delivery to apothecary shops throughout the city. The warehouse was too far from the barn where Nico and Massimo were concealed for them to tell whether the crocks were being packed with ginger or other spices.

Massimo said, "We'll need to track the cart to see what they deliver to their customers."

Nico ran a hand through his wet hair and glanced up at the dark sky. "I already feel as slippery as a lizard, so I guess chasing through the rain won't make it worse."

Polito's men, wearing cloaks to protect themselves from the rain, climbed aboard the cart and headed toward the San

Lorenzo district. Unable to match the speed of the horse-drawn cart, Nico and Massimo gradually lagged behind as they trotted after it. When the cart, a distance ahead, veered onto a side street, Nico stopped momentarily to catch his breath. Panting, he sputtered, "I know where they're going. There's only one apothecary in that direction." They walked the remaining distance to the shop, and reached it just as Polito's men, having made the delivery, came out of the shop, climbed onto the cart, and headed toward their next destination.

Following the routine he'd practiced during his time in the army, Massimo began each day with a run across the city, so chasing the cart a comparatively short distance hadn't tired him. After scanning his flagging companion, he offered, "I can follow the cart while you question the owner of this shop."

As a youngster, Nico had been a skilled athlete. Several times, he'd led his neighborhood pallone team to the city championship, but his studies at the university hadn't afforded him the time to maintain his physical prowess. Unwilling to admit any loss of stamina, he replied, "We can both track the cart and come back later to speak with the shop owners." He took a few deep breaths, then resumed the chase with a smiling Massimo trotting effortlessly alongside.

Polito's men made a second stop at an apothecary near the center of the city and a final delivery at a shop in the Santa Maria Novella district. Panting and soaking wet, Nico muttered, "I feel like a rat on a sinking ship," as he watched the empty cart heading back to the Martones' warehouse.

Inside the apothecary shop, an apprentice lifted the four newly arrived crocks onto shelves and set signs in front of each. The signs read peppercorns, cloves, nutmeg, and cinnamon. Massimo identified himself and Nico, then pointed to the newly placed crocks. "We need to inspect those spices."

The worried shop owner stammered, "Is there something wrong with them?"

The owner and his apprentice moved aside as Massimo came forward, removed the lids and announced, "Peppercorns, cloves, nutmeg, and cinnamon," as he sniffed the contents of each crock. Not wanting to reveal that he and Nico were investigating a tax fraud, he said only, "There's nothing wrong with the spices, but the delivery may be irregular. You may need to certify that you received these spices, so make a note of which spices you received and the date you received them." The befuddled shop owner stood staring at the spice crocks, unsure what to make of the incident after the members of the Security Commission left his shop.

Nico and Massimo retraced their route to the other apothecaries that had received the spice deliveries. In both shops, they found spices other than ginger. The first shop had received peppercorns, cloves and tumeric, while crocks delivered to the shop near the center of the city contained peppercorns, nutmeg, ginger, and saffron. "Now we know how the Martones increased their profits," Nico mused. "They bribed the tax inspectors to levy a low rate for all their imported spices by claiming all the shipments were ginger."

"These inspectors might be taking bribes not only from the Martones, but from other importers as well. And there might also be other inspectors who are taking bribes."

Nico nodded his agreement. "We need to tell the tax officials what we've found, so they can investigate further and discipline their men. Sergeant Grimaldi can have his men arrest Polito Martone."

Massimo said, "I wonder who in the Martone family, other than Polito, is involved in this scheme. I can't believe Daniela is aware of it."

"She may not know what her brother has been doing, but

the men transporting the spices and Polito's driver, and possibly others, are involved. Vittorio can question them. No one can apply pressure better than Vittorio."

Massimo asked, "Will you be prosecuting the case?"

"Since I'm a witness, I can't also be the prosecutor. If Luca Sasso is finished with Luigi Prizzi, he may be the one assigned to prosecute Polito,

"Would Sasso prosecute both the tax inspectors and Polito Martone?"

"Luca could prosecute the Martones, Polito certainly, and his father if we find that he's also involved, but the tax officials have their own lawyers who can bring charges against the inspectors."

Massimo suggested, "After you file charges against Polito, I can have Sergeant Grimaldi arrest him."

"Good," Nico agreed. "The tax officials' offices and the judiciary are both in the Palazzo della Signoria, so after filing charges against Polito, I'll visit the tax officials and tell them what we've found."

After filing tax fraud and bribery charges against Polito Martone with a judicial clerk, Nico dispatched a Chancery clerk to deliver a copy of the charges to Sergeant Grimaldi at Guardia Headquarters. From the Chancery, Nico made his way through a corridor on the palazzo's second level until he reached a room marked Tax Office. Dozens of desks crowded together filled the room, leaving barely enough space for the bevy of clerks to move about. The constant murmur of clerks discussing filing details with each other mimicked the sound of a beehive.

While low-level clerks processed a constant stream of tax

documents in the cramped, noisy space, the tax council officials reserved more opulent and spacious quarters for themselves. Nico continued along the corridor to the next room, an ante-room where a lone clerk sat behind a desk. Unlike the indus-trious clerks in the outer office, this man occupied himself by humming and drawing cartoon figures. He swiftly slid a blank sheet over the drawings to conceal his unproductive pastime when Nico stepped into the office and announced, "I wish to speak with a tax official."

"I'll find out if the official is available to meet with you. Can I inform him of the purpose of your visit?"

Seeing no reason to give specifics to the obtrusive clerk, Nico said simply, "To report an irregularity."

"Wait here," the clerk said and disappeared through a door at the rear of the room. He returned a moment later, handed Nico a sheet of paper, and said, "The official is currently occu-pied with an important task. You may report the irregularity in writing."

Nico set the paper down on the clerk's desk, leaned forward and locked eyes with the clerk. "Tell the official that two of his inspectors are taking bribes."

The clerk's eyes went wide, his jaw dropped, and again he disappeared into the adjoining room. The closed door couldn't contain the loud bellowing that erupted. "He wishes to see you," the clerk said when he returned.

Nico pushed the door open and entered the official's office. With his hands clenched tightly together on his desk, the offi-cial glared up at Nico and barked, "The purpose of the Guardia is to arrest criminals, not to harass tax inspectors."

"I'm not from the Guardia. I'm a member of the Security Commission."

The official slapped a hand down on his desk; the sound reverberating off the coffered ceiling. "An even worse dereliction. The Security Commission has no authority to arrest Florentines. You should be tormenting the Venetians or the Milanese."

Nico decided not to correct the man's misunderstanding of the Security Commission's authority; rather, he opted to pressure the official. "Two of your inspectors are taking bribes. I came here to apprise you of that situation and ask what action you intend to take against the offenders."

The official's face reddened. "You have been misinformed. We monitor the integrity of our inspectors, and none have ever been found guilty of taking bribes."

"Your monitoring must be flawed," Nico said defiantly. "I and another member of the Security Commission personally witnessed two inspectors engaging in fraud."

The official stood, and trembling with rage, said, "It is the responsibility of the tax officials to oversee the conduct of our inspectors, not the Guardia and certainly not the Security Commission. If you have a complaint, submit a form to the clerk." He pointed to the door. "Now, get out. I have important work."

Nico glared at the official. "Either you prosecute the inspectors who've been arrested and investigate possible corruption among the others, or I will see that this incident is brought to the attention of the Signoria."

The official snorted. "You foolish young man. The Signoria is busy with vital matters of the republic. You are mistaken to believe they care about tax collectors. I'll make sure the charges you filed are dismissed, and that will bring this matter to a close."

Nico said, "Now I understand. Impropriety in the tax office extends beyond two pathetic inspectors. Even tax officials are culpable." He turned and stomped out of the office.

34

Nico had almost reached Casa Argenti when a voice behind froze him in place. 'Good afternoon, Messer Argenti." His neighbor, a plump woman wearing an apron covered in flour, waddled toward him. "Pardon my directness, but will you be going to the guild dance?"

"Guild dance?" Nico echoed.

"Yes, the guild dance on Saturday."

"I hadn't thought about it. I've been rather busy lately."

Smiling broadly, the woman said, "Then you must take time away from work to experience life, and the dance is sure to be enjoyable."

Eager to end the encounter, Nico said, "I'm certain it will be." He turned and reached for the door handle.

"You know my daughter, Isabella. She's a wonderful dancer."

"Isabella," Nico mouthed reflexively, then nodded his head respectfully and said, "Excuse me, Signora, but I must go now." Inside, Nico exhaled in relief after getting away from his brash neighbor. Isabella, with her innocent charm, might become a devoted wife to someone in the future, although Nico saw her as a mere child who lacked many of Bianca's admirable qualities.

He climbed stairs to the casa's upper level and headed directly to the kitchen, hoping to find a sweet roll left from breakfast. Alessa, standing in the doorway behind him, said, "Donato ate the last pecan roll, but there's a raspberry torta on the side table."

Nico fixed a serious expression, walked over to Alessa, and gently took hold of her arm. "I've just come from the judiciary where I filed charges against Polito Martone for tax fraud." He guided her to a chair and sat next to her. "He's been bribing tax inspectors to avoid paying the full levy due on spice shipments. That's how Martone Imports has managed to increase its profits."

"How awful. Does Daniela know?"

"I don't believe she knows about the fraud. If she hasn't already heard that her brother has been arrested, word is sure to reach her soon."

Alessa placed a hand on Nico's. "The poor girl. She'll be devastated." Alessa gathered her resolve, stood, and said, "I have to go to her. She'll need someone to help her through this." As much to herself as to Nico, she added, "First Marco is lost to her and now her brother is found to be a criminal."

"I'll go with you."

"But you're the one who filed the charges against Polito. Won't it be awkward for her to see you?"

"It might be painful, but she needs to know the truth. Massimo and I were close-by when Polito bribed the tax inspectors. We watched him lie about the contents of the shipment, so I can tell her what happened. Whatever she hears from others could be half-truths, exaggerations, or lies."

Nico didn't reveal to Alessa his hope that by being at Casa

Martone he might learn whether Polito was solely responsible for the bribery or whether his father, Nozzo Martone participated in the scheme.

"Your friend Sandro Botticelli and I had planned to meet with Daniela tomorrow to renew her interest in painting. She was looking forward to it. It would have been a happy occasion. But now...."

Octavia, the housemaid at Casa Martone, answered Alessa's knock. She was visibly upset. Alessa embraced her, and speaking just above a whisper while holding the maid close, asked, "Has Daniela heard?"

"A man who works for Signor Martone came to the house. He said that Signor Polito has been arrested. I didn't hear why. They're all shaken, Signor Martone, Signora Martone, and Daniela."

"May I see her?" Alessa asked.

Octavia silently ushered Alessa into the house. Without being introduced or attracting Octavia's notice, Nico followed. Upon reaching the second level, they heard loud voices coming from a nearby room. A male voice, who Nico judged to be Nozzo Martone, fumed, "How could he do such a thing? It took years to build a successful, respectable business, and now the thoughtless fool has tarnished our reputation and brought shame to our family. We'll never recover from his stupidity."

As the visitors entered a hallway, they glimpsed Polito's parents in a nearby room. Nozzo and Lavinia Martone were moving about erratically, waving their arms and hands aimlessly as they struggled to grapple with the situation. "I don't believe it," Lavinia protested. "Polito wouldn't do such a thing. He's a good boy. It must be a lie. Someone wants to destroy our family."

Nozzo dropped onto a chair, his head in his hands. "It's my fault. I gave him too much responsibility. I should have known he wasn't ready."

"What will happen to him?" Lavinia asked her husband.

Before Nozzo could reply, Octavia quickened her pace and hurried the visitors away from Polito's fretting parents. At the far end of the hall, Alessa and Nico entered a salon where Daniela was sitting alone, silently staring into space. The room was small and minimally furnished. Daniela sat at the end of a reclining couch styled like the dining couches of the ancient Romans. Alessa sat next to Daniela, took her hand, and gently ran her fingers through Daniela's hair. For several minutes, neither woman spoke. Nico stood quietly to the side. Finally, Daniela said, "My mother and father are shattered."

"And you?" Alessa asked.

"Polito is my brother and I love him, but lately he's been distant. He keeps to himself and hardly speaks to me. I don't want to believe he could be a criminal; yet he's become hard. He rarely spends time with the family.

"The only time I'm with him is at church, and there he has a glazed expression and acts as though he's wasting his time. He only goes to church because my mother insists. Our parish priest tried to involve Polito in a charity project. He refused so abruptly and rudely that I felt ashamed for him."

Alessa asked, "Did the person who told you about Polito's arrest give you any details?"

"He said only that Polito had bribed a government official."

Alessa looked up at Nico, and Daniela followed her gaze. "Daniela, this is Nico, my brother. He witnessed the" — she stopped herself from saying crime — "incident. He can tell you what happened."

Daniela vaguely remembered Nico from the terrible day in
Calenzano when Marco was killed. With her eyes on him
expectantly, Nico explained. "As I'm sure you know, your
father's company imports a variety of spices. The more valuable
spices, like saffron and cinnamon, are taxed at a higher rate
than ginger. Polito was at the inspection station when the latest
shipment arrived. He claimed the entire shipment was ginger
and paid the tax official to pass the shipment without inspection. Later investigation showed that the shipment contained a
variety of spices and should have been taxed at a much higher
rate. Tax records show this deceit has been happening for
months. Polito has been arrested on charges of tax fraud and
bribery."

"What will happen to him?"

"The Guardia officers who arrested him will take him to a
magistrate who will schedule a trial. Given your family's
respectable standing, I'm certain the magistrate will release
Polito until the trial. He'll need to find a lawyer, one with experience in criminal trials."

"My father and mother need to know this," Daniela said.
She rose and left the room. Minutes later, she returned with her
parents. Looking at Nico, she said, "Tell them what you told
me." Nico repeated the information he'd given Daniela.

Nozzo said, "Months ago, I put Polito in charge of the shipments. He was eager to take on the responsibility, and he was
happy at first, but over time, he became withdrawn. We used to
chat about the business, but no longer. How long have these...
irregularities been happening?"

Nico replied, "Tax records show ginger as the only spice
imported for the past four months."

Nozzo grimaced. "That's not right. We import more than
just ginger. That explains how our profits have been rising." He
sank down onto a chair, his shoulders slumped. "Whenever I

asked Polito about the shipments, he brushed my concern aside. I should have kept watch over him."

Lavinia rested a supportive hand on her husband's arm. "Will he go to prison?" Nozzo asked.

"I can't say. That will be for a magistrate to decide, but if Polito is penitent and pays the evaded taxes, the magistrate might impose just a fine and forego a prison sentence."

Lavinia said, "You told us he'll be released until the trial, so he'll be coming home soon."

In a firm voice, Daniela said, "I don't think so. Polito won't come home because he'll be too ashamed. Not ashamed of what he's done, but ashamed that he got caught. He'll find somewhere to hide from us."

"How can you say that about your brother?" Lavinia snapped.

"He isn't the angel you'd like to believe him to be," Daniela countered, rose, and walked from the room. Alessa shot a quick glance at Nico, saw the slightest dip of his head, and followed Daniela from the room.

He might not be an angel, Lavinia thought, but he won't be sent to prison. Her son had caught the attention of the Guardia before, so this wasn't a fresh experience for her. Polito's first infraction was bloodying a man in a tavern brawl. When the Guardia learned the injured man was merely a common laborer in a woolen mill, they released Polito and apologized to Nozzo Martone for detaining his son. Polito's assault of a neighbor's housemaid had threatened to be a more serious matter until questioning of the neighbors revealed the maid was Croatian, not Florentine. The matter was settled swiftly by a modest payment to the girl's father in Dubrovnik.

However, tax fraud and bribery were more serious charges, ones the Guardia couldn't simply ignore. To vanquish those charges, Lavinia would need to prevail upon her second cousin,

Lucrezia Tornabuoni, the wife of Piero de'Medici, the patriarch of the Medici dynasty. Lavinia felt certain that Lucrezia's influence could convince a magistrate to waive a prison sentence. Aristocracy is entitled, she told herself.

Nozzo stood and faced Nico. "I want to see my son. Can you take me to him?" The two men left Casa Martone and headed to the judiciary, hoping to get there before Polito was released.

35

Vittorio stood beside a woodpile across from the Martone warehouse, the same woodpile that had masked Nico and Massimo the previous day. Since Vittorio wasn't known to the men moving spices in the warehouse, he stood in the open and didn't use the wood as a screen. The weather had improved. It was no longer raining, so Vittorio wasn't concerned with stepping in puddles.

The men in the warehouse were too busy to notice their observer. A short man with hair pulled back in a horsetail scooped spices from barrels into crocks. He marked each crock with the name of the spice it contained after filling it. His associate, a tall hefty man with a scraggly beard, loaded the crocks onto a cart. From Nico's description, Vittorio could tell these were the same men Nico and Massimo had chased through the city the previous day as they made deliveries to apothecary shops.

After filling the cart, the men came around the side and climbed aboard, ready to make the deliveries. Vittorio moved from the woodpile to the warehouse to intercept the two men.

They stopped suddenly, surprised by the sight of Vittorio standing beside the horse and holding its reins. Vittorio introduced himself as a member of the Security Commission. "I don't give a damn who you are; we gotta get to work," the short man growled.

"Before you go anywhere, we need to talk," Vittorio said calmly.

The tall man reached out as though trying to take hold of the reins. Vittorio grabbed the man's wrist, and, with a quick twist, pulled him forward, down from the cart, and sprawling onto the floor.

"Your boss, Polito Martone, has been arrested for tax fraud. You can either talk to me now or join him in the Stinche."

The tall man, having once spent a few days in the infamous prison, had no intention of going back. He pushed himself up, brushed the dust from his clothes, spread his hands in resignation, and said to Vittorio, "You needn't have done that." Flashing an icy glance at his companion, he added, "Our work can wait a bit while we answer the man's questions." The short man didn't respond.

Vittorio gestured toward the crocks stacked in the cart. "When these spices came into Florence yesterday. The tax inspectors were told that all the barrels contained ginger."

The tall man said, "Some are ginger, but not all."

"And you knew that when you brought them into the city, Vittorio asserted.

The man shook his head and held up a hand in protest. "We didn't bring them into Florence. We only deliver them to the shops. It was other men who brought them to Florence from Venice."

"Tell me about those other men. What are their names and where can I find them?"

The tall man shrugged. "We have nothing to do with them. I don't know their names and I don't know where to find them."

The short man spoke up. "One is called Cambio. I heard Polito call him that. I didn't hear a name for the other one, but I heard him say they were going to Pazzo Luigi's."

"Pazzo Luigi's," Vittorio repeated. What is that?"

"A tavern near the river."

"What can you tell me about Polito's driver?" Vittorio asked.

"His name is Goffo," the tall man replied. "I don't know how you can find him, but he keeps Polito's wagon at a stable on Strada Maestro outside the Porta la Croce gate."

Vittorio handed the reins to the tall man and stepped away from the cart. "Can we go now? Can we deliver these?" the tall man asked.

"These spices were brought into Florence illegally, so they are contraband. If you distribute contraband, you'll be committing a crime. Since Polito Martone is in prison and Martone Imports is guilty of tax fraud, it's doubtful you'll be paid for your work if you do deliver them."

"Shit!" the short man barked and pounded his fist on the wagon seat."

Vittorio walked away, leaving the two men wondering where they could find other work.

Dockworkers and crewmen on river barges were the usual patrons of Pazzo Luigi's. Cambio and his fellow driver Bindo frequented that tavern because both men had worked on barges before taking jobs as drivers for Martone Imports. Both had rewarding careers on the river, with Cambio even getting occasional jobs as a barge captain, until they swindled the son of a ship owner in Pisa and were banished from that city.

Although Polito Martone knew of their misdeed in Pisa when he hired them, he didn't ask about their offense. The story he'd heard suggested the men might be well suited to the scheme he had planned.

Vittorio didn't know the men's past, but he knew they were familiar with Venice and the cities between Florence and Venice along the Via degli Dei, the ancient Roman road that connected the two cities. That meant there was a risk the men might flee from Florence when he told them that Polito had been arrested. He couldn't detain both men by himself, so rather than taking the chance that the men might bolt, Vittorio stopped at Guardia headquarters and enlisted two officers to accompany him.

As they approached Pazzo Luigi's tavern, Vittorio said, "Everyone inside will become suspicious if three strangers enter the tavern together." He thought, but didn't say, the officers' huffish behavior would mark them as members of the Guardia, and no one speaks freely to Guardia officers. He said, "Wait out here while I find out if Cambio is inside." The officers agreed. They continued walking past the tavern to the waterfront and positioned themselves where they could view the building's entrance.

Four men were sitting at a table, and two were standing at the bar when Vittorio entered the tavern. All six had the muscular builds and shabby clothes of dockworkers. Vittorio set a soldo coin on the bar and ordered a beer. He took a swallow from his mug, wiped his mouth with the sleeve of his tunic, and declared, "I'm looking for work."

As he expected, his statement elicited no response because men in taverns rarely engaged with strangers. He took another swig, belched, then said, "I was told there's someone here called Cambio who might help me. Is one of you Cambio?"

At the mention of a tavern regular, the man to his right said,

"Cambio was here earlier. I don't know if he'll return, but he has a room across the way above the tailor shop."

Vittorio raised his mug in a gesture of appreciation, said, *"Grazie mille*, many thanks," downed the remaining liquid, and left the tavern.

Vittorio entered the tailor shop with the officers following. The tailor smiled broadly, "Gentlemen, how can I be of service?"

Vittorio didn't introduce himself, but mentioned the men with him were Guardia officers and they were looking for a man named Cambio. The genial tailor became doubly helpful when he realized the Guardia officers hadn't come to question him about his illegal gambling activity. "Cambio lives above my shop. His is the room on the right. His friend Bindo rents the other room."

Vittorio climbed to the second level trailed by the two Guardia officers. He knocked on the door and announced, "I've got a message for you from Signor Martone." Vittorio's duplicity brought smiles to the faces of the two officers.

Cambio swung the door open, growling, "How did he find where I live?" His mouth dropped open at seeing three men in the hallway.

Vittorio pressed a hand against Cambio's chest and shoved him backward into his room. A bed against one wall and a small fireplace for cooking filled nearly half the room. Cambio must have felt the cramped space was adequate since he spend most of his time traveling between Florence and Venice. The Guardia officers followed Vittorio into the room and stood alongside Cambio, ready to grab his arms if he resisted or tried to flee. Vittorio said, "The message for you is that Polito has been arrested for bribery and tax fraud."

Cambio managed a single word. "What?"

"You brought a shipment of spices into Florence that was

falsely declared to be ginger. The shipment wasn't only ginger, it contained a mix of spices, some subject to much higher taxes."

Regaining his composure, Cambio took a step back, away from Vittorio. "I just drove the wagon. I didn't know what was in the barrels."

"Lying will only make your situation worse. Two members of the Security Commission heard you talking with Martone. You saw the tax officials pass the wagons without inspecting them. That makes you an accomplice."

"I didn't know."

Vittorio raised his hand, his fingers spread in front of Cambio's face. "You can try to convince a magistrate that you are stupid." He let a long moment pass. "Or you can testify against Polito Martone."

Cambio raised his hands defensively. "No one will hire me if I turn against Martone."

"And no one will hire you if you are in the Stinche. You have a choice." Vittorio turned away and called over his shoulder, "Think about your options while I talk with your comrade, Bindo."

One of the officers stayed with Cambio; the other went across the hall with Vittorio. "Cambio needs your advice," Vittorio shouted as he pounded on Bindo's door.

Bindo pulled the door open, eyed two men facing him and another across the hall with Cambio. In an instant, he realized two of the men were members of the Guardia. Vittorio leaned close, eye to eye with Bindo, and said, "Tell your compatriot it will be better for him to testify against Polito Martone than to move from his comfortable room to a cell at the Stinche."

Bindo shifted his eyes between Vittorio and Cambio, hoping one of them would reveal why he'd been awakened from his afternoon nap. Vittorio explained the situation and offered Bindo the chance to testify against Polito Martone. He saw Bindo looking at his friend for a hint of how to respond and said, "You'll need to make your own decision because Cambio can't decide whether to be a witness or a prisoner." Vittorio's remark brought forth chuckles from the officers.

Bindo's eyes narrowed. "Are you saying if I testify against Martone, I won't be charged with a crime?"

"These officers are going to take you to the judiciary, where you'll be charged and detained so you can't flee, but if you agree to testify, I'll recommend to the magistrate that he waive your sentence. And the magistrates always accept my recommendations."

"Then I'll testify."

Vittorio turned and looked across the hall, where Cambio nodded vigorously. "Me too. I'll testify."

The officers escorted their captives out of the building. One faced Vittorio and asked, "Are you coming with us?"

"No," Vittorio replied. "I'm going to hunt for Martone's driver."

Two stables stood on the flat river plain outside the Porta la Croce gate, their isolated forms contrasted with the clustered buildings of the bustling city. Horses grazed in paddocks behind both stables. In front of one stable, a blacksmith fashioned horseshoes by repeatedly pounding his heavy hammer against iron shapes. A line of wagons and elegant carriages fronted the other stable. Vittorio reasoned that one wagon might belong to Polito Martone, so he approached that stable first.

Inside the stable, the stable master was brushing a chestnut colt and toward the rear of the stable, a boy was mucking the stalls. Outside, a boy was working to remove mud from the wheels of a carriage. He'd already cleaned one carriage. Another carriage and two wagons with caked on mud awaited him. Vittorio approached him and asked, "Do you clean them every day?"

"They need to be cleaned every day when we have rain that turns the roads into mud. I've cleaned them each of the past three days. In dry weather, they only need road dust brushed away. Usually I do that once a week."

"Does one of these wagons belong to Polito Martone?"

The boy hesitated and looked up at the mention of the name Polito Martone. Suspicious of the questioner's motive, he simply pointed at a wagon, one that still needed cleaning. The boy's reaction told Vittorio that word of Polito's arrest had reached the stable. Feeling no need to hide his purpose, Vittorio introduced himself and said, "I'm looking for the wagon driver. He's called Goffo. Do you know him?"

The boy nodded tentatively. "Do you know where I can find him?"

The boy glanced furtively at the stable, fearful that the stable master might object to him sharing information. In a wavering voice, the boy said, "He lives in a house by the river."

"Do you know the house?"

"I was there once."

Vittorio went into the stable and arranged with the stable master to borrow the boy. They entered the city through the Porta la Croce gate and followed the city wall south toward the river. As they neared the tanneries along the Arno river, the stinging smell of decaying flesh mixed with the acrid bite of tannin grew stronger. Vittorio wondered whether people who lived there ever became accustomed to the smell. Shortly after they turned onto Via dell Casine, the boy pointed. "That's his house."

Vittorio judged house to have two rooms, three at most. It was modest by Florentine standards, but beyond what a wagon driver could typically afford.

A quick glance showed no activity around the house. Vittorio asked, "Does he have a wife, or does he live alone?"

The boy replied, "I don't know. I never heard him mention a wife."

Vittorio let the boy return to the stable, then crossed the street and rapped on the door. His knock brought no response. Listening, he heard no sound inside, so he walked around to the side of the house and peered through a window.

"Are you looking for Goffo?" a voice called from behind.

As Vittorio turned, he found himself looking at a man with well-groomed hair, a fashionable tunic, and polished boots. "Yes," Vittorio replied curtly.

"He isn't here," the man responded, equally crisply.

The man looked too well dressed to be living in a neighborhood close to the tanneries. Vittorio approached him, identified himself, and asked, "Are you his neighbor?"

The man lost his stiff posture upon hearing of Vittorio's position as a member of the Security Commission. "I'm his landlord. I don't live here." He gestured toward the row of houses. "I own these houses. Goffo rents this one. I heard that his employer, Signor Martone, has been arrested. Is that why you want Goffo? Has he committed a crime?"

Vittorio avoided the man's questions and asked, "Do you know where I can find him?"

"He went to visit his cousin."

"Where?"

"He didn't say, but I can tell you the cousin is not in Florence."

Goffo had accompanied Polito Martone during the commission of his crime, but Goffo wasn't the one who bribed the tax collectors or lied about the contents of the spice barrels. His only transgression was knowing that a crime had been committed and not reporting it. Rarely did people get penalized for that offense. If the Guardia were to apprehend everyone who failed to report a crime, the tribunals would be hopelessly clogged with cases and the Stinche would be overflowing. Vittorio deduced that Goffo wouldn't expect the Guardia to be looking for him, so there must be another reason why he'd fled.

"Did he say when he'll return?"

"He didn't say, but his rent is paid for the next two weeks. If he isn't back by then, I'll be looking for a new tenant." The landlord reflected for a moment, then added, "Goffo seemed to be afraid. He wasn't speaking clearly, but he said he learned something that could put him in danger."

"Do you know Goffo's family name or his cousin's name?

"Zambini. His name is Goffo Zambini. He never mentioned his cousin's name."

"Goffo Zambini," Vittorio echoed as he headed back toward the city center. He had a name, but the driver could be anywhere and despite the landlord's expectation, Zambini might never return.

36

The tribunal chamber assigned to the Luigi Prizzi trial was deserted. A judicial clerk confirmed that the room had been scheduled for the Prizzi trial, saying, "The chamber was reserved today for the rendering of a decision in that case. I can't explain why the room is empty unless the trial has already concluded, but rarely does a trial end so quickly."

Nico guessed that if Luca Sasso wasn't in court, there were two places he might be: either his law office or the trattoria across the piazza. The trattoria was closer, so Nico opted to try that first. He left the Palazzo del Podestà crossed the piazza, and entered the trattoria, a favorite of lawyers because it was close to the courts. Lawyers kept the eatery filled throughout the day, stopping for drinks or snacks before trials began, after they ended, and during breaks prescribed by magistrates.

Even though it wasn't a customary meal time, the room was bustling with lawyers and notaries. Some lawyers were celebrating their courtroom victories; others could be heard commiserating with their notaries over their losses.

When Nico's eyes adjusted to the subdued lighting, he

spotted Luca sitting with his notary at Luca's favorite table at the rear of the room near the kitchen. "Brunello?" Giulia's lyrical voice asked when Nico passed her while threading his way to Luca's table. Giulia, the server, prided herself on knowing the favorite drinks of all the regular customers. In truth, Brunello, a dark red wine from the Republic of Siena, wasn't Nico's favorite. He'd ordered it a few times when he first came to the trattoria, so Giulia assumed it was his choice. He didn't want to dampen her enthusiasm, so he never corrected her.

Luca and his notary were engaged in a lively conversation, their animated gestures filling the air with energy. Nico placed a hand on Luca's shoulder and said, "From your joyous demeanor, I assume Prizzi's trial has ended and you've claimed another victory."

Smiling broadly, Luca said, "Indeed, my friend, you are correct on both points." Giulia passed beside Nico and set a glass of Brunello on the table. Nico reached for his coin purse, but Luca stopped him by placing his firm hand over Nico's. He held a silver coin out to Giulia and said, "My dear friend Nico arranged for me to prosecute the case I won handily today. And how could I not prevail with the irrefutable witnesses he brought me? Today, I'm delighted to treat him to his drinks."

Nico raised his wineglass. "I thank you, honorable prosecutor. You deserve an effortless win now and then, although your next case may present more of a challenge."

Luca's brow furrowed as he processed Nico's comment, but he discounted it for the moment as he recounted details of the Prizzi trial. "Vittorio is every prosecutor's ideal witness. He simplified the events and organized them into a clear set of facts that won the magistrate's favor. The Guardia officer who followed Vittorio strengthened my position, but I'm not sure his testimony was needed because Vittorio had already convinced the magistrate. As soon as Vittorio stopped speaking, I knew the case was won."

Nico asked, "Did Fornelli testify as he'd agreed?"

"He did, but his testimony wasn't very effective because the magistrate knew of Fornelli's reputation as a lowlife with a record of minor criminal offenses. The magistrate fidgeted impatiently the entire time Fornelli was speaking."

"But Fornelli was a principle in the case. You had to call him as a witness," Nico said supportively.

"Fortunately, the magistrate understood that, too."

"What was Prizzi's defense? Surely, he didn't claim to be innocent of the charges."

"No, he pleaded guilty. His lawyer, Garo Contadini, tried several approaches to gain the magistrate's sympathy. Ultimately, he claimed Prizzi was an upstanding businessman with no prior record, and that no one was hurt by the escapades. He kept referring to the crimes as escapades. His arguments had a measure of success by influencing Prizzi's sentence. The magistrate fined Prizzi and made him pay restitution for the damage done at the Ridolfi warehouse, but he didn't sentence Prizzi to prison." Sasso shrugged. "Neither Prizzi nor Fornelli were sent to prison. Sometimes I think our judicial system is too lenient."

Nico said cynically, "Maybe the magistrate's ruling is for the best. The Stinche is already crowded and the fine will enrich the Florentine treasury, the treasury that pays the magistrates' salaries."

Sasso laughed. "It pays our salaries too." Then, turning serious, he asked, "What did you mean earlier when you said my next case may present more of a challenge?"

Nico explained the bribery and tax evasion charges filed against Polito Martone. He described the tax records showing Martone Imports had made false claims about the spices they imported, and he told Luca how he and Massimo had collected evidence to prove the claims to be fraudulent.

Luca quipped incredulously, "You ran back and forth across the city chasing a horse drawn wagon? There was a time when a young Nico Argenti could race across a pallone field all afternoon, but you aren't that young man anymore."

"I know that, believe me. I felt like an old man next to Massimo. He ran like a gazelle and never gasped for breath. But I survived, and we have three pharmacists willing to testify that they took delivery of a variety of spices from Martone Imports, not just ginger."

"Will you and Massimo be witnesses at Polito Martone's trial?"

"Yes, Massimo, me, and the pharmacists. Also, Vittorio and two Guardia officers apprehended the wagon drivers who brought the spices into Florence. In exchange for granting them immunity to prosecution, the drivers are prepared to testify that Polito Martone bribed taxmen to pass the wagons without inspection."

"How could I refuse an appointment to prosecute such a solid case? What will be Martone's defense?"

"I can't guess, but I've no doubt he'll find a clever lawyer who'll think of something."

Luca signaled Giulia to bring a flask of vintage Chianti wine. "Isn't it premature to celebrate your next win already?" Nico asked.

Smiling broadly, Luca said, "Enough talk about court cases. I understand there's another reason to celebrate." Seeing Nico's puzzled expression, Luca added, "I heard that you finally proposed to Bianca, and it's long overdue." He refilled their wineglasses, raised his own glass, and announced, "Let me be among the first to wish you both a long, blissful and prosperous life together."

"How did you hear about Bianca and me? We haven't made a formal announcement."

"A magistrate told me. Your cousin Donato had mentioned it to the magistrate when he was dining at the Uccello restaurant." Luca laughed. "You don't need to make a formal announcement when you have a cousin who's eager to spread your joyous news. Have you picked a date for the wedding?"

"Not yet. Bianca is coming to Florence today to meet with a woman who is planning a visit to Rome. She wants Bianca to make a dress for her to wear when she meets His Holiness."

"She's meeting the pope?" Luca asked, with doubt in his voice.

Nico chuckled. "Every woman who goes to Rome thinks she's going to meet the pope. Perhaps this one will. After Bianca meets with the hopeful woman, we're going to look for loft space, so Bianca can move her dress business to Florence, and a place for us to live after we're married. Donato offered to let us live at Casa Argenti, and while I appreciate his generosity, I believe Bianca and I should be on our own."

Luca snickered. "Young marrieds need their privacy... so I've been told."

Nico let his gaze drift across the room to where Giulia set beer mugs in front of four spirited lawyers. She stepped aside, deftly avoiding a hand moving toward her backside. "And what about you, Luca? When are you going to act on your feelings for Giulia? She won't wait for you forever, not with all these men vying for her attention every day."

Luca followed Nico's gaze to Giulia, who was gracefully spinning away from one table and gliding elegantly back to the serving counter. The eyes of a half dozen men tracked her flow. "I sense you may be speaking the truth, my friend. Taking a leap forward with Bianca has brought you happiness; perhaps taking a small step with Giulia will bring me joy."

He raised a hand to signal Giulia. She acknowledged Luca's beckoning, and, after delivering an antipasti platter to a group of notaries, she came to his table. "The lawyers' guild is hosting an event, a dance, on Saturday to support the orphanage. Would you do me the honor of accompanying me?"

Her expression changed from a sweet smile to open-mouthed surprise. After a speechless moment while she processed Luca's request, her smile returned. Through trembling lips, she replied, "I'd be delighted to accompany you."

Nico winked at Luca, then rose and walked away, leaving Luca and Giulia to arrange the details of their rendezvous.

37

The convener of the Officials Over Orphans lived in an historic three-level building that predated the Florentine Republic. One legend alleged it was the place where Countess Matilda of Canossa entertained Pope Gregory when he visited Florence. Others might have referred to the building as a palazzo, but not the convener. He was a private person who eschewed the attention craved by other wealthy Florentines. Following the death of his wife several years ago, he lived a solitary life in the large house, relying on a cook for his meals and a housemaid to ensure its tidiness.

The convener stood on the second-level balcony gazing at the sun glinting off the nearby cathedral when his eye glimpsed the Officials Over Orphans prospective new member, Nico Argenti, coming to meet with him. He waved to Nico, then trotted down to open the door and welcome his guest. "Thank you for coming here to meet with me," he said cheerfully.

"I was certainly surprised to receive your invitation, Signore."

"There is no need for formality. Call me *Locatore,* everyone does," he said as he led Nico past the anteroom to the modestly furnished room that he used as an office. Could the name Locatore, landlord, refer to his administrative function at the orphanage, Nico wondered, but didn't ask.

Soft, warm afternoon sunlight painted the wall of books behind Locatore's desk. He opted to sit in front of the desk alongside Nico. "When the Signoria originally established an authority to oversee the operation of the children's orphanage, they named five members with lifetime appointments. My predecessor believed the Officials would benefit by having broader input, so, with the approval of the Signoria, two new positions were added for members with one-year terms. This year, Chancellor Scala suggested, and the Officials agreed, to invite you to serve in one of those positions."

"I'm honored to be asked, but my position on the Security Commission often has me away from the city."

Locatore waved a hand dismissively. "That should not be a problem. Each of our five permanent members dedicates time to overseeing different aspects of the orphanage's operation, but you would only be expected to attend meetings held every other week where we gather to discuss and evaluate progress being made in caring for the children in the city's care."

"I should be able to do that," Nico consented, hoping nothing would disrupt his time in Florence for extended periods like his recent assignments to Bologna and Pisa.

"The Officials know well you that were instrumental in ridding the orphanage of a corrupt administrator, so we'll be delighted to have you join us. It embarrassed us that his lies and behavior had escaped our notice. We've added safeguards to guarantee that such a failure will never occur again. If you have time now, we can visit the orphanage and I can show you the changes we've made."

"Thank you for the invitation, but maybe we can plan a visit for another day since I have a prior commitment. Bianca, my future spouse came to Florence today so we can search for a place to live after we are married."

Locatore clapped his hands together and flashed a broad smile. "Congratulations, Nico. How wonderful for you! Have you already found rooms to consider?"

"No, we haven't, but I've been told pharmacists are excellent resources for finding available rooms in their neighborhood because people tend to share gossip with them."

"I've heard that said about pharmacists as well, but I might also be able to help you. I'm called Locatore because I own buildings throughout the city, and some of them always have rooms available."

Nico said, "We have an additional consideration.

Bianca has her own dressmaking business, so we also need to find a loft where she can operate her business."

Locatore's brow furrowed. "Is your future spouse from Siena? Did she make a dress for the wife of the Venetian ambassador?"

"Yes, Bianca has made dresses for both Signora Emo and her daughter."

"Last week, I attended a reception hosted by the Venetian ambassador. His charming wife wore a stunning gold colored gown. I don't recall the name for the gown's style, even though she mentioned it repeatedly. She received compliments from all the guests and all the women wanted to know the style and who made it for her. I remember her saying it was made for her in Siena by a talented dressmaker who is familiar with all the new fashions popular in Paris."

"That would be Bianca. She has a friend in Paris who apprises her of the latest Parisian fashions."

"From their reactions at the ambassador's reception, I'm certain many Florentine women will be delighted to learn that your fiancé is moving to Florence. They'll surely keep her busy." Locatore leaned back in his chair. "I have a property in the San Giovanni quarter near Piazza San Marco. An artist had been living there until he left for Rome. I also have a loft a short distance from the piazza where the artist painted. He liked that loft because it has large windows that make the space bright. San Giovanni is a pleasant neighborhood, close to the city center, yet quieter than the area around the cathedral."

Locatore told Nico how to find the rooms and the loft. They agreed to meet the following day at the orphanage so Locatore could show Nico the new procedures the Officials had instituted.

Nico met Bianca and her uncle at the mercato. It wasn't proper for a woman to travel alone, so Bianca's uncle always accompanied her when she traveled from Siena to Florence. He enjoyed perusing the mercato in Florence, where he could find fruit from Sicily that wasn't available in Siena. He happily scoured the stalls of fruit vendors while Nico and Bianca went to the San Giovanni neighborhood to examine the rooms and loft owned by Locatore. When they turned onto Via San Gallo, the street where the rooms were located, Bianca said, "This neighborhood is much quieter than the city center." Joking, she added, "It's almost as quiet as Siena."

The rooms were above a tailor's shop. The tailor's apprentice led them up to the second level and unlocked the door. As Bianca entered the closed rooms, she detected a slight musty smell, evidence that the rooms had been closed since the artist had moved out. A couch and a side table were the only furnishings in the sitting room. A painting of a Biblical scene hung on one wall, perhaps a sign of appreciation left for Locatore by the previous tenant.

Nico walked the room's perimeter, pulled the window covering aside to let in the soft afternoon light and said, "This room is spacious and clean, but sparse. It will need a few things to make it feel comfortable."

Without asking whether Nico had specific things in mind, Bianca said, "I have some furniture in Siena that we could bring here."

They moved through to the bedroom that had only a washing table and a bed large enough for one person. After surveying the room, Bianca said, "There is ample space for two clothing chests, a larger bed, and possibly a small table next to the bed."

Nico said, "My clothes fit into a single chest, but I thought women's clothes needed more space. Alessa fills two chests with her clothes."

Smiling, Bianca said, "You are astute, dear Nico. My room in Siena is only large enough for one chest, so I keep the rest of my clothes in two other chests at my loft. Since I'll have a loft in Florence, I'll only need one chest in the bedroom."

The kitchen had a small fireplace along one wall, a table, and two chairs. Bianca said, "We'll have to acquire some items, but these are suitable rooms, certainly larger than my rooms in Siena. But will they be adequate for you, Nico? Now, you're living in spacious Casa Argenti."

"For years while I was at the university, I shared rooms hardly bigger than these with three other men." He reached out and hugged Bianca, kissed her, and said, "I'm sure I'll be much happier sharing these rooms with you."

Bianca stood motionless for a minute, enjoying the warmth of Nico's touch, then said, "I'm eager to see the loft."

They walked a short distance along Via San Gallo to the

building Locatore had described as a space used to store lumber for a nearby carpentry shop, and they climbed to the loft on the second level. Opening the door, Bianca laughed. "It's colorful," she said as she scanned the paint splatters dotting the floor, "and it's larger than my workspace in Siena."

She pulled aside the linen sheets covering each of the windows. "Bright lighting is essential when doing fine sewing, and this lighting is excellent." She paced the length of the room. "I could use this space now. The woman I met with earlier, the one who is going to Rome, asked me to make three dresses for her and she's leaving for Rome in only three weeks. That time is hardly enough to complete the dresses, and I'll also need to schedule fittings. It would be nearly impossible to finish if I had to travel between Florence and Siena. The task would be much easier if I were to make the dresses here in Florence."

Delighted that Bianca was pleased, Nico said, "It sounds like we've made some decisions." He came close behind and when he wrapped his arms around her, she said, "Now all we need to do is pick a wedding date."

38

Nico entered Piazza della Signoria heading toward the Chancery to update Chancellor Scala on the Security Commission's efforts at finding Marco Ridolfi's killer. Off to his right, near the center of the piazza, he spotted a crowd of men and women shifting their gazes from one building to another as though caught in a vortex and unable to escape its pull. Their brightly colored clothing suggested that they were visitors to Florence, perhaps from the south, but as Nico passed close, he overheard them speaking an unfamiliar language. Almost simultaneously, each of them caught sight of a man across the piazza waving his arms frantically to attract their attention. They trotted off in his direction like a flock of sheep, their speech quickening and growing louder as they moved. Florence, the world's wealthiest city, drew people from throughout Europe, all hoping to share in its prosperity. Watching the group disappear around the corner, Nico pondered whether they would find the success they envisioned or swell the city's population of beggars.

A clerk called out to Nico as he passed through the

Chancery office on his way to meet Chancellor Scala. "Messer Argenti, a messenger from Messer Sasso's office delivered this note for you."

Without slowing, Nico reached out and snagged the note, nodded his appreciation to the clerk, unfolded the paper, and read.

Nico,

The tax officials have declined to file charges against their inspectors for taking bribes from Polito Martone. This will not affect my prosecution of Martone because I have other credible witnesses, but I'm sure you'll be displeased by this news.

Luca

Nico's stomach churned. "Those bastards," he muttered. "How can they condone bribery?"

Nico halted in the doorway of Scala's office, uncertain whether to disturb the First Chancellor who was sitting on the edge of his desk staring at an array of note cards filling the wall in front of him. Cards at the top of four columns identified concerns raised by Florentine diplomats. The cards below each contained information pertaining to the issue. Scala's task was to assess the facts and determine whether the concerns might become threats to the Florentine Republic. If he perceived a threat, he would initiate measures necessary to protect the republic. Nico read the column-heading cards and wondered which of the problems might eventually demand action by the Security Commission.

"Would you prefer we meet later, Chancellor?" Nico asked.

When Scala turned towards his visitor, the signs of his strenuous job became evident in his slow movements and the wrinkles on his forehead. Gesturing toward the wall, he said,

"These matters haven't yet grown into crises and stepping away from them for a time will help clear my thinking, so let's meet now." He moved to his conference table. Nico followed and sat across from the Chancellor.

Nico spread his hands in resignation. "I'm sorry to report that we haven't yet found Marco Ridolfi's killer, but another crime might help advance our investigation. A notary returning home from his office late at night was attacked and left for dead. The Guardia found him and brought him to Santa Maria Nuova hospital. Robbery wasn't the motive for the attack. The man was stabbed twice, but nothing was taken from him. His coin purse was still at his belt when the Guardia found him."

"Could this have been an act of callous barbarism?" Scala speculated. "Thankfully, our city becomes more civilized every year, but we may never eradicate brutality completely."

"We do have crimes born of hatred, but this one is significant because the notary had recently been retained by Marco Ridolfi to delve into the tax filings of Martone Imports. Vittorio sees the connection to Marco Ridolfi as an unlikely coincidence."

Scala leaned back in his chair. "Signor Colombo has exceptional instincts; if he believes there might be a link, it's worth exploring further."

Nico said, "The assailant left behind the knife used to stab the notary.

It's a type commonly carried by artisans and aristocrats, making it a challenge to find its owner, but, as you know, Vittorio is relentless."

"That he is," Scala said. Changing the subject, he asked, "How are Nozzo and Lavinia Martone coping with the fact that their son is facing criminal charges?"

"Signor Martone carries the burden of blame upon

himself for not monitoring his son's activities. Signora Martone holds her feelings close, so it is difficult to know her thoughts."

Scala asked, "Will you be prosecuting Polito Martone?"

"Luca Sasso will be the prosecutor. Massimo and I will be witnesses, along with pharmacists who received deliveries of contraband spices."

Scala said approvingly. "I'm familiar with Messer Sasso. He's a capable prosecutor."

Nico continued, "Polito's wagon driver could be a key witness. He fled after Polito was arrested. Once we find his whereabouts, Vittorio and I will persuade him to return to Florence to testify against Polito."

Expressing his frustration with a grunt, Nico said, "There is another crime not being addressed. The Convener of the Tax Officials seemed annoyed when I reported to him that two inspectors had been taking bribes." Nico held up the note he received from Luca Sasso. "This note says the tax officials have declined to take action against the inspectors."

Scala nodded knowingly. "Sadly, it's happened before. Government officials appoint their hapless relatives to minor positions, then disregard matters when their relatives commit minor infractions."

With a bitter tone, Nico said, "The inspectors can't continue to take bribes without consequence. Since the Officials refuse to file charges, then I must."

Scala held up a hand. "Doing so won't achieve the result you desire. This instance is one example of how our justice system fails to meet the ideals you learned at the university. Whenever charges of malfeasance are filed against government workers, the judicial clerks consult with the supervising officials, in this instance the Tax Officials. If the Officials don't support the filing, the charges are dismissed. "

Nico's jaw dropped in disbelief. "Is there nothing to be done?"

"Someday our judicial system may reach Justinian perfection, but we haven't yet achieved that ideal. So, you have no recourse as a prosecutor, but I can tell you something that might give you a way to proceed.

Scala displayed a sly smile. "In Florence, many women accept that their husbands reserve certain affections for their mistresses. The arrangement frees the wives from acts that some find displeasing. However, jealousy makes it unacceptable to those women for their husbands to bestow more than passion alone on their *innamorate.*"

Scala leaned forward, folded his hands on the table, and paused a moment to recall the details. "While you were at the university, or maybe even before that, an event occurred that disturbed the social order of Florence. The wife of a Mercanzia official had a chance encounter with her husband's mistress and found the lady of pleasure wearing a dress of the finest silk, expensive perfume, and jewelry so conspicuous that it tested the limits of our sumptuary laws. Through conversation, the wife discovered her husband to be the source of the extravagances. The finding unleashed within the woman a fury to rival that of the Roman goddess Ultio. She embarked on a campaign to shame and humiliate her husband. She was relentless, applying pressure until he was driven from public office and made a subject of public disgrace. His former friends now pass him on the street without even a civil acknowledgement."

Nico nodded slowly as he absorbed the implications of Scala's tale. "Does the Tax Officials' convener have a mistress?" Nico asked.

Scala replied, "He does, and he treats his lover well with gifts that would surely rouse his wife's hostility were she to know of them."

Nothing of importance happened in Florence without the Chancellor's notice, so Nico didn't inquire how Scala knew of the convener's treatment of his mistress. After pondering Scala's suggestion, Nico said, "I'm curious how the convener would resolve the dilemma if given a choice of punishing his corrupt relatives or having his wife made aware of the extravagant favors given to his mistress.

39

Nico paced back and forth across the small Security Commission office, studying the note cards pinned to the wall. The only sound, other than his footsteps, were birds fussing outside the window. Their activity had intrigued Massimo, so he'd climbed onto the roof, leaned over the edge and discovered the birds had built a nest under the roof overhang.

If the count of cards filling the wall were a measure of progress, Nico should have been pleased because each day the count grew; yet he felt they still weren't close to finding Marco Ridolfi's killer. Movement in the hallway of a Chancery clerk walking toward the office caught his attention. Rarely did clerks climb to the building's top level, the level they called the attic, except to deliver a message from Chancellor Scala. Panting slightly from the climb, when he reached the office doorway, the clerk said, "There is someone in the Chancery conference room who wants to speak with you. She said it is urgent."

"She?" Nico echoed with surprise. He never recalled a woman being in the conference room. "Is the Chancellor with her?"

"No, she's alone."

"Who brought her to the conference room?"

"No one. She went there by herself."

"And none of the clerks questioned her or tried to stop her?"

The clerk simply shook his head. Nico flashed a smile. He knew only one woman who would be so bold and presumptuous. "We'd better hurry. The woman will expect me to be prompt." Nico pulled the office door closed and trotted toward the stairway with the clerk trailing behind.

Stepping into the conference room, Nico said, "Francesca, I believe you've intimidated all the clerks."

Nico had barely entered the room when Francesca rushed past him and swept out of the room. "A crime is happening now. Come with me and I'll explain. My carriage is outside."

The fearless woman left the clerks even more awestruck when she raced past them and out of the building with Nico at her side. Her carriage waited on a narrow street behind the palazzo. Crossing the piazza, Nico spotted a young Guardia officer and called to him, "Come with us. We have to stop a crime."

After completing the Guardia training course two weeks earlier, the recruit had been assigned to patrol the piazza in front of the Palazzo della Signoria because his superiors thought it would be good for government officials to see the law enforcement agency's presence whenever they entered and exited the building. The recruit had once spent a summer picking peas on his uncle's farm and had thought that was the most boring experience possible until he was given his current assignment. He'd never spoken with Nico Argenti, but knew him to be a member of the Security Commission, so the recruit didn't hesitate before sprinting after Nico and Francesca.

The carriage door had barely closed when the driver

signaled the horses to move and Francesca explained, "Signor Marchionne, the foreman at the Ridolfi's sugar warehouse, has been stealing sugar and selling it. His buyer is at the warehouse now taking delivery of another shipment."

The carriage sped through the city's normally calm streets, sending people jumping aside for fear of being trampled. It raced past two Guardia officers who shouted for the vehicle to halt, but the driver ignored them and encouraged the horses to charge ahead. Passengers in the coach clung to their seats to avoid being thrown to the floor as it bounded over rough cobblestones. When they reached a smooth stretch of road, Nico asked, "How do you know about the theft?"

Francesca replied, "Giuliana and I were questioning men at the warehouse about Marco Ridolfi's murder. As I told you, men share information freely with attractive women. To keep our attention, the men in the warehouse chatted incessantly."

Nico scowled. "Why were you questioning warehouse workers? You said you would only talk with people whom Marco and Daniela had invited to the betrothal celebration."

"We started with the invitees, but they knew nothing, so we expanded our inquiry." Nico wanted to scold Francesca for putting herself at risk, but held his tongue, fully aware that his words wouldn't temper her behavior.

The carriage slowed and stopped in an open area near the Ridolfi warehouse. Giuliana stepped out from behind a copse where she had been secreted. "They're still in the warehouse," she announced to the trio as they climbed down from the carriage.

No sooner had she spoken than a wiry man exited the building and headed toward a horse-drawn cart. He had straight black hair reaching down to his shoulders and wore a rumpled tunic that was missing a couple of buttons. "He's the buyer," Giuliana said, keeping her voice low even though the man was too far away to hear her.

Looking at the Guardia officer, Nico said, "We need to arrest him before he drives away."

Puzzled by Nico's directive, the recruit said, "How can we arrest him? He hasn't committed a crime."

"I'm confident we'll find the casks in his cart contain sugar. That makes him a buyer of stolen merchandise."

Still fazed, the recruit asked, "How do you know the sugar is stolen?"

Nico smiled, patted the officer on the back, and replied in jest, "Because Francesca said it is stolen." Then, with a serious tone, he added, "And I have no doubt that her assertion will be proven true. Since you're the Guardia officer, you should be the one to arrest him."

Buoyed by Nico's conviction, the officer seized the buyer by his arm and announced, "You are under arrest." His first arrest since joining the Guardia. Every evening at Guardia headquarters, the recruit had remained in the background, listening as other officers recounted their escapades. Tonight, he would be the one with a story to tell.

The buyer tried to wriggle free, but the recruit held him fast. "I did nothing wrong," the buyer protested.

Nico said, "You're trading in stolen merchandise."

"I stole nothing. I paid for the sugar."

Gesturing toward the casks in the cart, Nico asked, "How much did you pay for these?"

"Two soldi. I paid a soldo for each of them," the buyer stated defiantly.

Nico snorted and poked a finger against the buyer's chest. "Don't waste our time with your lies. We both know it isn't possible to buy casks of sugar for one soldo unless the sugar is stolen."

Nico turned to the recruit and said, "Let's go inside where you can make another arrest."

When the recruit pushed the buyer through the doorway into the warehouse, Marchionne was sitting behind the crude construction that served as his desk, a wide board suspended between two barrel heads. His feet rested atop a cask and his arms were folded across his chest. A smirk played across his face, suggesting he was contemplating where to spend the money he'd received from the sale of sugar he'd pilfered from the Ridolfi's inventory.

Marchionne's jaw dropped at the sight of the men and women parading into the building behind the buyer. He recognized Giuliana immediately, and he vaguely recalled having seen Nico, but the others were strangers.

Marchionne stood. He was a short man who came only to Nico's shoulders. He wore a worker's smock and shoddy shoes. His greasy hair needed brushing. Nico approached him, and pointing to the buyer, said, "This man claims you sold him two casks of sugar. We'd like to see the transaction entry in the sales register."

"Who are you? I don't have to show you anything," Marchionne said bitterly.

Before Nico could answer, Giuliana bolted forward and faced the foreman. "You work for my father. Show me the sales register." Marchionne wasn't allowed to make sales, so he had no register. He sat with a blank expression as he struggled to find a response. "How long have you been stealing our sugar?" Giuliana demanded. Still, Marchionne remained silent.

To the Guardia officer, Nico said, "You can arrest Signor Marchionne for theft and selling stolen merchandise, but he may also be guilty of murder."

The recruit's eyes went wide. Marchionne bellowed, "Murder? What are you saying? I didn't murder anyone!"

Nico pointed an accusing finger at the supervisor. "You were at Marco Ridolfi's betrothal celebration. Maybe you killed him because he discovered you were stealing sugar."

In a brittle voice, Marchionne blurted, "I was at the villa, but I swear I didn't kill Marco."

"Your denial isn't convincing because you were present where the murder was committed and now we find you could have had a reason to kill Marco. The theft charges will hold you until an investigation can show whether you are a murderer." The officer led the two criminals out of the warehouse and secured them in the bed of the buyer's cart; a tight space, but the officer wasn't concerned with their comfort.

Nico reiterated his plea for Francesca and Giuliana to exercise caution. "Marchionne might not be the only one involved in the sugar theft, and arousing an accomplice could put you in danger." Their half-hearted acknowledgement of his warning as they boarded Francesca's carriage gave Nico no comfort. "I pray you live long enough to become an old woman," he called after her as the carriage rode away

Nico and the officer drove the cart to the Stinche prison to incarcerate the prisoners and then proceeded to the judiciary to file charges against the two criminals.

Leaving the officer in Piazza della Signoria, Nico said, "A judicial clerk will inform you when Marchionne's trial is scheduled, and the prosecutor will notify your sergeant to arrange a time for you to give your testimony."

The overwhelmed officer, still struggling to grasp the fast-paced events, said, "Those two women... One said her father owned the warehouse."

"She's Giuliana Ridolfi," Nico explained. "Her father owns the sugar importing business."

"And who was the other woman?"

"Her name is Francesca Pitti. You may have heard of her

father, Luca Pitti. He's a banker who's held various positions in government."

The officer asked timidly, "Is she a member of the Security Commission?"

Nico laughed. "No, she's just a very assertive woman." He patted the officer on the back, said, "I appreciate your cooperation and hope we didn't disrupt your assigned duties," and walked away.

40

Nico headed to the office of the Tax Officials. Chancellor Scala's story gave him a way to pressure the official using knowledge of gifts from the official to his mistress. The official's extravagant treatment of his lover was so egregious that it hadn't taken Nico long to gather enough information to challenge the official. He climbed to the second level of the Palazzo della Signoria and strode through the corridor to the office of the Tax Officials. "Stop! Where are you going?" a hapless clerk stammered.

Nico ignored the clerk, swept past him, and continued to the tax official's inner office. He pushed the office door with such force that it swung open, stopping only when it slammed into the wall, dislodging a painting and sending it crashing to the floor. The startled official dropped the pen he'd been holding, splattering the papers on his desk with a spray of ink. "Damn it!" he shrieked before looking up at the intruder. Then, upon recognizing Nico, he snarled, "You again! You have no right to charge in here like a barbarian. Have you no respect for my position?"

"I have admiration for your position. It is you I disrespect.

Your inspectors are corrupt. They're taking bribes; yet you dismissed the charges against them. Your actions make you a more serious offender than the inspectors. Florence needs government officials with integrity, not men who abuse the laws for their own personal gain."

Shaking an accusing finger at Nico, the official snorted, "I know about you. My brother-in-law graduated from the University of Bologna. It's a fine institution, but it doesn't teach the intricacies of Florentine law, so let me school you. Under our laws, I am the one who decides what behavior is acceptable for tax inspectors, not the Guardia and not the Security Commission."

Alerted by the boisterous exchanges coming from the inner chamber, the clerk peeked into the office, unsure whether he wanted to become involved in the fracas. Seeing his underling's head appear in the doorway, the official bellowed at the clerk. "Get this man out of here!"

The clerk took only a single step into the office and scrutinized Nico, who stood a head taller than him, had broad shoulders and an athletic build. Knowing he would be overpowered should he engage the intruder, the clerk tensed, afraid to move. Nico raised a hand and warned, "Stay back while your boss and I have a conversation." Turning to the official, Nico said, "A conversation about Maria Falcone."

The official cringed at the mention of Maria Falcone's name, thought it a matter that should remain private, and wagged a hand at the clerk. "Leave us. Go back to your desk." Without hesitation, the clerk happily fled the room.

Nico began, "It so happened that I was at the tailor shop when Signora Falcone arrived to receive her new bright yellow *giornea* overdress. When I complimented her on how beautiful she will look in it, she told me the giornea and the lace *gamurra* she was wearing were gifts from her generous lover. 'He showers me with luxuries,' she said and displayed her silver brooch as another example of your kindness."

Nico placed his hands spread apart on the desk and leaned forward to look directly at the official. "Your wife is of an elite family and I'm told she appreciates elegance; yet you don't shower her with the same bounty you lavish on Signora Falcone. I've also been told your wife is unaware of your relationship with Signora Falcone."

The official bellowed, "You bastard! I'll see that the inspectors are punished, if that's what you want."

Nico stood up straight. As he turned to leave, he said, "You rejected that proposal. Now it will be your wife and your father-in-law who rid Florence of them... and you, the dishonorable tax official who protected them." Nico slammed the door closed as he left the inner office. The clerk kept his head down when Nico strode past him.

41

Nico was met with a bustling atmosphere and hardly an empty seat in sight when he entered the Uccello's dining room. The tantalizing aroma wafting in from the kitchen confirmed that the evening's menu featured roast grouse with the chef's special chestnut and wine sauce. Grouse had become a favorite of the Uccello's patrons. Whenever grouse was served, the dining room would always be packed with hungry patrons.

Across the room, Donato, the Uccello's owner and Nico's cousin, moved among the tables chatting with patrons. Nico weaved his way among the crowded tables to reach the chaotic kitchen. He jumped aside to avoid colliding with Joanna, Donato's wife, who was leading servers carrying antipasti platters to one of the private dining rooms. A server with a tray of roast grouse brushed past him, heading to the dining room. "Add more wine," the head chef admonished one member of the kitchen staff. "Thicker slices," he instructed another.

Nico slipped into a storage alcove where there was always an open bottle of wine. He poured a glassful and sipped, pleasantly surprised by its delicate fruity fragrance. He sat on a crate enjoying the wine when Joanna dashed in, carrying a plate of the roast grouse entrée. "You looked hungry," she said and handed the plate to Nico. "I can't join you now. Grouse has become a favorite of our patrons. Whenever it's on the menu, the dining room is filled and the kitchen is hectic. Tonight, we also have two private parties." She rushed back out to oversee the private events.

As the guests transitioned from their main courses to desserts and after-dinner drinks, the bustling sounds from the kitchen gradually diminished. Nico had just swallowed the last morsel of grouse and fungi sauce when Donato came into the alcove, poured himself a glass of wine, and sat near Nico. "A busy night," Nico said.

"It was busy, but fortunately, the service proceeded smoothly with no problems. The chef manages the kitchen like a conductor leading an orchestra. He's a master at predicting how much food to prepare and the servers moved like rabbits." Donato opened another bottle of wine and beckoned Nico to follow him. "The small private room is empty and it will be more comfortable than sitting on crates." The small private room had seating for eight, ideal for mid-day meetings of business associates and evening family celebrations. Each of the larger reserved rooms could comfortably accommodate twenty.

Donato said, "Men in the dining room were curious about Polito Martone. Has his trial date been set?"

"It's been delayed an unusually long time because the magistrates' schedules have been full."

Donato snickered. "Are we experiencing a surge in criminal activity in our beautiful city?"

"Two magistrates had been on holiday. They've returned, so I expect the judicial clerk to schedule the trial soon."

"Will Polito be found guilty?"

"I would never wager on the outcome of a trial. Luca Sasso

is a skilled prosecutor. His prosecution should be convincing since he has tax records and credible witnesses."

"Including you."

"Yes, Massimo and I will be among the witnesses. Luca will be able to prove without a doubt that tax fraud had been committed. But Polito's lawyer is a clever weasel. He will probably argue the tax inspectors are culpable and Polito did no wrong in paying the tax amount levied by the inspectors."

Donato countered, "Polito watched the inspection. He saw his wagons weren't properly inspected."

"Again, Polito's lawyer can claim that inspection procedures are purview of the tax officials, so Polito can't be held responsible if the inspections are not performed properly." Seeing Donato's unease, Nico added, "Capable defense lawyers can always find ways to support their clients' positions. That's why trial outcomes can never be predicted with certainty."

Seething at the injustice, Donato said, "So, Polito might escape any penalty and the tax officials have dismissed the charges against their inspectors. This will be one more example of crime going unpunished in our republic because of flaws in our justice system. You're a lawyer, Nico. Can't you fix this?"

"Learned scholars have been improving our legal system since Justinian authored his code six hundred years ago, yet despite their efforts, I doubt the system will reach perfection in another six hundred years. Nico smiled, took a sip of wine, and said, "However, Chancellor Scala showed me a way to compensate for the flaws in our legal system until we gain the wisdom to improve it. He recounted Scala's tale. The two tax inspectors and the corrupt official who appointed them vanished after the official's wife learned of the sumptuous gifts he bestowed on his mistress."

"You told the wife?"

"The mistress had no reservations about telling me about

the clothes and jewelry she had received from her lover. I merely detailed them in a note to the official's wife."

"Not the approach I would have expected from you... or from Chancellor Scala."

"The morality weighed on me, too. Ultimately, I decided the proper outcome was for the wife to learn the truth."

Donato pondered the issue for a moment, then asked, "Has any progress been made toward finding Marco Ridolfi's killer?"

"A new suspect came to light briefly. Signor Marchionne, the Ridolfi warehouse manager, had been stealing and selling sugar. If Marco Ridolfi had uncovered the thefts, it would have given Marchionne a motive for murder. When Vittorio went to interrogate Marchionne at the Stinche prison, he immediately determined that Marchionne couldn't be the killer. The angle of the bruises on Marco's neck meant they were made by someone much taller than Marchionne."

"Wasn't Francesca Pitti the person who discovered that Marchionne was stealing sugar?"

"Yes, Francesca and Giuliana Ridolfi."

Donato shook his head. "Francesca certainly is a unique woman. Even our society's strict norms can't contain her."

Nico said, "She is strong willed, and she's intent on questioning people about Marco's murder. I worry that she'll be in danger if she uncovers the killer."

Nico held out a paper to Donato. "Someone left this note for me at the Chancery."

Donato unfolded the sheet and read,

I saw the kiler leave Marcos room. Later I found out Marco was kild. The kiler was dressed fancy like a gest. He has brown hair and a dark blu tunic. I only saw his back.

Donato asked, "Do you know who wrote the note? Or why he waited more than a week to send it?"

"He didn't leave his name. I imagine he's a member of the villa staff who may have just come to Florence today. If the man he saw was indeed the killer, we can narrow our search by focusing only on the guests." Nico shrugged. "Although we've always considered it unlikely that the killer was a member of the villa staff. I intend to talk to the Chancery clerk who received the note to see if he can guide me to the person who wrote it."

Donato asked, "Does it help to know the killer wore a dark blue tunic?"

"Perhaps. Bianca is attentive to how people dress, both men and women. If she were at the celebration, she would probably remember which men wore blue tunics. I certainly don't remember the color of every man's tunic, and blue is a popular color, so there could have been several men wearing blue tunics."

Half in jest, Donato said, "Maybe Francesca would recall who wore blue."

"I'm hesitant to get Francesca more involved, but she also has an eye for style, so to be thorough, I should ask for her input."

After refilling Donato's glass and his own, Nico said, "Bianca and I found a place for us to live after we are married, rooms for us and a loft for her business."

With a hint of disappointment in his voice, Donato said, "I thought you'd be staying at Casa Argenti. There's ample space for both of you."

"I appreciate the kind offer, but we think it would be best to rely on each other as we start married life. The rooms are in the San Giovanni district. It's a pleasant neighborhood. The rooms are spacious and the loft is nearby. Bianca agreed to make dresses for a woman who is leaving for Rome in three weeks, so she'd like to rent the loft immediately. The woman who wants the dresses lives in Florence, so it will be more efficient for Bianca to work in Florence rather than Siena."

"And when will you need the rooms?"

Nico laughed. "I don't know. We've both been too busy to discuss a wedding date."

———

42

Nico walked from the Uccello to the Chancery. The streets were filled with Florentines enjoying the warm spring evening. Shops stayed open later than normal to cater to the cheerful walkers. In a few weeks, the same folks would be complaining about the oppressive heat and those with means would flee to a refuge in the countryside. The Chancery lacked its usual commotion when Nico entered. Almost all the clerks had departed, except for the man Nico was searching for. He consistently remained late. "I'm Nico Argenti. I understand you're the man who accepted a note on my behalf yesterday."

The clerk responded defensively. "I took the note, but I didn't read it."

Nico waved a hand dismissively. "I'm not interested in whether you read the note. I want to find the man who delivered it."

"He didn't give his name."

"Can you describe him?"

The clerk closed his eyes. "He had a boyish face, round with puffy cheeks. His face reminded me of my young brother, although my brother is only eleven years old, and this man was older. He was dressed simply like a mill worker."

"Did he smell like a mill worker?"

"No, he didn't have the vinegar smell of mill workers. His stink was the same as everyone else."

"Was he tall? Short? Thin? Fat?"

"Thin. Not short or tall, about the same height as me." The clerk's eyes brightened. "He had a mark on his chin. The kind of mark men are born with. It was reddish and mostly round with a tail that reached down to his neck." I didn't think to ask his name."

"I'm sure you were busy at the time and I appreciate your accepting the note."

If he works at the villa, Signor Ridolfi will know him, Nico reasoned.

Walking from the Chancery to Casa Ridolfi, Nico scrutinized the men he passed on the street. Many of them fit the clerk's description of thin, medium height, and wearing workers' clothes. The only distinguishing characteristic was the mark on the man's chin.

A housemaid answered Nico's knock at Casa Ridolfi and led him to a salon where Antonio Ridolfi sat behind a desk, staring at papers splayed across the desktop, rubbing his temples, and mumbling to himself. Nico stopped in the doorway, hesitant to intrude. Moments later, Antonio grunted and looked up, surprised to see a figure looking at him. "Messer Argenti. Did I forget that we have an appointment?"

"No, we didn't have an appointment and I apologize for calling on you without notice. You seem to be troubled."

Ridolfi gestured at the papers covering his desk. "These are invoices from shippers in Venice. I'm struggling to determine whether they are correct. Marco always interacted with the shippers." He pushed the papers aside. "Surely you aren't here to discuss the import business. Have you found Marco's killer?"

"Not yet, Signore, although we are making progress. A worker from your villa could have information to help us. I believe he came to Florence yesterday from Calenzano. I'm hoping you might know where I can find him."

"Inns are expensive for the villa workers, so we let them stay at the warehouse. Two men came to Florence yesterday to collect a statue that I had commissioned for the peristyle at the villa." Drifting in thought, he said, "It was probably a mistake. My wife believes the villa is cursed and I should sell it. She may be right." Recovering his attention, he asked, "What is the name of the man you are searching for?"

"I don't know his name, but I was told he has a boyish face and a mark on his chin."

Ridolfi echoed, "A boyish face and a mark on his chin. That would be Loro. He'll be returning to the villa after the sculpture is delivered to the warehouse. If it hasn't been delivered yet, Loro should be at the warehouse."

Two men were securing a statue into a wagon when Nico arrived at the Ridolfi warehouse. When he got closer, he realized the statue was of Athena, the Greek goddess of reason. It would make a fine addition to the statuary in the peristyle at Villa Ridolfi. The men finished roping the statue in place and headed toward the warehouse. Nico called, "Loro!" and a man with a boyish face turned toward him. "I'm Nico Argenti. You left a message for me at the Chancery. The information in your note was very helpful, and I'm hoping you might remember more about the man you saw."

"I only saw him from the back. I put that in the note."

"You said he had brown hair. Was it light brown or dark brown?"

"Dark brown."

"Straight or curly? How long was it?"

"Straight. It came straight down but didn't quite reach his shoulders."

"You said he wore a blue tunic. Did you notice anything else about his clothes? Did he wear a hat? What style of shoes was he wearing?"

"No hat. I didn't look at his shoes."

"Close your eyes and try to picture him."

Loro closed his eyes and wrinkled his nose. "He was turning away from me when he came out of the room. I saw the side of his face for an instant." Nico was about to ask whether the suspect had any facial hair when Loro exclaimed, "His ear! He had a pointy ear." Unconsciously, Loro rubbed his own ear. "Most people have rounded ears. This man had a pointy ear."

It was a bizarre question, but Nico had to ask, "Would you be able to identify him if you saw him again?"

Uncertain he'd heard correctly, Loro said, "Identify him by looking at his ear? I don't think so."

Nico laughed at himself, wondering whether he would have the courage to stand before a magistrate in a murder trial and present a witness who claimed he could identify the killer by the shape of his ear. To Loro, he said, "You've been very helpful. Knowing that the man has straight dark brown hair shorter than shoulder length and pointy ears will let us narrow our search."

Nico had learned to inquire about physical descriptions by watching Vittorio conduct investigations. While heading home to Casa Argenti, he contemplated whether Vittorio had ever asked witnesses about the shape of a suspect's ears.

43

Nico was alone when Lazo Ridolfi, Marco's closest friend and intended groomsman, entered the Security Commission office. Lazo glanced around at the modest quarters and said, "I imagined the esteemed Security Commission would have been granted a more spacious accommodation."

Nico said, "We are only three members and we spend little time here, so the space is adequate."

He noticed Lazo giving him an odd look. "Is something wrong?"

"Before you went to the university, you played pallone. You were the captain of your neighborhood team."

Nico said, "I was. Thinking back, it feels like that was in a different lifetime."

Lazo said, "When I played on a neighborhood pallone team after you left for the university, men still talked about your escapades, about how you tricked the opposing teams."

Nico laughed. "I didn't initiate most of the antics. I simply followed along. The real trickster on our team was my friend Bluffo. His stunts earned him the tag *deceiver*. He was often accused of cheating, but no one ever caught him breaking the rules."

Lazo's eyes settled on the cards pinned to the wall at the front of the room. He began reading names from the cards at the head of each column. "Berto Lenzi. Angelo Lenzi. Luigi Prizzi." He stopped reading abruptly and said, "If these names are your suspects, I'm pleased that mine isn't among them."

Nico asked, "Should there be a Lazo Ridolfi column?"

"I was Marco's loyal friend, his only genuine friend other than his love, Daniela."

Nico nodded. "There is no doubt in my mind about that. Your name isn't absent by chance. Our investigation was swift in ruling you out as a suspect." Nico folded his arms across his chest. "You intended to speak with Daniela, believing she would reveal things to you she would tell no other. Is that why you've come here? Has she shared critical knowledge with you?"

"I spoke with the poor woman. Among the many things she shared with me was that your sister's visits bring her a great deal of comfort." Lazo paused to study the cards. "She also told me that Marco had hired a notary named Bernardo." Lazo touched one of the cards. "I see she also shared that information with you."

"Not me. One of my colleagues. If that is your reason for coming here, I appreciate your thoughtfulness, although, as you can see, we already had that information."

Lazo stepped away from the wall. "That was not my reason for coming. Daniela told me she had given that information to your associate, Massimo. I'm here for a different purpose. I understand you wish to locate Polito Martone's driver, Goffo Zambini." Noting Nico's surprised expression, Lazo said, "Your investigations aren't confidential. Your interest in Zambini is widely known. You're aware that

Zambini left Florence to visit a cousin, but you don't know where to find him."

"And you do?" Nico asked.

"I do and I'll tell you, but I ask one favor in return." Nico stared at Lazo, waiting for him to continue. "I want to go with you when you capture him."

Nico coughed. "You're saying that you'll tell me where to find Zambini if I agree to take you with me?"

"Exactly."

Nico chuckled. "I think you'll tell me in any case because you want justice for Marco."

"I could accomplish justice by going myself to apprehend Zambini and bringing him back to Florence."

Nico waved his hands dismissively. "That would be foolish. You have no authority and you would be setting yourself against Zambini and his cousin. You may be fit, but you'd be outnumbered."

Lazo said, his intensity fading, "Take me with you."

"Why are you so intent on capturing Zambini?"

"I was Marco's closest friend, so I feel compelled to help bring his killer to justice."

'We have no reason to believe the driver is Marco's killer. He wasn't at the villa and he has no motive for killing Marco. We want him only as a witness at Polito Martone's tax fraud trial." Nico studied Lazo while he considered the request for a moment, then asked, "Did Marco always want to join his father's business?"

The surprise question caused Lazo's shoulders to slump as tension left him. "Marco had an uncle who enjoyed a measure of success as an artist. At the height of his career, the uncle was commissioned to paint a portrait of Clarice Orsini, the consort of Lorenzo de' Medici. When Marco was young, he saw his uncle's life as exciting and wanted to become an artist himself."

Lazo laughed. "Fortunately, Marco soon came to appreciate that he had no artistic talent."

Nico stepped close to Lazo and locked eyes with him. "You may come to with Massimo and me, but you must do exactly what we say. If you cause us any problems, we'll find a reason to send you to the Stinche."

Lazo said, "Goffo Zambini is with his cousin in Arezzo.

Nico asked, "Where in Arezzo?"

"I don't know, but Arezzo is a small city. I'm sure we can find him."

Nico laughed. "You say Arezzo is a small city. Have you ever been there?"

Lazo flashed a mischievous smirk, his eyes sparkling with amusement. "No, I haven't been there, but I've heard it's a mere village compared to Florence."

"I've been there. It's not a village," Nico countered. "We'll leave this afternoon."

44

Nico, Massimo and Lazo set out on horseback toward Arezzo along the Via Cassia, the ancient Roman road that passed through the Valdarno, the wide river valley named for the Arno River that the road paralleled. Farms producing goods for hungry Florentines spread off into the distance. Thanks to gentle rain during the spring that year, crops flourished, so farmers were already in the fields harvesting peppers, zucchini and other mid-season crops.

The men had departed from Florence in mid-afternoon and spent the night at an inn in the town of San Giovanni Valdarno. The following morning, Nico's eyes went wide in surprise when the innkeeper's wife came into the dining room bearing a platter of sausage and eggs. He remarked, "In Florence, my morning fare in usually a sweet roll baked by my sister."

The woman said proudly, "You might have seen chickens running around. They lay enough that we can serve eggs most mornings."

Not only had Nico seen hens, he'd been awakened by a

rooster's crowing in the dark, while the sun was still debating whether to rise.

Dipping her head reverently, she added, "It's not often we have sausage. Our farrow gave birth to a litter. Most are healthy, but one piglet was blind and didn't survive."

Massimo took another patty from the serving platter and said, "The tasty sausage you've made honors the ill-fated piglet."

After a restful night and a hearty breakfast, the men continued their journey to Arezzo. As they rode, Massimo asked Nico, "Do you have news of Polito Martone? Has he remained in Florence, or has he fled the city?"

"Polito is with his family. His father holds himself responsible for his son's waywardness. What I know of Polito is from my sister, Alessa. She and Daniela have become close. Several months ago, Signor Martone took Polito with him to Venice, where they met with ship owners who transport spices from Asia and the Levant. Polito had been pressing his father for a greater involvement in their import business. Since Polito engaged well with the shipowners, his father gave him responsibility for tracking the imports. Polito was pleased, and the spices continued to arrive without incident, so Signor Martone stopped monitoring Polito's activities. He considers his neglect as the instigator of Polito's crimes."

"Bah," Lazo objected. "Polito is no child. His father shouldn't treat him as one."

"And what of Signora Martone? Does she share her husband's sentiment?" Massimo asked.

"From what Alessa has seen, Signora Martone avoids judgment and blame. She continues to support her son."

The men arrived at Arezzo in mid-morning. As they approached the San Lorentino gate, Nico said, "I've come to see Arezzo as a fine city, but my initial encounter here was quite unpleasant. I, and the man I was meeting, were attacked outside a tavern by rogue mercenaries. We were assaulted and left stranded in the forest outside the town."

"We'll do our best to prevent a recurrence of that experience," Massimo remarked dryly. For Lazo's benefit, he added, "To find Signor Zambini we might need to ask at taverns, but we shouldn't mention that we're members of the Security Commission. There are men pushing for Arezzo to gain its independence from Florence. Thus far, they haven't become violent like the insurrectionists we encountered in Pisa, but we've nothing to gain by provoking them."

Massimo's words reminded Nico of the caution Alessa had given him about going to Arezzo. "You've been wounded there once already," she'd said. "At least this time you'll have Massimo to protect you."

Nico pointed to a building across a field to his left. "We can begin our inquiries at that stable. If Zambini rode to Arezzo on horseback, he might have left his horse there."

The pungent scent of fresh hay reached the men before they rounded the barn and saw a man unloading bales from a wagon. "Are you the stable master?" Nico asked.

"He's in the barn," the man said crisply, without slowing his work.

A lone man was whistling casually while repairing a bridle when Nico and Massimo entered the barn. Lazo remained outside with the horses. Alerted by their shadows on the bench in front of him, the stable master turned around. From their appearance, he could tell the two men before him had been riding. "You have horses to be stabled? Two denari each to brush them. Four denari per day in the paddock with feed and water; more if you want them kept in a stall in the barn."

Nico held out a soldo coin. "We have three horses. They can go in the paddock. If we're successful in finding the person we're looking for, we'll return this afternoon. Perhaps you've seen him. He came from Florence two days ago and might have left his horse here."

"People always come from Florence and leave their horses here."

"His name is Goffo Zambini."

"Some people like privacy, so I don't ask names when they leave their horses."

Thinking quickly, Massimo said, "He owes us money. He lost a bet and ran off without settling his debt. He has a cousin here in Arezzo. Is there a family in Arezzo named Zambini?"

"Zambini? I don't think there's a family with that name in this city."

"The man we're looking for arrived in Arezzo two days ago, and he's still here. How many men left horses here two days ago and haven't come back yet?"

The man scratched his head, thinking. "Two men. One is a peddler who comes often to sell soap. He can't be the one you want. The other man I've never seen before."

"What did the other one look like?"

Glancing at Nico, the stable master said, "Like him, but heavier and not as tall. Older too. His arm was wrapped close to his chest. He claimed the arm was injured when he was thrown because a small animal startled his horse."

Nico said, "That could be Zambini. He could have gone to a barber to get his wound tended. Where can we find the barber?"

"There are two barbers in the city. The closest one is near the San Francesco church. Go past the church and head down the hill. You'll see his sign."

Nico declared confidently, "I can guide us to the church."

They entered the walled part of the city through the San Lorentino gate, headed south, passed the church of San

Francesco, and saw the barber's sign ahead. As they approached, a piercing scream emanated from the shop. Lazo startled. "Some poor soul must be getting more than a haircut."

"Perhaps that's Zambini getting his arm set," Nico speculated, as he pulled the shop door open.

A muscular man wearing a gray apron triumphantly displayed a pair of tongs, holding the tooth he had just extracted from the man who was moaning in the chair in front of him. The barber patted the man's shoulder and said, "This one won't trouble you anymore." He pushed a sponge soaked with a medicinal liquid into the man's mouth. "Bite down on this. It will stem the bleeding and ease the pain."

The barber washed his hands, removed his blood-spattered apron, and turned his attention to his visitors. "Tooth extractions are never pleasant. It'll take time before he's recovered and active again. How may I help you, Signori?"

Massimo fabricated a different story than the one he told the stable master. "A friend of ours came to Arezzo from Florence two days ago. We heard he injured his arm during his journey. We're concerned about him, but we're unsure where he is staying. Might you have treated him? His name is Goffo Zambini."

The barber nodded vigorously. "Yes, yes, Signor Zambini. I remember him. He came here fearing his arm might have been broken, but it wasn't. He just suffered a bad sprain." Raising a finger to emphasize his point, he added, "I don't mean to understate his situation. Sprains can be more painful than breaks; fortunately, they heal more quickly. Be assured, your friend sustained no long-term harm."

Nico asked, "Did he say where he'd be staying in Arezzo?"

"He said he had a cousin who lives in town, but he didn't tell me the cousin's name." The barber scrunched up his nose in thought. "Ah, but he did mention that his cousin is a lumberman. You could ask at the lumber mill." Seeing the expectation in Nico's expression, he said, "You came from Florence, so you must have passed through Porta San Lorentino."

Nico nodded his agreement.

"Shortly before you reached the city, you crossed a stream. From there, you can take a road heading north, which will lead you to the sawmill."

The men retrieved their horses from the stable, rode to the stream the barber had described, and headed north on a road deeply rutted with wagon tracks. In less than a mile they reached the mill, where two sawyers were struggling to maneuver a massive log onto the saw's platform. The Florentines tethered their horses and grabbed hold of the back end of the log. All five men strained to raise the log into position. One sawyer pushed a lever that set the toothed blade in motion while the others drove the log forward. Sawdust flying into the air showered the two sawyers. Nico and Vittorio, at the back end of the log, escaped the spray. Lazo, standing closer to the sawyers, had his hair liberally dusted.

With the log finally cleaved in two, the older of the two sawyers brushed the dust from himself and greeted his visitors. "Thank you for the help, signori. My other son is sick today. He's a bear who can lift twice as much as me. Without him, we can barely handle the big logs." He scanned his visitors. "How can I be of service to you?"

Nico explained they were looking for a lumberman who had recently been visited by a cousin from Florence.

"Yes, the one-armed Florentine came here yesterday. He said he was a wagon driver, so I gave him a job. He's hauling logs from where the men are cutting. Despite having only one useable arm, he handles the wagon surprisingly well. You can wait here for him to bring the next load, or you can ride up to where the men are cutting."

They opted to ride to the cutting site. Shortly after leaving the mill, they saw a wagon piled high with logs coming toward them. Nico stared at the oncoming vehicle. Its bouncing through deep ruts made it difficult to identify the driver at a distance, but eventually Nico declared, "That's him. That's Goffo Zambini." He moved his horse to the middle of the road and signaled for Zambini to stop. Massimo and Lazo eased their horses to positions alongside the wagon, where they could wrest the reins free if Goffo refused to stop. Nico shouted, "Goffo, we want to talk to you!" Goffo eased the wagon to a stop. Nico declared, "You are Polito Martone's wagon driver."

"I was his driver, but no longer. As you can see, I now work for the mill."

"Why did you leave Florence?"

In an acidic tone, the driver replied, "To visit my cousin. But it's not your business if I leave Florence. Why are you questioning me?"

"We're members of the Florentine Security Commission," Nico replied.

His voice becoming even more agitated, Zambini said, "I've done nothing wrong. Move aside and let me pass."

Massimo turned his horse to let him face Zambini directly. He snarled, "Stop lying. You knew Signor Martone was arrested for tax fraud and bribery. That's why you left Florence."

"Yes, I knew he was arrested. He no longer needed a driver, so I had no reason to stay in Florence."

"You were driving him when he bribed the tax officials."

"I didn't..." Goffo began to protest until Nico interrupted him by raising a hand.

"I saw you in the wagon when Polito Martone paid the tax men. You witnessed the crime and didn't report it. That makes you complicit."

Shaking his head frantically, Zambini countered, "No. No, I did nothing wrong."

Nico said calmly, "Hear us before you say anything more. You can avoid charges by testifying against Polito Martone."

"You want me to go back to Florence. I can't do that. I wouldn't be safe."

Nico looked puzzled. "What do you mean? Why wouldn't you be safe?"

Zambini ignored the questions and said, "I need to think. Let me deliver these logs."

Still confused by Zambini's remarks, Nico and Lazo slipped their horses aside so the wagon could move ahead. Massimo drew close to Nico and said, "There is fear in Zambini's eyes."

"He must be worried that we're going to take him back to Florence, to prison."

Massimo replied, "There's more troubling him than the fear of arrest." Massimo moved forward to ride ahead of the wagon. Nico and Lazo rode behind. When they reached the mill, the sawyers began unloading the logs, none large enough for them to need assistance. Goffo unhitched the horses and led them to the stream to drink. While they were taking their fill, Goffo sensed Nico's presence behind him and asked, "Is Polito in prison?"

"He's still with his family. He'll be free until the trial."

"You're confident that he'll be found guilty and sent to prison?"

"Another member of the Security Commission and I saw Signor Martone pay the tax men to let his wagons pass into the city without proper inspection. We will testify against him, and I'm sure the magistrate will accept our statements as truthful."

Goffo scoffed. "You don't know Polito as I do. He's a clever bastard. He'll claim he can't be faulted because the tax men were derelict and didn't do their jobs. Your testimony will mean little."

Goffo's words struck Nico. He shared the view Martone's lawyer would take that approach to construct his defense. How would Luca Sasso counter? How would he counter if he were the prosecutor? Getting a conviction might not be as straight-forward as Nico had assumed. Rather than challenge Goffo's assertion, Nico said, "Three pharmacists will testify that they received spices not declared on Martone Imports' tax statements."

Goffo shrugged. "I know nothing about that. I'm not privy to tax information. All I did was transport Signor Martone. I'm a wagon driver."

Massimo came forward, close enough to feel Goffo's hot breath. "If you know nothing, why did you flee from Florence?"

Goffo took a step backward. Another step and he would be in the stream. "I already told you. Polito no longer needed me, so I came to visit my cousin," he said, his voice tentative.

Massimo sneered, "You're spouting dung. If you're only going to lie to us, we'll take you back to Florence and charge you as an accomplice to tax fraud. You knew the spice wagons should have been inspected. When you heard Martone had been arrested, you fled to Arezzo to save your ass."

Massimo reached out to seize Goffo's arm. "Let's go. I'm tired of listening to your lies."

Goffo wriggled free. "I can't go back to Florence if Polito is walking around like a free man."

This time it was Nico who moved close and locked eyes with the wagon driver. "What are you afraid of?"

Goffo lowered his gaze. "I won't be safe. He'll kill me."

Doubting what he'd just heard, Nico asked, "You think Polito Martone will kill you? Why would he do that?"

"I heard something."

"What!" demanded Massimo.

"When he was released after his arrest, I drove him from the judiciary to his house. Polito was livid and ranting. He said if he'd been successful in killing the notary, no one would have uncovered his tax scheme. He said he'd tried to kill that notary and failed. And if he'd succeeded like he did with that bastard Marco Ridolfi, his arrangements with the tax men would still be secret. In his rage, he admitted to killing one man and attempting to kill another. When he realizes he told me about the killings, I'll be his next target."

The statement startled Nico. Goffo claimed Polito Martone had killed the man his sister loved, the man she intended to marry. In his mind, Nico visualized Alessa consoling Daniela, the poor woman who still grieved over Marco's loss. Her suffering was greater even than his parent's pain. Would Daniela ever recover from that horrid experience?

Lazo eyed Nico and declared, "You must make the murderer pay for his crime."

Goffo said weakly, "I heard Polito confess his guilt, but who will believe me? There's no proof."

"I believe you," Nico said, then raised a hand before Goffo could speak. "But you are correct; it will take more than your words to persuade a magistrate."

Nico turned away, ambled along the stream bank, paused for a minute, then walked back and faced Goffo. "So far, we haven't come across any evidence that leads us to Marco Ridolfi's killer, and it's doubtful that we'll find any in the future. The only way to convict Polito Martone will be for him to confess his crimes again in the presence of trustworthy witnesses. And we'll need your help to make that happen."

45

The lawyer that Lavinia Martone recommended to her son had an office in the heart of the city, on a street leading to Piazza della Signoria. His two clerks were sifting through papers when Polito Martone entered the elegantly appointed office. "He's expecting me," Polito snapped as he brushed past them. He swatted the interior door aside and pushed his way into the inner office where the lawyer sat behind a large wooden desk, its expansive top engraved with images of lilies, the venerable symbol of the Florentine Republic. Polito announced, "My mother says you're the best."

Messer Orazio Fenzi gestured toward a chair. "Lavinia is a wise woman. You can trust her instincts." Chuckling, he added, "Although I lost a case once, but that was in the distant past."

Polito dropped onto a chair, leaned his elbows on the desk, and looked across it at the lawyer. "I'm accused of bribery and tax fraud."

"Yes, I know. I have a copy of the charges filed against you."

"Does it matter whether I'm guilty?"

Fenzi leaned back in his chair. "It's commonly believed that guilt is paramount, but in reality, that's seldom true. I once had a client charged with murder. Four reliable witnesses said they saw my client stab the victim; yet I managed to get that man exonerated."

"How did you..." Polito began when Fenzi raised a hand to quiet him.

"That was a different case. We are here to discuss your situation. You are charged with bribery. Tell me, who can swear that they saw you pay a bribe?"

"Two members of the Security Commission saw me pay the tax inspector."

"Did they count the florins? Can they vow the payment included a bribe, and that it was not just the proper tax assessment?"

That hint of the lawyer's strategy for his defense spread a grin across Polito's face, but it lasted only moments before fading when Polito said, "They claim I imported spices not reported on the tax documents. They have the tax records and pharmacists who will say we delivered other spices to them."

"There are ways to disparage that claim. The optimum approach will depend on which magistrate is assigned to your case. We can meet again after a magistrate is named. For now, enjoy your status as a free man."

Fenzi leaned forward, his expression rigid, and raised a foreboding finger. "Talk to no one about your case, not your family, not your friends, and especially not lowlifes you meet in taverns."

Despite the lawyer's warning, Polito left the office eager for a beer to punctuate the newly found belief that he might escape conviction. He was so intent on reaching the nearest tavern that he overlooked the wagon ahead, his wagon piloted by his driver, Goffo Zambini. It was understandable in his excited state that he hadn't noticed the wagon, but even if he were alert, he wouldn't have spotted Vittorio and Massimo hidden beneath a heavy covering in the wagon bed.

"Signore!" Goffo called out when Polito came abreast of the wagon.

Polito looked up, puzzled at first, then suspicious. "Goffo, I was told you'd disappeared... run away to save your sorry ass. How did you know I was here meeting with a lawyer?"

"How I found you matters not. The Security Commission is hunting me. They want me to share the blame for your crimes, but I'm not going to the Stinche while you hire a clever lawyer and go free. I didn't benefit from your tax scheme and I bear no responsibility for killing Marco Ridolfi and the notary."

Polito swiveled his head, looking around, fearful that someone might have been close enough to hear. "Quiet, you fool. What do you know of Marco Ridolfi?"

"Only what you told me, that you killed him so he couldn't marry your sister."

Fuming, Polito growled, "You *stronzo,* I never said that. My actions had nothing to do with my sister. Whoever lies in her bed is of no concern to me. I had to kill Marco because he discovered an irregularity in my business and he wouldn't stop probing until he found enough to destroy me."

Polito's face reddened, and a vein popped in his neck. Through clenched teeth, he said, "That self-righteous bastard was an easy kill. I didn't even need a weapon, just my belt. I twisted it tighter and tighter until his last sound was a pitiful gurgle."

Now shuddering, Polito continued, "Marco hired the notary to investigate my tax records, so I had to get rid of the notary, too. Damn him. I left him in a pool of his blood with my knife slicing deep into his back. I don't know how he survived. Damn them both."

Goffo turned his head enough to call over his shoulder. "Is that enough?"

Massimo pulled the covering aside. He and Vittorio stood in the wagon bed. "More than enough," Vittorio replied.

"You bastard," Polito barked at his driver. Reflexively, he reached for his knife and tightened his grip on the hilt, ready to thrust it into his driver until reason regained control of his thoughts. Slowly, he let his fingers uncurl. He tensed and reached for the side of the wagon. Could he escape from these two commissioners? Where would he go?

Massimo had seen other fugitives try to avoid custody by dashing away. He leaned close to Polito's ear and said softly, "I run two miles every morning, so it's only just that you have an advance start. I'll wait here in the wagon until you reach the corner before I give chase, then we'll see how much farther you get before I throw you to the ground." Polito pulled his hand away from the wagon rail and slumped down, defeated.

Vittorio said, "Goffo, take us to the judiciary. Nico is there, prepared to file murder charges against Signor Martone."

When they reached the judiciary, Nico was standing outside in the piazza waiting for them. Vittorio grabbed Polito's arm and, pulling him down from the wagon, said, "Men like you never know when to stay silent."

Massimo gave Nico a friendly slap on the back. "I had doubts about your simple ploy, but if worked perfectly; Polito never suspected that Vittorio and I were hiding in the wagon bed. You're a clever man, my friend. Someday, someone might write a book about you."

46

Octavia, the housemaid at Casa Martone, opened the door and found herself face-to-face with Vittorio, Sergeant Grimaldi, and two of Grimaldi's officers. Grimaldi introduced himself as a member of the Guardia and said, "We are here to search Signor Polito Martone's rooms and possessions. Take us to his room."

Overwhelmed by the men and Grimaldi's pointed instruction, Octavia responded in a trembling voice. "I must ask Signor Martone."

In a compassionate but firm voice, Grimaldi directed, "First take us to Polito's room, then you may speak with Signor Martone. One of my men can go with you to explain our purpose if you wish."

Having no choice, Octavia led the men past the anteroom to the main staircase. At the second level, the men's resounding footsteps brought Signora Livinia Martone out of the dining salon into the hallway. She cried out, "Octavia, what are you doing? Who are these men?"

Grimaldi signaled for his men to continue climbing to the third level while he crossed the hallway to explain their mission to Signora Martone. Frightened by his approach, she shouted, "Nozzo! Nozzo! There are intruders in our house."

Nozzo Martone dashed out of his study and ran to his panicked wife. Color drained from his face at seeing the strange men. Grimaldi held up a hand. "I'm Sergeant Grimaldi of the Guardia. Your son Polito has been accused of a serious crime. My men are here to search his possessions for evidence."

"I'll tend to these men. Don't worry," Nozzo said and guided his wife toward his study. Then he called, "Octavia, come here. I'll bring these men to Polito's room."

Vittorio moved close to Octavia and said, "You needn't be afraid. Go to Signora Martone."

At the third level, Nozzo pointed. "That's Polito's room."

The two Guardia officers were not trained investigators, so they waited in the hallway for their sergeant to give them direction. Vittorio stepped in front of Nozzo. "Are all of Polito's possessions in this room?"

Nozzo rubbed his eyes. "He has a chest in the storage area. I don't know what he keeps in it. What do you expect to find in your search?"

Vittorio ignored the question and moved into Polito's room. One chest sat on the floor across the room next to a desk. Vittorio opened the second chest located at the end of the bed and began emptying its contents onto the bed. Grimaldi, his officers, and Nozzo Martone stood aside and watched. After removing several items, he lifted out a dark blue tunic and carried it to the window where he could examine it closely in brighter light. The tunic had one loose clasp and a stain on the left sleeve near the wrist. Vittorio sniffed the stain and announced, "It is most likely wine." He gave the tunic to Grimaldi who passed it to one of his men.

Nozo protested. "It's just a tunic. Why are you taking it?"

Grimaldi replied, "A witness reported that Marco Ridolfi's killer wore a dark blue tunic."

Shocked by Grimaldi's statement, Nozzo muttered, "A witness? There was a witness to the killing?"

Lavinia Martone came into the room, saw the contents of the chest strewn across the bed, and bellowed, "You can't do this. Those are Polito's clothes. You have no right." She moved toward Vittorio as though she intended to stop him. Grimaldi stepped in front of her and said to Nozzo, "Take your wife from the room." His forceful tone implied that if Nozzo could not remove his wife, a Guardia officer would do so. Nozzo embraced his wife. She lost her bluster, dropped her head onto his shoulder, and whimpered, "Polito's a good boy."

Vittorio opened the second chest and carried shoes, hats, and other accessories to the bed. The chest held two belts, but both were unadorned cloth. Neither had decorative studs. When he finished with the chest, Vittorio turned his attention to the desk. The only item of interest was a notebook. Skimming through it, Vittorio saw entries pertaining to the quantities of various spices being imported, and comments about employees, including Polito's driver, Goffo Zambini. He handed to notebook to Grimaldi. "The prosecutor of the tax fraud case will want this in the event the lawyer claims that Polito never knew what spices were being imported." Vittorio's comment brought forth a moan from Lavinia Martone.

Vittorio asked, "Where is the storage area?" Nozzo led the men to a room at the end of the hall filled with boxes, chests, and assorted furniture.

Nozzo pushed aside a table with a loose leg, pointed and said, "That chest belongs to Polito." Unlike other items in the room, it was not covered with a thin layer of dust.

The two Guardia officers pulled the chest into the middle of the room and opened it. Sitting atop the pile of clothes haphazardly stuffed into the chest was a white silk belt decorated with diamond shaped studs. Vittorio took out a paper and placed it next to the belt. The markings on the paper corresponded exactly to the distance between the studs on the belt, and the sketches Vittorio had made of the marks on Marco's neck matched the design of the studs on the belt. Near one stud was a trace of blood. Vittorio pointed to the bloodstain as he passed the belt to Sergeant Grimaldi, and said, "This is undisputable evidence."

Nozzo Martone followed Vittorio and the Guardia officers out of the storage area and watched them descend the staircase. He wanted to ask what he might do to lessen the charges against his son, but he knew nothing could diminish the severity of the crime.

47

Nico was at Luca Sasso's favorite table sipping a beer when Luca entered the trattoria. Luca smiled warmly at Giulia and whispered something as he passed by her on his way to join Nico. Giulia returned the smile, and her cheeks flushed slightly at Luca's greeting. Luca slid into a chair opposite Nico and said, "Before we get mired in discussing legal issues, I want to thank you for encouraging me to ask Giulia to the guild dance. We spent a wonderful evening together."

"Did Giulia's mother accompany her? The woman's facial expression gives the impression that she's constantly in a gloomy state. I hope her attention didn't dampen your inner fire."

"I too feared that Giulia's mother might have spoiled the evening. Just having her sitting nearby watching us would have been unnerving, but fortunately, it was Giulia's brother who accompanied us. He spent the entire evening dancing with the eligible daughters of every member of the guild and hardly noticed his sister was at the event. His neglect gave Giulia and I ample opportunity to talk. In all the time I've been coming to this trattoria, she must have served me more than a hundred mugs of beer, yet we were never more than strangers. A single evening of dancing and conversation unveiled the remarkable woman who's always rushing to and from the kitchen."

"Your enthusiasm tells me you'll be looking for other occasions to enjoy her company."

"Certainly, although I have nothing planned yet." Luca waved a dismissive hand. "Now to business and how to proceed with Polito Martone. I read the charges you filed against him for the murder of Marco Ridolfi. Is the case against him strong?"

"Yes, it is. Three witnesses, Massimo, Vittorio, and Polito's driver, heard Polito admit to killing Marco Ridolfi. In addition, Vittorio and Guardia officers searched Casa Martone and found, among Polito's possessions, a belt that matches the one used to strangle Marco Ridolfi."

"You are not a witness?"

"No. I filed the charges based on the statements of the witnesses, but I wasn't present when Polito was apprehended."

"Since you're not a witness, will you be prosecuting the case?"

"I could, unless the magistrate or Chancellor Scala has reason why I shouldn't. However, I have a suggestion for you to consider. Polito committed murder because he thought that Marco Ridolfi was on the verge of uncovering his tax fraud scheme. Since the tax fraud and murder cases are connected, I suggest merging them into a single trial that we prosecute together. You can interrogate the witnesses about the tax fraud charge and I'll question the witnesses related to the murder charge."

Luca tilted his head slightly, pondering Nico's suggestion. "Having different prosecutors for each of the charges would be a novel approach. I like the idea, but combining the two cases would create a complication because I intended to call you as a witness at the tax fraud trial."

Nico's face broke into a cunning grin. "I'm not aware of any legal limitations that would prevent me from being a witness."

"I'm not aware of any restrictions either, but I'll be eager to see the defense lawyer's reaction when I call my co-prosecutor as a witness. Since you filed both the tax fraud and murder charges, you should be the one who delivers the introduction."

Nico and Luca left the trattoria and crossed the piazza to the office of the judicial scheduling clerk. The clerk's brow furrowed at hearing their proposal. "Do I understand this correctly? You're asking to have the tax fraud and murder cases addressed at the same trial and you both want to be named as prosecutors?"

Both men replied, "Yes."

The clerk scanned the charge documents. "Messer Argenti, you're listed as a prosecution witness in the tax fraud case."

Nico asked, "Is that a problem?"

The perplexed clerk replied, "Being a prosecutor and a witness at the same trial? To my recollection, it's never been done."

"Is it forbidden?"

"I don't know. Let me ask a magistrate." The clerk left the room to speak with a magistrate who was preparing for trial.

The clerk returned a few moments later, shaking his head and said, "He's never encountered that situation, but he said it is permitted. Since one charge is for murder, the trial must be adjudicated by a panel of three magistrates." He opened the scheduling folio, leafed through the schedule sheets, and said, "The earliest date that a panel can be convened is six days from now. Will any of the witnesses be testifying in secret?"

In Florence, witnesses could provide their testimonies in a confidential session with the magistrates if they believed revealing their identities would put them at risk. In those situations, the defendant's lawyer would be furnished with a transcript of the testimony, with the identity of the witness omitted.

Luca replied, "None of my witnesses have asked for privacy."

Nico said, "I have one witness who wishes to testify in secret."

The clerk noted Nico's request and said, "Signor Polito Martone has entered the name of his lawyer as Messer Orazio Fenzi. I will see that Messer Fenzi is told of the trial date and that the two charges against his client have been combined."

Nico and Luca spent the days preceding the trial preparing their witnesses. Vittorio, Massimo, and Sergeant Grimaldi had extensive experience in court, so they required no guidance on how to present themselves. The lawyers met with them only to review the questions they would be asked during the trial. Luca divided his time among Cambio and Bindo, the wagon drivers who brought the spices from Venice, and the pharmacists who received the imported spices.

Nico met multiple times with Loro, the villa worker who had seen the killer, and Polito's driver, Goffo Zambini. He stressed to each man the importance of restricting their statements to facts and only answering questions directly. "Cases have been lost by witnesses straying into irrelevant information," Nico told them. That had never happened in Nico's experience, but his professors at the University of Bologna law school had assured students it was so.

Nico told each man the questions he would ask them

during the trial. He instructed, "The magistrates may also ask you questions. They are not enemies. Answer them with facts if you can. If you're unsure what is being asked, tell the magistrate you don't understand. The defense lawyer should not interrupt your testimony, but defense lawyers don't always behave properly. Some intentionally try to intimidate witnesses, so disregard their comments. If the lawyer disrupts your testimony, stop and wait until a magistrate or I tell you to continue. If the defense lawyer asks you a question, do not answer him. He is not allowed to question you."

Nico devoted the last day before the trial to preparing the accusation. The accusation statement presented at the trial's outset was crucial because it detailed the crimes allegedly committed by the defendant. To secure a guilty verdict, the prosecution had to convince the magistrates that the defendant acted in accordance with the accusation. Any claim made in the accusation that was not addressed or substantiated during the trial could cause a verdict of not guilty.

One morning of the trial, Nico sat in the dining salon of Casa Argenti ignoring a freshly baked lemon tart while making final tweaks to the accusation. Alessa filled Nico's water glass and observed, "This case is weighing heavily on you." Her comment elicited no response, so she flicked a few water droplets in Nico's direction.

Nico looked up. "I heard you and yes, the case is weighing on me. Signor and Signora Martone are God-fearing people. Signor Martone belongs to a confraternity that provides food and shelter for indigents. And I'm about to prove that their son is a murderer, a crime that could have him put to death."

Alessa touched Nico's hand. "Magistrates will pronounce the consequences for Polito if they find him guilty. You won't decide Polito's guilt or prescribe his punishment, so don't feel those burdens rest on you. But I can understand your misgivings. You aren't the only one who is conflicted. Yesterday, I visited Daniela. Her brother is accused of killing the man she had planned to marry. It was painful for me to watch her struggling to cope with the two tragedies, but it is Polito who bears the responsibility for Daniela's distress and her parents' suffering, not you. They need the resolution of knowing whether he is guilty and you can help bring that to them."

Nico walked around the table and embraced Alessa. "Your wisdom often leaves me in awe, little sister, and this is one of those times."

48

TRIAL DAY 1: PROSECUTION

With Alessa's encouraging words echoing in his mind, Nico walked briskly from Casa Argenti to the Palazzo del Podestà where the criminal courtrooms were located. The warm morning sun further lifted his spirits. His meticulous preparation of the accusation let him feel ready to fulfill his role as prosecutor. Nico entered the tribunal chamber and joined Luca Sasso who was seated at the prosecution table reviewing his notes.

The court clerk readied the positions on the raised platform at the front of the room for the three magistrates. Each position had a padded chair and a small desk holding a glass of water and writing materials so the magistrates could make notes. Satisfied the positions were properly prepared, the clerk left the room. A short time later, he returned and informed the prosecutors. "All of your witnesses have arrived and are in the holding rooms."

A growing murmur filled the trial chamber as observers entered and found their seats in the gallery at the rear of the room. Nico turned and glanced briefly, only long enough to notice Signor and Signora Martone. He pulled his gaze away, not wanting to make eye contact with Daniela or members of the Ridolfi family.

The gallery buzzed as Polito Martone, accompanied by his lawyer, entered the chamber. They had barely taken their places at the defense table when a side door opened and three men wearing the black robes and wide red sashes of senior magistrates entered the chamber and took their positions on the dais. As soon as the magistrates were seated, the clerk stepped forward and announced, "Under the authority of the Eight of Guard, this tribunal is convened to hear accusations against Signor Polito Martone by Messers Luca Sasso and Nico Argenti representing the Republic of Florence."

The highest ranking magistrate said, "Messer Argenti, you may begin. Nico stood and read the accusation.

Honorable Defenders of Justice, on behalf of the Republic of Florence, we bring before you this accusation against Signor Polito Martone, a citizen of the parish of San Procolo of Florence. Witnesses will swear testimony and evidence will be presented to prove that Polito Martone evaded the payment of levies justly imposed on the importation of spices into the Republic of Florence. And further, upon realizing that his fraudulent scheme was about to be discovered and exposed by Signor Marco Ridolfi, a citizen of the San Marco parish of Florence, Signor Polito Martone murdered Signor Ridolfi by means of strangulation.

Nico sat. Luca Sasso stood and said, "Honorable Magistrates, with your permission I will call the first witness." The senior magistrate gestured for Luca to proceed.

Luca called Nico, who walked to the witness stand. The clerk came forward to swear in Nico as a witness when defense lawyer Orazio Fenzi jumped up and shouted, "He can't be a witness! He's a prosecutor!"

A smirk spread across the face of the senior magistrate. He asked, "Messer Fenzi, can you enlighten us as to which statute in the legal code of our republic prohibits a prosecutor from testifying?"

Fenzi's shoulders slumped. He replied, "I cannot, Honorable Magistrate," and slunk down onto his seat.

The magistrate gave Luca a quick wave of his hand, signaling for him to proceed. At Luca's request, Nico presented copies of tax documents showing the tax levies applicable to various spices and the amounts paid by Polito Martone. Luca then called upon Nico, followed by Massimo, to describe their observations of spices entering through the Porta San Gallo gate without proper inspection. Both men recounted how they tracked the wagon as it delivered the spices to pharmacies. Next, Luca called Cambio and Bindo, the wagon drivers who brought spices into Florence. They testified Polito had been present when the tax inspectors had passed the wagons without careful inspection. Finally, the three pharmacists described the spices they had received, varieties different from those listed on the tax report Nico had displayed earlier. It was nearly noon when Luca summarized his case. Except for his initial outburst, defense lawyer Fenzi had made no objections.

In the afternoon, Nico began his presentation by calling Vittorio, Massimo and Goffo Zambini. All three men testified to hearing Polito Martone boast about strangling Marco Ridolfi and attempting to kill the notary, Bernardo Vernacci . Vittorio described his examination of Marco Ridolfi's body and his determination that the victim had been strangled. He displayed the paper on which he had recorded measurements taken of bruises on Marco's neck and stated his conclusion that the injuries had been inflicted by a belt.

Next, Nico asked that the courtroom be cleared so a witness could testify in secret. After the court clerk had escorted Polito Martone, his lawyer, and the gallery observers out of the chamber, Nico called Loro as his next witness. The nervous youngster was brought to the witness stand and sworn in by the clerk. In response to Nico's questions, he described what he had seen at the villa on the day of the murder. When he mentioned that the person he had seen had pointy ears, the senior magistrate interrupted Loro and asked Nico, "What are we to do with this information unless you intend to call an expert on ear shapes as your next witness?"

Addressing the magistrate, Nico said, "I believe this witness can help us with that." He turned to Loro and asked, "Have you seen the defendant, Signor Polito Martone?"

"Yes, I have seen him."

"Do the shapes of Signor Martone's ears match what you have referred to as pointy ears?"

"Yes, the tops of his ears are pointy, not round."

"Do the shape of Signor Martone's ears match the recollection you have of the person who left the room where Marco Ridolfi was murdered?"

"Yes, they're the same shape."

After Loro finished testifying, Polito, Fenzi, and the observers were allowed to reenter the chamber. As his final witness, Nico called Sergeant Grimaldi, who described the search of Polito's possessions at Casa Martone. He displayed the blue tunic and the belt that had been seized. Using the paper that Vittorio had introduced earlier, he showed that the position and shape of the studs on the belt matched the bruises on Marco Ridolfi's neck. He pointed to one spot on the belt. "This mark has the distinct color of a bloodstain." He handed the belt to the court clerk, who passed it to the magistrates.

When Nico indicated he had no more witnesses, the clerk

ended the session saying, "This tribunal is adjourned until tomorrow, when the defense may present its case." Nico remained at the prosecution table until the gallery had been cleared. He did not notice his sister Alessa sitting next to Daniela Martone.

49

TRIAL DAY 2: DEFENSE

Polito Martone and Orazio Fenzi were conferring at the defense table when Nico entered the tribunal chamber. Fenzi tried to review his notes, but Polito kept distracting him with questions. "Fenzi is early today. He must be eager," Luca said when he joined Nico at the prosecution table.

Lavinia Martone strode up the room's central aisle, walked to the defense table, and handed something to her son. The clerk spotted her and rushed to her. "You can't be here," he said with desperation in his voice. "You must return to the gallery." He reached out to grasp her arm and shepherd her away, but thought again, lowered his hand, and merely repeated, "You can't be here." Lavinia glared at the clerk and said a few additional words to Polito before returning to the gallery.

The three magistrates, their faces expressionless, entered the room and took their places on the raised platform. The senior magistrate nodded to the clerk, who announced, "This tribunal bearing charges against Signor Polito Martone brought by representatives of the Republic of Florence is in session."

Cued by the senior magistrate, Orazio Fenzi stood. "Honorable magistrates, in the matter of tax payments made by Signor Polito Martone on behalf of Martone Imports, the prosecution has not demonstrated that Signor Martone paid anything less in taxes than the amounts demanded by the tax inspectors." The statement prompted two magistrates to make entries in their notes.

Fenzi continued. "Prosecution witnesses contended Polito had observed improper inspection of his wagons when they entered the city. I ask you to consider, honorable magistrates, that the prosecution introduced neither evidence nor testimony defining the criteria for a proper inspection. It is the tax inspectors' responsibility to determine what constitutes a proper inspection, not the person whose goods are being imported. Signor Martone did exactly what was expected of him; therefore, the defense asks that you find Signor Martone not guilty of the charge of tax fraud."

Luca leaned toward Nico. "Fenzi's defense was exactly as you predicted."

Nico responded, "The case would have been solid if we could have proven that Polito bribed the inspectors, but they would never admit to taking bribes."

Fenzi cleared his throat. "Now let me address the murder charge. Signor Colombo and Signor Leoni claim to have heard my client admit to killing Marco Ridolfi. But consider, at the time, both men were ensconced under a heavy covering in the back of a wagon moving along a noisy street. My client, when he spoke, was facing toward the front of the wagon, away from the witnesses. Those are not satisfactory conditions for overhearing conversations. I ask you, honorable magistrates, to consider that those witnesses were mistaken. Maybe they heard Signor Martone confess because that is what they wanted to hear."

Fenzi shot a sideways glance at the prosecutors, then continued. "The motive they advanced for the crime was nothing more than speculation. But we do not need to speculate. The Ridolfi family has real enemies and at least one of them attempted to harm and possibly kill family members and their guests at the villa on the day Marco Ridolfi was murdered."

Fenzi called his witness, Ugo Fornelli. "Signor Fornelli, were you at the Ridolfi villa on the day that Marco Ridolfi was killed?"

"Yes, I was."

"Tell this court your reason for being at the villa."

"I was paid to taint the wine."

"What do you mean, taint the wine?"

"I put petals of the Scopa Fiori Giallo flower in the jugs that were used to serve the wine."

"Are Scopa Fiori Giallo flowers harmful?"

"They have been used as a poison."

"I understand the guests left the villa before the wine was served, but villa workers did consume the poisoned wine. Tell us what happened to those villa workers."

"They got sick. Some got so sick they had to be treated by a physician."

"Might they have died if they had not been treated?"

Nico stood to raise an objection. Before he spoke, Fenzi raised a hand and told Fornelli, "You need not answer the question. You couldn't know what might have happened to the men if they were not treated."

Fenzi dismissed the witness and returned his attention to the magistrates. "Honorable magistrates, Signor Fornelli is just one person hired to strike against the Ridolfi family. I ask you to consider that any number of people might have acted against Marco Ridolfi."

Fenzi looked down at his notes. "Now let me address the purported evidence. Fenzi reached down under the defense table, withdrew a belt, and held it aloft, visible to everyone in the room. "I purchased this belt from one of our city's respected tailors. If you compare the studs on this belt with the markings on the paper that Signor Colombo entered as evidence, you will find the design and spacings match perfectly. This belt and the one owned by my client are not unique. Dozens or even hundreds of men in our city might own identical belts. We can give no credence to the claim that my client is a murderer because he owned a particular style of belt."

Fenzi set the belt down onto the defense table and scanned the three magistrates as he said, "I submit the arguments I presented provide ample reason to reject the murder charge against Signor Martone."

When Fenzi sat, the senior magistrate announced, "This session is adjourned while we deliberate. The clerk will inform you when we have reached a verdict."

Nico waited until the magistrates left the room, then said to Luca, "Fenzi presented a commendable defense. I hadn't expected Fornelli to be called as a witness, but I guess he'll do anything to earn a payment."

Luca gave Nico a reassuring pat on the shoulder. "Fenzi didn't address Gofo Zambini's testimony." Chuckling, he added, "or Polito's pointy ears."

Nico said, "He did the best he could since we know Polito is guilty."

An hour later, the court clerk dispatched couriers to inform the prosecutors and defense lawyer that the magistrates had reached a verdict. The gallery observers had been milling in the street. When they saw the lawyers file into the tribunal chamber, they followed close behind.

The senior magistrate scanned the room, scowled, and asked, "Messer Fenzi, where is your client?"

Fenzi shrugged. "I don't know. I haven't seen him since the session was recessed. Perhaps he didn't receive word that the session has resumed."

With an obvious display of disgust, the senior magistrate pounded his fist onto the desk forcefully enough to cause his water glass to teeter on the table's edge. His associates moved to join him. With frustration in his voice, he said to them, "Why do we even try to charge men like Polito Martone with serious crimes? Trials become a farce when wealthy men can escape punishment by choosing exile to a place where they use their riches to live a lavish lifestyle beyond the reach of our justice system."

One associate responded, "We've indulged that practice for centuries, yet our republic flourishes. And it rids us of criminals without the cost of incarcerating them."

The other associate scoffed, "Bah. There is no justice if men are not held accountable for their actions. The Guardia should be allowed to pursue criminals even beyond the boundaries of the republic, and men on trial for serious crimes should have their assets impounded pending the outcome of their trial so they can't flee."

The senior magistrate slapped his hand down onto his desk to draw the attention of those in the tribunal chamber. In a loud, forceful voice, he announced, "We have reached a verdict." The chamber became as silent as a tomb. "For the charge of tax fraud, we find Signor Polito Martone not guilty." Nico believed he could hear Lavinia Martone exhale. "For the charge of murder, we find Polito Martone guilty." An undertone of excited whispers erupted from the gallery.

Before storming out of the room, the magistrate turned to face Sergeant Grimaldi, who was standing at the side of the room. "Sergeant, have your men apprehend Signor Martone and confine him until such time that we announce his sentence." It was a perfunctory directive. Both the magistrate and Sergeant Grimaldi believed Polito had fled beyond the jurisdiction of the Florentine Guardia.

50

Polito pounded on Cambio's door with both fists. Inside, it sounded like a team of oxen were about to burst into the room. "Open the door, damn you! Open the door!" Polito shouted.

Cambio was making steady progress at consuming his second bottle of wine and wondering where he would find work if Polito were sent to prison when he heard Polito's voice. He pulled the door open blubbering, "They forced me to testify. I had no choice."

Polito barged into the room, waving his hands and snarling. "Forget about that. Those snake-bitten magistrates are going to find me guilty. I can tell by the way they looked at me. You've got to help me get away. I need to leave Florence."

"Leave? To where?"

"Maybe Bologna. Bologna's close." Polito stomped across the room. "No, not Bologna, Venice. I know people in Venice and I can get money there."

Cambio said, "The horses and the wagon we use to transport spices are at the stable. You can use those."

"Don't be a fool. I'm not going alone. I don't know the road. You're coming with me."

Lavinia Martone shook uncontrollably upon hearing the pronouncement that her son had been found guilty of murder. With support from her husband and her sister, she hobbled out of the courtroom. Vittorio and Massimo waited until the others had left the gallery, then they went to join Nico and Luca at the defense table. Massimo asked, "Do you think Polito intends to leave Florence?"

Nico replied, I'd be more confident in making a prediction if you were asking about someone other than Polito. From what I know of him, his decision-making process isn't always rational."

Massimo said, "Should he choose to leave, there may be belongings he'd want to take with him. I can go to Casa Martone and ask Octavia whether Polito went there to collect things."

"I'll join you," Nico said. "If Signor and Signora Martone have means to influence their son, I want them to know his sentence will be much harsher if he becomes a fugitive."

Deep in thought, Vittorio stroked his chin, contemplating what Polito might do next. "Polito's knowledge is limited. Apart from Florence, the only city he knows is Venice, and I doubt he would know how to get to Venice on his own. He'd need help, and the two men he'd likely seek assistance from are Cambio and Bindo. I'm going to question them." Nico, Massimo, and Vittorio agreed to meet later at the Chancery.

Octavia answered the door when Nico and Massimo arrived at Casa Martone. Unlike the other times when she greeted Massimo, her mood was somber. Massimo asked, "Have you seen Polito? Did he come to the casa to pack a bag with clothes or other things?"

"I saw him early this morning. Not since then."

Nico and Massimo exchanged glances. Might Polito have been planning an escape even before Messer Fenzi had presented the defense?

"Was he carrying anything when he left?" Massimo asked.

"I don't know. I didn't see him leave."

Nico said, "I would like to speak with Signor Martone." He noticed Octavia tense, and added, "It's important." She led Nico and Massimo to the anteroom, where they waited while she went to find Signor Martone.

Minutes later, Nozzo Martone shuffled into the anteroom and dropped onto a chair. Nico said, "I know this is a difficult time for you and your wife."

"She's with her sister. She can't... we can't believe any of this." He looked up at Nico. "Octavia said you have something important to share with me."

"The magistrates have not yet decided on a sentence, and it hinges on how Polito conducts himself."

With a perplexed look, Nozzo uttered, "I don't understand."

"Magistrates have broad discretion in administering sentences. Let me give you an example. Last month, I attended the trial of a mill owner who came to Florence from Milan to kill a competitor. After his brutal attack, he returned to Milan. He was tried in absentia in a Florentine court and sentenced to decapitation. The magistrate said that given the circumstances of the crime, the man would have been confined in prison for five years had he been willing to undergo the ordeal of a trial in Florence.

"That case was not unusual. If Polito were to remand himself to the custody of the Guardia, his punishment would most likely be confinement, otherwise he might receive a death penalty."

Nozzo nodded his understanding. He said, "Polito's whereabouts are a mystery to me. I don't know how to reach him."

Massimo said, "Your family has a villa outside the city. Might he have gone there?"

"Our villa is in the Chianti hills. It's close to the Sienese border, but still in the Florentine countryside, so there would be no benefit for him to go there."

Massimo asked, "Where else might he have gone?"

Nozzo squinted, then rubbed his eyes. "Venice. It's the only city, outside Florence, that Polito has visited. If he's left Florence, he must be going to Venice."

Vittorio rapped on Cambio's door. The force of his knock pushed the door inward. "Cambio," he shouted. Hearing no response, he entered the room. Seeing no one, Vittorio moved past the open bottle of wine and half empty glass sitting on a table and stepped into the bedroom. Soiled clothing lay in a heap next to a chest at the foot of the bed. Using his investigator's keen eye, Vittorio meticulously scanned the room. Nothing hinted at where Cambio had gone or when he might return.

He crossed the hallway and banged on Bindo's door. Footsteps inside grew louder, then stopped, and the door opened enough to show Bindo's round face and crooked nose. Bindo's jaw fell open upon recognizing the tough-minded investigator. Vittorio said, abruptly, "Cambio's door was unlocked, and he isn't in his room. Where is he?"

"I don't know. Earlier I heard a noise in the hallway, and when I looked out, he was leaving. Polito Martone was with him."

"How long ago did you see them?"

Bindo bit his lower lip, thinking. "Not long ago, but before the church bells sounded nones."

"Is your wagon at the stable?"

"The wagon belongs to Martone Imports, and yes, we left it at the stable."

Vittorio reasoned that if Cambio and Polito were heading north toward Bologna in the wagon, he could overtake them on horseback before they reached the border, but he had agreed to meet his colleagues at the Chancery.

Nico and Massimo were in the Chancery conference room when Vittorio burst in and announced, "I believe Polito and Cambio have ridden off in a wagon heading to Bologna and eventually to Venice. If we leave now on horseback, we can catch them before nightfall."

Nico said, "Massimo and I have been discussing whether it is proper for us to apprehend Polito."

Vittorio's eyes widened in disbelief as he looked at Nico. "Polito is a convicted criminal. He committed murder. Why would we not want to capture him?"

Nico replied, "If you believe Polito is still in Florentine territory, we should tell the Guardia where to find him. He would be their responsibility."

Vittorio, still standing, leaned forward and rested both hands on the back of a chair. "What if he's already crossed into the Province of Bologna? The Guardia isn't permitted to follow him across the border."

Nico responded, "I'm not sure it is our duty to pursue him."

Vittorio shook his head. "Polito's a convicted criminal. By what reasoning can you think we shouldn't pursue him?"

Massimo stood and said, "We would benefit from the Chancellor's guidance." He left the room and returned minutes later with Chancellor Scala.

Vittorio summarized his position. "Polito Martone has been convicted of murder and is most likely attempting to thwart the tribunal's judgement by fleeing from the republic. The Security Commission is authorized to operate beyond our boundaries, so I believe we should bring him to justice."

Scala said methodically, "You are correct in saying that the Security Commission may operate outside our republic." He turned to Nico. "On what grounds do you object to pursuing Polito Martone?"

"The Security Commission was formed with the purpose of opposing threats to the republic. Polito Martone is a criminal, but I don't believe he can be considered a threat to the republic. Admittedly, Polito's crime is serious, a capital offense, but if our mission is expanded to include pursuing criminals, which ones would we chase? Would we soon find ourselves tracking pickpockets?"

Vittorio asserted, "We targeted the corrupt orphanage administrator when he fled to Bologna."

"True," Nico reasoned, "but he was conspiring with a rogue band of mercenaries and they were a threat to the republic."

Scala faced Massimo. "You haven't ventured an opinion."

"My experience derives from the army. The army is constrained. It can operate outside the republic only when sanctioned by the Ten of War." Massimo eyed Scala. "You've been a source of Security Commission assignments, so it would seem this is a matter for you to decide."

Scala leaned back in his chair. "I have done so as a surrogate for Andrea Mozzi. When the Commission was formed, the Signoria deemed it should report to Signor Mozzi in his capacity as First Chair of the Ten of War. The question you men are raising is profound and therefore rightfully is one for Signor Mozzi to resolve.

"However, at the moment, a crucial matter is consuming his attention. Word has not reached the public yet, but Venice is readying an army of over ten thousand troops to go against Milan. Signor Mozzi is in Milan, forming a coalition to resist the Venetian assault, which could come as soon as summer.

"We can't know when Signor Mozzi will return to Florence, but when he does, I will ask him to clarify the Security Commission's mission. I realize this may not be satisfying, but from what you've uncovered, we can expect Polito Martone to be in Venice when Mozzi returns. If Signor Mozzi determines that Polito Martone's capture fits within the Security Commission's mission, I'm sure you men will be able to find him in Venice."

The meeting ended with Vittorio visibly dissatisfied with the outcome. Massimo, accustomed to military discipline, accepted the situation without hesitation. Nico left the conference room and strode out into the piazza. With his gaze cast down to the dull gray cobblestones, his mind wandered to thoughts of the future. For sixteen years, the Treaty of Lodi had been the cornerstone of peace among Venice, Milan, and Florence. Is that peace about to end? Might we be sent after Polito Martone into a warring Venice? Is this a time to plan a wedding?

⁓

Dear Reader,

My deepest gratitude to you for taking the time to read

Deadly Rivalries. Whether you found yourself lost in its pages for hours or simply enjoyed a brief escape, I am truly grateful for your time and attention.

If you've enjoyed the twists, turns, and characters in *Deadly Rivalries*, I kindly invite you to share your thoughts by leaving a review. Reviews are the stars that light up the night sky for self-published authors. So, whether it's a few words or a heartfelt paragraph, your review matters!

Warmest regards, Ken ken@kententarelli.com

ABOUT THE AUTHOR

Ken Tentarelli is a frequent visitor to Italy. In travels from the Alps to the southern coast of Sicily he developed a love for its history and its people. He has studied Italian culture and language in Rome and Perugia. At home he has taught courses in Italian history spanning time from the Etruscans to the Renaissance. When not traveling, Ken and his wife live in New Hampshire.

* * *

What was life like at a Renaissance university?

Get your FREE download of Nico's Story, a recounting of Nico's path through the University of Bologna by signing up for our newsletter at

https://www.KenTentarelli.com/nicos-story

ALSO BY KEN TENTARELLI

The Nico Argenti Series

The Laureate: Mystery in Renaissance Italy (book 1)

When Nico Argenti returns from the university, he is drawn into the turmoil gripping his beloved city of Florence.

The Advisor: Intrigue in Tuscany (book 2)

Nico uses his legal training to help a small mountain town threatened by a vindictive knight.

Assignment Milan (book 3)

Nico races to uncover the plot targeting the Florentine Republic when a Florentine banker goes missing in Milan.

Conspiracy in Bologna (book 4)

Nico is dispatched to Bologna to thwart a vengeful renegade and rogue mercenaries.

Rebels in Pisa (book 5)

Nico confronts insurrectionists in Pisa.